FINDING HOME

JAMEY MOODY

Live This Love

© 2020 by Jamey Moody. All Rights Reserved.

Edited: Amanda Laufhutte

Cover: Lucy Bexley

This is a work of fiction. Names, characters, places, and incidents are the product of the author's imagination or are used fictitiously. Any resemblance to actual person, living or dead, business establishments, events, or locales is entirely coincidental.

This book, or parts thereof, may not be reproduced in any form without permission.

ebooks are not transferable. They cannot be sold, shared, or given away as it is an infringement of the copyright of this work.

Thank you for purchasing my ebook! I hope you enjoy the story.

If you'd like to stay updated on future releases, you can visit my website and sign up for my mailing list at:

www.jameymoodyauthor.com

As an independent author, reviews are greatly appreciated.

I'd love to hear from you!

Email: jameymoodyauthor@gmail.com

❀ Created with Vellum

CONTENTS

Also by Jamey Moody	v
Chapter 1	1
Chapter 2	12
Chapter 3	18
Chapter 4	26
Chapter 5	38
Chapter 6	47
Chapter 7	56
Chapter 8	65
Chapter 9	79
Chapter 10	89
Chapter 11	100
Chapter 12	111
Chapter 13	124
Chapter 14	135
Chapter 15	144
Chapter 16	151
Chapter 17	162
Chapter 18	174
Chapter 19	188
Chapter 20	203
Chapter 21	216
Chapter 22	227
Chapter 23	237
Epilogue	247
About the Author	251

ALSO BY JAMEY MOODY

Live This Love

The Your Way Series:

Finding Home

Finding Family

Finding Forever

1

Somedays you're the windshield, somedays you're the bug. At this moment, Frankie Dean felt like the bug. She was going through the mail of Your Way, the fitness center she owned with her two best friends.

"Whatcha got there?" asked Desi. Desdemona Shaw had been Frankie's best friend since kindergarten 40 years ago and one of her partners in the gym. She had short dark hair with hazel eyes that were full of mischief.

"The mail," replied Frankie flatly.

"Duh, I know it's the mail. What are you looking at so intensely?"

Frankie handed Desi the wedding invitation she had been holding.

Desi read it and exclaimed, "What the hell! You have got to be kidding me! She invited you to her

wedding?"

"No, she invited all of us, I guess. It's addressed to the gym," Frankie said showing Desi the envelope.

"I can't fucking believe her!" Desi said with fire in her eyes. "Are you all right?" she asked looking at Frankie.

Frankie sighed and said, "Yes, I'm okay. It was a punch to the gut but, I'm over it already." Frankie ran her hand through her short brown hair then continued sorting the mail.

"Are you sure? I'd like to go kick her ass!"

"I'm sure. I promise, I'm over her but, it still pisses me off that I was so stupid. I know better than to date someone that's never been with a woman. It's happened to me twice now and I'm never doing it again!"

"It seems like it's only been a minute since you broke up."

"It's been six months. She'd been seeing him for a month before she told me."

"Typical, they find out what sex is supposed to be like and lose their fucking minds. Now that she knows she'll be telling him what to do but, you just wait, she'll be crawling back."

"Stop, Des, it wasn't like that," Frankie said, her green eyes softening. "Now that it's been six months and I can look at it from a distance, I think Laura really just needed a friend at the time and was lonely. Then I came along and well, you know what happened."

"Yeah, I know. You were kind to her as you are to everyone. I wonder what she would do if we showed up at the wedding?"

"We're not going to the wedding. In her own way I'm sure she was just trying to be nice."

"What wedding are we not going to?" Stella asked walking into the office. Stella Morris was the third partner in the gym and at 52 looked like a fitness model. Her auburn hair was pulled into a pony tail as she was just finishing teaching a yoga class for beginners.

"Laura sent the gym an invitation to her wedding to the guy she cheated on Frankie with," Desi said, filling Stella in.

"Easy Des," Stella said while placing her arm around Frankie's shoulder. She met Frankie's eyes with her own soft brown ones full of compassion. "Wow, sorry Frankie, I'm sure that had to sting."

"I'm all right, really, you two," Frankie said looking at them both. "I'm happy for her."

"Of course you are because that's the kind of person you are," Stella said.

"Anyway, it's been six months, I've moved on and that's that," Frankie said handing each of them their mail.

"Moved on? You haven't had one date since you broke up," said Desi.

"Exactly, taking a break is a good thing," answered Frankie.

"Maybe for Ross and Rachel but, how is it a good thing for a beautiful, kind, successful, hot lesbian like you?" asked Desi.

"You happen to be a beautiful, kind, successful, hot lesbian, too and I don't see you dating anyone," countered Frankie.

"Oh you two, it doesn't do any good to compare your lesbian hotness," Stella said chuckling. "Besides, Frankie has a strength class in 10 minutes. Go throw some weight around - it always makes me feel better."

"Yep, I'd better go set up," Frankie said walking toward the door. "See y'all later."

"Was that your last class today?" Desi asked Stella.

"Yep, I'm done. Nat has the evening dance class, aren't you doing the evening spin class?"

"Yes, I haven't seen Natalie this afternoon, have you?" Natalie Stevens was their all-around instructor that taught the classes that Stella, Frankie, and Desi didn't cover. She had been with them since almost the beginning. In the 10 years that they had been open, Your Way had become one of the premier fitness centers in town. They specialized in making everyone feel welcome no matter their fitness level, experience, or coordination. There was something for everyone at Your Way.

"She opened this morning, had the afternoon off, and is coming back for that last dance class. That girl would work all day and evening if we'd let her," said Stella.

"That's why I haven't seen her. Frankie and I are closing tonight so I didn't get here until afternoon. Do you think we should go to Laura's wedding?"

"Why would we do that? I know Frankie says she's over her but still, that woman hurt our friend. And I don't care if she didn't mean to."

"I agree. I just don't get it. Frankie is the best girlfriend anyone could have. Laura's crazy for letting her go. I guess I thought she'd see that if we were there."

"It doesn't matter, she's out of Frankie's life and ours too. I'm going home. I've had enough of this place today."

"I expect folks to come by for tours tomorrow, our special with three free one-on-one sessions expires in two days," Desi said, reminding Stella.

"Got it. I'll be ready. See you tomorrow."

～

Olivia King stepped off the scale and sighed. She then got in the shower to get ready for work. That number kept rolling through her mind over and over, it reminded her of a slot machine and when it stopped, she wasn't a winner.

As she looked at herself in the mirror she decided today was the day. She'd been hiding all winter and now it was April. One thing she did like about living in Dallas was the weather; not too cold but hot in the summer. She couldn't imagine wearing shorts the way she looked now. She'd had enough.

She finished drying her shoulder length dark blonde hair and pulled her best friend Sofia's name up on her phone, tapped it and waited. This was a good hair day, so at least she had that.

"Good morning," Sofia answered cheerily.

"Hey, I need a favor."

"Okay, OK. Did you get that? OK, your initials," Sofia said chuckling.

"For the millionth time, that is not funny," Olivia responded, rolling her eyes in the mirror.

"Yes it is! Anyway, what do you need?"

"I need you to come with me after work and take a tour of that fitness gym that's running the special," Olivia explained.

"What gym?

"The gym I've told you about the last two weeks," Olivia said sighing. "Do you ever listen to anything I say?"

"Yes, I just needed a reminder. I seem to recall you mentioning something about it."

"Good. I'll pick you up after work."

"Wait, I have plans after work," Sofia said quickly.

"You owe me. I'll be by after work," Olivia said firmly.

"Owe you, why do I owe you?"

"Two weeks ago you begged me to go to that wine bar with you so you could ogle the bartender... who you later disappeared with leaving me there. Or how about this past Saturday when you drug me to karaoke with your co-workers so you could sneak out early with your boss' assistant and no one would notice."

"I'll be ready, what do I need to wear?"

"Your work clothes are fine, we're just taking a tour, not working out."

"Yippee, I can hardly wait," Sofia said sarcastically.

Later that day as Sofia got in Olivia's car she said, "Tell me again why you're doing this."

"Have you looked at me lately? I'm tired of carrying around this extra weight."

"You might need to lose a few pounds but, you don't look bad," said Sofia.

"Gee thanks. I'm never going to get a girlfriend if I don't do something, so I'm joining a gym and losing this weight." Olivia said matter-of-factly.

"You don't expect me to join with you, do you?"

"No. I just wanted you to go with me for the tour."

They walked through the door of Your Way and Frankie greeted them.

"Welcome to Your Way, I'm Frankie, would you let me show you around?"

Sofia eyed Frankie up and down and whispered to Olivia, "I'd let her do more than show me around."

Olivia ignored her and reached out her hand, "Hi, I'm Olivia and this is my friend Sofia."

"Hi Olivia," Frankie said, taking her hand. She looked into the most beautiful brown eyes she'd ever seen. Suddenly realizing she'd been holding Olivia's hand a little longer than she should, Frankie turned to Sofia and said, "Hi Sofia."

"We'd like to take a tour and were interested in the special you're running," said Olivia. What a beautiful woman she thought, her hand tingling where Frankie had held it.

"Great, right this way. We named the gym Your Way because that's exactly what we want you to do, make it yours. Fitness isn't one size fits all, everyone is unique so your plan has to fit you. What do you like to do? We have several different classes, group and individual sessions, as well as sports too."

"Actually, I'm not really sure. That's why I wanted the tour," explained Olivia.

"With the special you get three one-on-one training sessions so I'm sure we can find something you like. And you're welcome to try all the classes to see which you like best or take a different one every time you come in depending on how you feel."

"I know what I'd like to feel," Sofia whispered as they walked to the treadmills.

"Would you stop," Olivia whispered glaring at her friend.

"This area is for the treadmills. If you'll notice, there are TV's at every machine and you can watch whatever you want as you exercise. Right back here is the free weight area. We have plenty of weights, bars, benches and squat racks. Have you ever lifted weights before?" Frankie asked them.

"Not really," Olivia answered.

"No problem. We'll make sure you know how to use these safely so you can get the most from your workout," Frankie said, smiling at Olivia.

At the end of the free weight section was a wall of windows looking into a workout room. "This is where several of our classes are held," Frankie said as Desi walked out of the room.

"This is Desi Shaw, one of the owners," Frankie said introducing her. "Des, meet Olivia and Sofia. They're taking a tour."

"Hi Olivia, Sofia," Desi said nodding at each of them. "This is one of two workout spaces that we hold classes in. We have spin classes, kickboxing, HIIT workouts, boot camps, dance, and yoga. When there isn't a class you're welcome to work out in the room with the other equipment."

"Dance?" asked Olivia.

"We have dance fitness classes. They are so much fun. I can't dance to save myself but, I feel like I can when I'm teaching or participating in dance fitness class," said Frankie.

"It's all true, I've seen her dance," Desi said chuckling. "But really, you have to try it at least once. It's a lot of fun. And if there is some other activity that we don't offer, tell us about it, we'll see what we can do."

Desi noticed Frankie looking at the front door intently and turned to see what was happening. In walked Laura, Frankie's ex. Before Desi could stop her she reached the group.

"Excuse me, could I talk to you a minute, Frankie?" Laura asked nervously.

Frankie could feel her face reddening. She hadn't seen Laura in six months and certainly didn't think she'd ever walk back into Your Way. She looked at Olivia and Sofia and smiled.

"Would you excuse me for just a minute? Desi will show the workout room and I'll be right back," Frankie said trying to be professional.

"No problem," said Olivia smiling back. She could see that something was going on between Frankie and the woman that just walked in and she noticed how tense Desi had become.

As they walked away Desi realized she was staring a hole through Laura's back and snapped out of it. "Sorry about that," she said to Olivia and Sofia.

"That was tense," said Sofia. "I don't think you like her much."

"Not one of my favorite people," Desi said, taking a deep breath. "That was unprofessional of me, I'm so sorry. Please, let me show you our workout room. And don't think our gym is full of drama because that couldn't be further from the truth."

"Drama can be fun," Sofia said thinking she liked this place.

They looked around the workout room that had mirrors on one wall and equipment on the other. There were spin bikes, weighted balls, jump ropes, foam rollers, and just about any kind of equipment to customize a workout.

As they walked out of the room Desi explained there was another workout space just like it across a hallway that led to the back of the building. When they entered the hallway Frankie caught up with them.

"Do you have any questions? Did Desi explain all the classes and extra equipment in the room?" she asked hurriedly.

"She did," Olivia said, turning around, their eyes meeting. Frankie's green eyes showed a flicker of pain and just as quickly it was gone. Olivia felt the strongest urge to reach out and take her hand but, the moment passed.

As they made their way down the hall, she pointed out the restrooms and dressing rooms. "We'll stop in the dressing room on our way back to the front but I wanted to show you the gym first," she said, walking through double doors and holding them open.

They walked into a gym with basketball hoops and volleyball nets. The court was split so one end was for volleyball and the other for basketball.

"We have a volleyball league and a basketball league at different times during the year. Right now it's set up for both games but we can have two volleyball games or two basketball games going at the same time. You're welcome to shoot baskets or work on volleyball skills when there isn't a game going on," explained Frankie.

"Wow, this is nice! I didn't expect there to be a gym," said Sofia. "Why do they call workout places gyms anyway?"

"Great question that I don't really have an answer to," said Desi. "It seems that fitness centers, health clubs, and gyms are synonymous."

"I think I call it a gym because that's where I started. When I was a kid, we went to the gym to play volleyball and basketball indoors," said Frankie.

"Me too," added Olivia.

"Did you play sports?" asked Frankie.

"Yeah, I did in high school but, I haven't in years."

"I think that's why we have the leagues because Frankie and I still like to play games and you have to have people to make up a team," Desi said.

"Maybe you'll get back into it and play with us," Frankie said to Olivia.

"Oh, I don't know about that. I've got to get some of this weight off before I can even think about that," Olivia answered.

"I keep telling her she looks fine," said Sofia.

Frankie smiled and said, "There are lots of reasons to work out and losing weight is certainly one of them but, I like to look at it in a different way."

"What do you mean?" asked Olivia.

"Exercising has been proven not only to improve physical health but, it also improves mental and emotional health. You hear a lot about self-care these days and I think exercising should be included in that. I want a workout to be joyful. Don't get me wrong, it is work, but after just a few minutes your mood will elevate," explained Frankie.

"Wow, you're passionate about this," said Sofia.

"I know. Sometimes I can get a little carried away but, I want you to get all you can out of every class. I want you to have that joy," said Frankie, eyes sparkling.

Olivia was mesmerized by how passionately Frankie spoke. It made her want to join the gym and start her first workout but, it also made her want to get to know Frankie better. Those green eyes were so bright when she was speaking that way Olivia got lost in them.

"Oh, I forgot to mention that we have training plans too. We can train you one-on-one after identifying your goals or we can make a training plan for you to do on your own. There is always someone here to answer questions or assist you with equipment or whatever you need," said Frankie.

Olivia glared at Sofia before she could whisper something else.

Instead, Sofia looked at Frankie then Desi and said, "Wow, you've convinced me and I wasn't planning on joining."

"You weren't?" Frankie said looking at Sofia confused.

"No, I'm here to support my best friend."

"Oh, I get it. I don't like to go into places by myself for the first time either. We want you to feel comfortable and safe. I'll give you my number so the next time you're by yourself, text me and I'll come out and walk in with you," Frankie said with the kindest eyes looking directly at Olivia.

Olivia smiled nodding her head, "I do feel comfortable."

"Let's go back up to the front so we can show you the recovery area," said Desi. "That's really just a fitness term for a place to sit, relax, and have something to drink or a cup of coffee."

On the walk back to the front Olivia took a minute to walk through the different areas again while Sofia and Desi went to the drink area. Frankie stayed with her and gave her space to look around.

"Are there any questions I could answer for you?" Frankie asked.

"Do you teach classes?"

"I do. Desi, Stella, and I own Your Way. You haven't met Stella yet but, you will. We can teach every class we offer. There are some that I'm better at than others but, we believe it's important that we all can step in wherever needed. Natalie is our other instructor that takes care of interns that we have from time to time."

"Do you teach the one-on-one sessions, too?"

"Yes, we all do that too. Are there any classes that you're interested in or did a training plan appeal to you?" As they walked Frankie realized that there was something about Olivia that made her hope she would join the gym. It was her eyes, she could see the kindness in them and they were the most beautiful brown eyes she'd ever seen. Not just brown, but soft and warm and welcoming.

"I don't want to appear pushy. I want you to know everything about us and that there's a place for you here. Oh man, that didn't sound creepy, did it?" Frankie said cringing.

Olivia laughed, "No, that didn't sound creepy and you haven't been pushy. I can tell that you really love this place and what you do and want your members to, also."

"That's true."

"Why don't we go have one of your fancy recovery drinks and you can tell me about your different membership plans," Olivia said smiling. She did feel comfortable here and hoped she'd gain more than just good health from Frankie.

2

Olivia walked into Your Way and made her way to the dressing room. She had thought about texting Frankie with her offer to walk her in and the thought made her smile. To her surprise, Sofia had decided to join too, so she hadn't needed an escort. Today they were meeting there because Olivia came straight from work. As she walked to the dressing room, Desi waved at her and yelled hello.

She sat on the bench in front of a locker and changed clothes. As she was tying her shoes Frankie walked in.

"Hey Olivia, how are you?" Frankie asked, picking up a towel and throwing it into the basket.

"Actually, I'm still sore from that kickboxing class you taught a couple of days ago," Olivia replied smiling.

"Yeah, but I bet it's a good sore because it means you're getting stronger," Frankie said smiling.

"A good sore, hmm, I'll have to think about that one," Olivia said getting her clothes together and putting them in her bag.

"What class are you taking today?"

"I thought I'd take Stella's yoga class to help some of this soreness."

"It will, good choice. How are the classes, is there one in particular you like?"

"I haven't tried them all yet but, I plan to. Are you about to teach a class?'

"No, I'm cleaning up in here a little. Sometimes these towels seem to miss the basket," she said chuckling.

"I wanted to ask you about the strength class I saw offered."

"That's one I'm teaching," she said excitedly. "It's a six week plan three times a week using free weights. It's offered in the morning and evening. Have you done your one-on-one sessions yet?"

"No. I wanted to be more familiar with everything before I did them."

"Please take advantage of them, they're one of my favorite things."

"Really?"

"Yeah, I can help you with specific things that I'm not able to in the group setting."

"Ok, I'll make sure and schedule them soon."

"Good," Frankie said smiling. "Maybe I'll be able to do them for you."

"Maybe," Olivia said, quietly thinking she'd like that. She had taken a couple of Frankie's classes and thought she had caught Frankie looking at her in a way other than her instructor but, she knew there's no way she'd be interested in someone like her.

"Oh no, did that sound bad? I meant as your trainer," Frankie looked embarrassed.

"I know, why would you think different?" Olivia asked, feeling like Frankie had read her thoughts.

"Trainers and gyms in general get a bad reputation sometimes."

"For what?"

"Well, there's a stereotype that people hook up with their instructors," Frankie said looking away embarrassed.

"Oh, I didn't think that. Besides, I'm not the kind of girl you'd ask out anyway," Olivia said.

"Why would you say that?"

"Because, look at me. I'm overweight and out of shape. That's why

I joined; I want to lose this weight so maybe someone would be interested in me."

"That would have nothing to do with me asking you out!"

"Oh, come on Frankie, you know how important appearance is. That's what people see first," she argued.

"Yeah, but just because someone looks good isn't going to determine whether I ask them out or not. There's a lot more to it."

"Maybe, but aren't you in the appearance business, really?"

"No. I'm in the health and fitness business. I want to help people improve their health and live their best life. Do you really think I'm like that? That it's all about looks?" Frankie said, becoming upset.

"You are a personal trainer, Frankie. That's changing the way people look. And it's easy for you, you're fit and gorgeous."

"It's so much more than that, Olivia. Please tell me how I have given you that impression," Frankie said looking hurt.

"You haven't really, Frankie. I know you keep saying we get more from exercise than just losing weight but ..." Olivia said, not finishing her sentence.

"You know what, let's pick up this conversation after a month and see if you still feel the same way. And just so you know, I ask women out that are kind and that makes them beautiful to me," Frankie said walking toward the door. Over her shoulder she said, "There's a lot more to you than your weight, Olivia. Your yoga class is starting." And with that, she walked out. She couldn't decide if she was angry or hurt or maybe both.

Olivia walked into Stella's yoga class thinking about what Frankie said. She felt like maybe she'd hurt her feelings and should apologize.

"Hey, over here," Sofia said waving at Olivia.

Olivia walked over and took the mat beside Sofia, "Hey."

"What's with you? Why so serious," Sofia asked.

"I think I messed up," replied Olivia.

"What did you do?" Sofia asked, eyeing her friend.

Olivia replayed the conversation she had with Frankie.

"Hmm, that kind of was a shitty thing to say to her about appearances," Sofia said. "Is that what you believe, that she wouldn't ask you out because of the way you look?"

"I guess part of me does. No way she will ever ask me out now."

"What's got into you? Where did your confidence go and why all of a sudden this desire for a girlfriend?"

"I don't know, I just feel like I'm overweight and no one would be interested in me like this. Have you noticed how many dates I've been on lately?"

"Well, I have noticed that you've been working a lot the last few months so how could you have time to date anyway? And what's stopping you from asking someone out, like Frankie?"

"It's been really busy at work, you know that. This subdivision is a big deal. And there's no way she'd go out with me now."

"*You* are a big deal, Olivia. You're a successful architect and anyone would be lucky to go out with you. Answer me this, why are you so confident when it comes to your job but not when it comes to women?"

Stella walked in and said, "Welcome. Let's get started."

Olivia was glad she didn't have to answer that question. She was confident in her job because she was damn good at it but, women were a whole other thing.

Meanwhile Frankie walked around the gym putting weights back on racks, picking up towels and tidying up the area while muttering to herself. She couldn't believe Olivia thought she was so shallow. Surely she didn't act like that. Why did it upset her so much? Actually, she knew why, she liked Olivia and wanted to ask her out but had hesitated until she got to know her a little better.

"Hey, who are you talking to? Yourself?" asked Desi.

"Why can't people put their weights back and pick up their towels? Is it so hard to pick up after yourself?" replied Frankie sighing.

"Well, you and I both know there are always a few that think they don't have to. So, why is that bothering you? We do this every day," replied Desi wondering what was going on with her.

Frankie sighed, "Let me ask you something, Des."

"Shoot."

"Do I act like the way someone looks is important to me?"

"What? I'm not sure I understand what you mean."

"I was talking to Olivia King and she said she wasn't the kind of woman that I'd ask out."

"Yes she is. Do you want to ask her out!" Desi said getting excited.

"Not now, there's no way she'd go out with me. For some reason she thinks she needs to lose weight, that she isn't pretty enough or fit enough for me."

"How did that happen?"

"I don't know! I encouraged her to schedule her one-on-ones and thought it came out wrong, she said it didn't because she wasn't the kind of girl I'd ask out," Frankie said, shaking her head.

"Hmm," Desi said thinking about all Frankie had told her.

Frankie continued, "The bad part is she's taken a couple of my classes and I couldn't keep my eyes off her."

"Wow. She must have body image problems because you're not like that. You know that."

"I know but, it threw me," Frankie said, looking miserable.

"So what ended up happening?"

"We had a conversation about appearance and working out and I told her we'd have another conversation in a month and see if she felt the same way."

"So what are you going to do if she's in your classes?"

"I'm going to make sure she hears me about the benefits of exercise besides losing weight."

Desi paused for a moment, "You know that sometimes it takes people a while to come around. They want instant results."

"Of course I know that, I've only been doing this for twenty fucking years!"

"Dang Frankie, calm down. Let me finish this, you go home."

"Sorry, this is bothering me more than I thought. See you tomorrow." With that Frankie left.

She had ridden her bike back after lunch because she wanted to get a good ride in today. The local triathlon Your Way helped sponsor was coming up in a few months and she planned to enter. There was nothing better than being out on the bike; she rode down to a new subdivision that was being built not too far from the gym. This time of day the workers had gone home and she didn't have to worry about traffic. One of her favorite things was to walk through houses as they were being built and imagine what they'd be like when finished. She'd always wanted to have a house built with her ideas and preferences.

As she rode down the streets, several houses were in the process of being built and others getting ready to start. She could tell how some were going to look on the outside and was surprised that this didn't look like one of those cookie cutter planned subdivisions where all the houses were similar. Whoever was designing these houses had a different idea what a neighborhood looked like and Frankie appreciated it. Who wants their house to look exactly like the one next door? She certainly didn't.

3

This was Olivia's third week at Your Way and she was starting to feel a sense of belonging and ease when she walked through the door. However today she was a little nervous because she was starting the strength program that Frankie was teaching. She had taken classes that Frankie taught since their conversation, and Frankie didn't seem to be upset with her, but this class was different because there would be some one-on-one time adjusting form as they lifted weights. Thank goodness Sofia was doing this with her.

As she made her way to the free weight area she noticed Sofia waving at her from a treadmill, "Come warm up a little with me."

Olivia stepped on the treadmill next to her and said, "Look at you turning into an athlete."

"Haha, not hardly," Sofia said. "Are you ready for this?"

"Yep. I'm looking forward to an actual program planned by someone that knows what they're doing. All these classes have been fun but, you know me, I like a plan."

Sofia laughed, "Says the architect. I actually meant are you ready for the one-on-one attention from Frankie?"

"Yeah, I still feel like I should apologize to her."

"I did my last free one-on-one session yesterday."

"Who did it?"

"Natalie. I did one with Stella and one with Frankie. They were all good. Have you done yours yet?"

"No, I need to schedule them," Olivia said sighing.

"What are you afraid of?"

"Nothing. My work schedule has been crazy again and I didn't want to have to cancel once I scheduled it."

"Right," Sofia said, looking skeptical. "Come on, we'd better go."

They walked over to the weight area and joined six other women. Frankie walked up smiling, "Welcome. We're going to start with a few measurements. Everyone wants to lose weight but there are other ways to know that your body is changing," Frankie said looking right at Olivia. She couldn't hold Frankie's green eyes and looked away but not before smiling slightly.

"I have tape measures and forms to put your results on. In a month we'll do this again and compare the results," she said handing out the forms. "If you'll partner up this will be easier."

As everyone spread out by twos Frankie said, "Ok, I want you to measure your upper arms, chest, waist, upper legs, and calves."

"Where exactly on our upper arms?" Sofia asked.

"Let me show you," she said, taking the tape and turning to Olivia. "Do you mind, if I demonstrate?"

"Sure, go ahead," Olivia said, her heart starting to beat faster.

"You want to hold it up with a bend at the elbow, like this," Frankie said gently raising Olivia's arm. Olivia could feel her cheeks reddening and she could feel her pulse in her ears.

"Measure around the bicep at the largest point. Don't flex, just relax the muscle," she said her fingers grazing over Olivia's arm as she measured. Olivia thought her heart might beat out of her chest.

"Here," Frankie smiled, handing her the tape to measure Sofia's.

"Now, do the other arm," Frankie said, walking around helping people where needed.

"Next is the chest," Frankie said, turning to Olivia. "May I use your tape?"

"Sure," Olivia said, handing the tape to her.

Frankie wrapped the tape around her own chest and turned, "Would you pull that up my back, please." Olivia took the tape and did as Frankie asked. She turned back around and pulled the tape tight across her chest. "You don't want to pull it too tight," she said. "Just until it's snug right across your nipples."

Olivia forgot to breathe as Frankie looked directly at her. She could feel her nipples getting hard simply looking at the tape across Frankie's chest. When Frankie handed her the tape their fingers brushed and Olivia couldn't look away, her eyes burning into Frankie's.

Frankie lost herself in Olivia's beautiful brown eyes for a moment and then came to when Sofia asked, "Where next?"

"Next we'll do the upper thigh," she said looking at Olivia questioning if she could demonstrate again. Olivia gave the slightest of nods and Frankie took the tape and kneeled in front of her.

"You want to measure a little higher than mid-thigh," she said, reaching behind Olivia's leg and bringing the tape to meet in the front. Olivia's eyes were glued to Frankie's hands. Thank goodness she had on capri workout pants because she thought if Frankie touched her skin there she wouldn't be able to swallow the moan forming in her throat.

"Not too high and again don't pull the tape too tight," Frankie said, her voice a little lower. She handed the tape to Olivia to measure Sofia's leg after she recorded the measurement.

"Careful with those hands," Sofia said, breaking the tension. The group chuckled and Olivia shook her head.

"As if," she said, writing down the number.

"Ok, that leaves your calves," Frankie said bending down in front of Olivia again.

"Wait, what about our waist, didn't you want to measure that too?" Sofia asked.

"Sorry, I did," Frankie said a little flustered. "To make it a little easier I want you to measure right across your stomach where your belly button is. That may not be your actual waist but it will be easy to measure in the same place again." She waited while everyone finished and recorded their measurements.

"Now, the calves. Olivia if you'd turn around," said Frankie as she crouched down and looked up at her. Olivia turned around and closed her eyes as Frankie pulled the tape around in front of her leg and measured to the back part of her calf. "Try to measure at the largest part of the muscle."

Knowing Frankie was kneeled behind her with her head at butt level caused Olivia to hold her breath and when Frankie's fingers touched her calf it took all Olivia had not to turn and find her lips with her own. She slowly released the breath she was holding and opened her eyes; Sofia was looking straight at her with a smirk on her face.

"Don't say a word," Olivia said softly but firmly to Sofia. She still had the smirk on her face when Olivia measured her leg.

When they all finished with the measurements Frankie started the class. It took the rest of the time to find starting weights for each individual for the different lifts. The next class would start the actual program. Olivia was thinking this might be the time to schedule her one-on-one sessions with Frankie. If she hadn't felt it before she certainly did today. There was no denying the connection between them.

"Looked like you were enjoying the measuring," Sofia said as they left the gym.

"Was it obvious?" Olivia asked cringing.

"No, but if you didn't notice Frankie was enjoying it just as much as you."

"You think so? I swear Sof, I feel like there's something there but, I know there's no way she'll ask me out after what I said to her."

"Then you ask her out," Sofia suggested.

"Why would she possibly go, after what I said?"

"You'll never know unless you ask, you might be surprised."

"No, when she turns me down it will make classes awkward and then what will I do? No way," Olivia said shaking her head and unlocking her car.

"Ok but..."

Olivia held up her hand, "No buts." Changing the subject she said, "Several of our classmates are getting together at that little bar down the street. Do you want to go?"

"Sure, nothing like a drink after a workout," she said laughing.

They walked into the bar and saw three of the women that were in their class at a table in the corner. Veronica, Stacy, and Alice made room for them to sit.

"Hi ladies, it's Olivia and Sofia, right?" asked Stacy.

"That's right, I'm Sofia and this is Olivia," Sofia said, taking a seat next to Veronica.

"Hi everyone," said Olivia sitting next to Sofia and Stacy.

Across from them Alice said, "So, what did you think of the class?"

"I can't believe I joined the gym in the first place. Olivia dragged me with her the first day to get some information and I joined," Sofia explained chuckling.

"That's great," said Veronica. "I've been coming almost since they opened and I love this place. Stella, Frankie, Desi, and Natalie are the best!"

"We've only been coming for a little less than a month but I can already see changes," Olivia said, surprising herself. She thought about it and sure she'd lost a couple of pounds but she definitely could see improvements in her fitness and energy levels at work. Damn Frankie would really give me a hard time now, she thought smiling to herself.

"I'm sure you can, it doesn't take long if you're consistent," said Stacy.

"I don't know about you ladies but, I like the gym because I've made new friends. Even if I only see them here, it's nice to know someone is around to work out with me," said Veronica.

"That's true. I actually met my girlfriend in the volleyball league at the gym," Alice said smiling.

"Wow, really," said Sofia. "I guess I'm not surprised, this is a great place to meet people," she continued sliding her eyes over to Olivia. "What about the owners, what's their story?" she added looking back at Veronica.

"Stella was married for years, she lost her wife 4 or 5 years ago," said Veronica.

"That's so sad," said Olivia.

"It really was, I'm not sure what was wrong with her but, it hit Stella hard, she was gone for a while."

"Wow, I had no idea. She's so calm and thoughtful," Alice said the others nodded in agreement. "And beautiful. You know, she's one of those people that are beautiful inside and out."

Veronica nodded in agreement, "Desi is single, I think. I haven't seen her at the gym with anyone. And Frankie doesn't have a girlfriend either. I heard her and the woman she'd been seeing broke up a few months ago."

"They both could have anyone they wanted. They're gorgeous," said Stacy.

Olivia was getting more and more uncomfortable as the conversation continued. She didn't feel right gossiping about Stella, Desi, and Frankie. I guess it wasn't really gossiping but, something didn't feel right about it. She turned to Sofia and said, "Hey, you ready to go. I have an early start tomorrow."

"Sure. Ladies, thanks for inviting us. It's nice to know someone else will be groaning from soreness along with me tomorrow," Sofia said laughing.

"It was nice to meet you all," Olivia said. "See you in a couple of days."

"Are you two sticking with the evening class or the morning?" asked Stacy.

"I may have to switch back and forth depending on when I can get to the gym," Olivia answered.

"Me too," said Sofia.

"See you later," Veronica said and Alice waved.

They walked to the car and Olivia said, "I think I'll go back by the gym and schedule a one-on-one class tomorrow with Frankie."

"Don't be afraid, OK. Ask her out!" Sofia said getting into her car. Olivia smiled and waved and drove back to Your Way.

She went inside but couldn't see Frankie anywhere, so she walked to the back and looked in the gym. Stella was putting away balls that were lying around. Olivia picked up a basketball that was nearby as she walked to where Stella racked them.

"Hi Olivia, thanks for helping," Stella said smiling.

"Sure. I was looking for Frankie."

"She left after her last class. Anything I could help you with?"

"I was going to see if I could schedule a one-on-one session with her tomorrow. I need to do the ones that came with my membership when I joined.'

"Let's go up to the front and we'll see what she has scheduled for tomorrow," Stella said.

On the way to the office Olivia said, "Are you the last one here?"

"No, there are a couple people in the workout room. It's been kind of a slow night. Did you like the strength class tonight?"

"Yeah, there wasn't much lifting tonight, but I think I'm really going to like it."

"Good. That's a great class. You might want to hit a yoga class in between strength sessions."

"I will, thanks for the advice."

"That's why I'm here, to make your fitness dreams come true," Stella said smiling.

"I like that. Who knew I'd ever have fitness dreams!"

"Let's see, Frankie has a class at 5:30 tomorrow evening so she should be able to help you after that. Does 6:30 work for you?" asked Stella.

"That will work."

"Okay, I've got you down," Stella said entering Olivia's information into the schedule on the computer. "Hey, look at that Olivia King, OK. I never noticed that before."

"Yeah, Sofia likes to call me OK sometimes. It's kind of confusing if anyone else is around," she said chuckling.

"I like it," Stella said.

"Thanks Stella, see you tomorrow," she said, smiling. As she made her way to her car, Olivia realized she liked coming here more and more. Sure, she liked that she was getting healthy but, she really liked these people and this atmosphere. Who knew!

4

Frankie looked at her schedule and frowned. "Hey, did one of you add a session with Olivia King after my class tonight?"

"I did," replied Stella. "Is there a problem?"

"I need to leave right after class. I should have blocked it off and forgot about it."

"I can cover for you," said Desi.

"It's not that. I'd really like to do it," Frankie said, sighing.

"What's the big deal, we switch out and cover one-on-ones all the time," said Stella.

"I know, but Olivia is different," answered Frankie.

"Oh?" questioned Stella.

"She's kind of special to me."

"Uh-huh, you want to elaborate?"

"Well, at first she was here to lose weight and we had a conversation about appearance and," Frankie said, becoming flustered. "It's hard to explain."

"Are you interested in her? I mean besides her fitness goals," Stella said, raising her eyebrows.

Desi interrupted, "The first day she came to look us over I saw sparks fly."

"You did?" said Frankie.

"Yes. Surely you felt it. I didn't say anything because that's also when Laura came by."

"So, what's going on Frankie?" asked Stella. "Is there something you need to tell us?"

"It's not like that, Stel. She made the comment that I would never ask her out because of her weight. It really bothered me. Since then I've tried to make sure she understands there's more to us, meaning Your Way, than losing weight and there's more to her than a number on the scale," Frankie tried to explain, albeit poorly. "Anyway, I'd really like to do the session."

"I think I get it; you'd like to ask her out but can't because she won't believe you're genuine," Stella said.

"Not exactly, if I don't show up, I'm afraid she'll think I'm avoiding her because we kind of had a moment in class yesterday."

"Well, she did ask specifically for you," said Stella pausing. "Let me do it. I'll make sure she knows it's my fault and not yours."

"'Thanks, I appreciate it."

"But Frankie, you need to be careful. She's a client and that comes first."

"I know, nothing inappropriate has happened."

"No one said it has; I'm glad you're finally interested in someone," said Desi.

"I didn't say that. Besides, a lot of good it does me. She thinks I'm a shallow personal trainer helping people look good."

"No one could think that about you. If anything your heart is too big," Desi said.

"Anyway, Stella please tell her I'd be glad to work with her another time and I'll see her tomorrow in class," Frankie said.

"I will, Frankie," Stella said. "And sorry for the mix-up, it'll be alright."

Frankie smiled, "I hope so."

∼

OLIVIA WALKED into Your Way dressed in a new pair of leggings and a coordinating tank top. Since joining the gym she'd bought several workout bottoms and tops and actually thought about what she would wear to each workout. She knew it was because she hoped to see Frankie. But she also knew she wasn't Frankie's type so why care at all. She looked around but didn't see Frankie anywhere. Then she noticed Stella walking toward her.

"Hi OK," Stella said with a twinkle in her eye.

"Hi Stella," Olivia said, chuckling and shaking her head.

"I messed up yesterday. Frankie won't be able to do your session so I'd love to fill in if that's alright with you."

Olivia was noticeably disappointed, "What do you mean you messed up?"

"I didn't know Frankie had to leave early tonight. She's really sorry because she wanted to do it."

"Is she all right?" asked Olivia.

"Yes, I'm not sure why she had to leave but, I told her I'd fill in. If you'd rather we can schedule another time."

She probably didn't want to be near her after last night and left early on purpose Olivia thought. It was dumb to schedule with her anyway. She took a deep breath and said, "No problem Stella, I'd love to work with you."

On the walk over to the workout room Olivia thought about Frankie's touch, replaying it in her head since last night. Veronica said she was single but Olivia thought Frankie could have her pick of any woman she wanted. Why would she be interested in her? She may have been torturing herself with these mental gymnastics about Frankie, but she couldn't deny the spark she felt whenever they were together and thought Frankie felt it too. Stop, she told herself firmly!

"That is quite an intense look on your face. What's going on in that head of yours, OK," Stella asked.

Olivia snapped out of it. "Sorry, I've just had a lot going on lately with work," she said which wasn't untrue, she had been busy with the new subdivision.

"I'm not sure I know what you do," Stella said, getting them both a workout mat.

"I'm an architect."

"Wow, that's interesting," said Stella nodding her head. "Was there something in particular you wanted to work on in this session?"

"I thought maybe my lifting form, but the yoga stretches you mentioned last night sounded good too," answered Olivia.

"Has work been stressful lately?"

"Yeah, it's always somewhat stressful. I'm designing the new subdivision just down the road from here."

"Wow that does sound stressful. Designing a subdivision! That's amazing, what does it involve?"

"Well, you have a few different house plans but what I'm trying to do is not make them all look the same or each a variety of one another. That's what most planned subdivisions look like and I want this to be different. Of course, that makes things a little harder too, but I think it's worth it."

"I always wondered how they were planned. Have you ever meditated? It's a wonderful stress reliever."

"I haven't much. I've tried a couple of times with little success."

"Here, sit," Stella said pointing to the end of one mat and sitting on the other end. "Let me show you a couple of easy techniques that you can do anywhere."

"Okay, what do I do?"

"Find a comfortable position to sit, relax your arms, shoulders, and face. Close your eyes and take a deep breath in and release it slowly out your nose. Let's take three big breaths and release them."

Olivia did as she was instructed and found she relaxed more and more with each breath.

"Good. Now think of the tension in your body and with each breath you're releasing a little more of that tension until you feel relaxed. Think of blowing it out of your body with each breath."

When Olivia had taken and released three more breaths she did feel more relaxed.

"Do you feel relaxed?" asked Stella.

"I do," replied Olivia.

"Do you ever find you have thoughts flying in and out of your head and simply want to calm them down?"

"Yes! That happens to me all the time," Olivia exclaimed.

"It happens to me too. Sometimes you just want to turn them off and breathe."

"Exactly!"

"This breathing technique we're using can help. Want me to show you how?"

"Absolutely!"

"Okay, close your eyes and we're going to breathe in and out as before, but this time I want you to focus on your breath. Follow it into your chest and out again through your nose. If you want, you can place one hand on your heart and the other on your stomach. Feel your chest and stomach rise and fall as you follow the breath in and out."

Stella paused for Olivia to take several breaths. Then she continued, "Now keep breathing in and out and when a thought enters your mind simply release it and focus on your breath again. Imagine it as if the thoughts are bouncing off your stream of breath as you focus on in and out."

Olivia concentrated on what Stella said. Sure enough thoughts of work came and went through her mind. And then there was Frankie. Thoughts of why she wasn't here to do this session came and Olivia let them bounce off. The same thing happened with thoughts of last night at their strength class and even thoughts of their conversation that Olivia still thought about apologizing for. But then there was nothing. Just her breath. In and out, taking all the thoughts and tension with it.

"Okay Olivia, let's take one more deep breath and open your eyes," Stella said.

Olivia did as Stella said and opened her eyes. Stella was smiling at her.

"So, do you feel a little less stressed and more relaxed?"

"I do. That was as good as a workout," replied Olivia. "I mean, I've noticed that after a workout I feel a lot better, less stressed than before."

Stella smiled and thought to herself that Olivia was definitely learning there's more to Your Way than losing weight. "That's how it's supposed to work. Exercising, whether high intensity or low, is one of the best stress relievers out there. A lot of people don't realize that."

"I would be one of those people. I've learned to love working out, not just because I've lost weight but because it makes me feel good." The more she thought about it, the more she owed Frankie an apology. She was right, there's more than just losing weight.

"You can use this breathing exercise anytime. At work, in traffic, here. Simply take a moment and three deep breaths. I think it'll almost cure anything," Stella laughed.

"Thanks Stella. I will use this, especially at work."

"Good. I'm glad I could show you something new. Tell me, Olivia, I know you're taking Frankie's strength program; do you have any goals that you're working toward?"

"Not specifically. I know that's something I should do, set goals. I think I know more now and have looked at the other programs you offer."

"Sometimes it helps to have something to train toward, like a race, a game, or an event."

"I stop in occasionally and watch a basketball or volleyball game in the gym, but I don't feel good enough to play yet. I mean, eventually I might want to try."

"Do you know how to swim?"

"I do," Olivia looked at Stella questioningly.

"How about biking, can you ride a bike?"

"Sure I can, I love to ride bikes. I just haven't done it in ages. Why?"

"Well, we help sponsor a triathlon every year. That would be a great goal to train toward."

"A triathlon? Are you crazy? Me?"

Stella laughed, "My wife used to ask me that all the time. And no,

I'm not crazy." For a moment happy memories flashed through Stella's mind and across her face.

"Oh no, I'm so sorry, Stella," Olivia said, obviously upset.

"Don't be," Stella said, reaching out and putting her hand on Olivia's arm. "These are nice memories, I loved it when she called me crazy."

They were both silent, Olivia didn't know what to say.

"Olivia, really, it's all right. She died almost five years ago. Some days are still very hard but that was a really nice memory and I'll go to bed happy tonight. So, thank you," Stella said smiling.

"You're welcome, I think..."

Stella laughed, "Now, back to this triathlon."

"You really think I could do a triathlon?"

"Of course you can. I wouldn't have suggested it if I didn't think you could do it."

Olivia looked at her skeptically.

"Do you have a bike?"

"Actually, I do. My ex left hers and never came back to get it. It's a pretty good one too."

"Would it bother you to ride it since it was hers?"

Olivia scoffed, "Not at all! We didn't break up on the best of terms."

"I'm not sure there are many break-ups that are on the best of terms. Relationships are hard and so is breaking up. I don't care how adult we all try to act."

"Isn't that the truth!"

"Okay, you know how to swim, you've got a bike, and I've seen you run on the treadmill so you're all set."

"Wait, hold up!"

"Come on OK, we were talking about a goal, something to work toward."

"Yeah but, a triathlon is big. I've never done anything like that before."

"Oh Olivia, you can do so much more than you think you can. Believe me, you can do this. I'll be right with you, we're all doing it."

"All?"

"Desi, Frankie, Natalie, and me. We sponsor it and we also participate. The beauty of this is that yes, it's considered a race but, it's really about completing something you've worked toward. I can't tell you how proud you're going to be when you cross the finish line," Stella said beaming.

"Okay," Olivia said shakily. "But I don't know anything about training for a triathlon."

"We have a beginner program that I'll email to you before you leave tonight."

"Wow, I guess I'm doing this," Olivia said with a little more confidence.

"Yes, you are," Stella said raising her hand for a high five. Olivia slapped hands and a huge smile began to grow on her face.

"We'll all help you train. I swim just around the corner at the Y. The membership is cheap to swim only. I sometimes bike around here in-between classes. If the weather is nice, I run outside. If not there's always the treadmill. See, you can do this."

"Now, if my work schedule will cooperate," said Olivia.

"You have plenty of time. Come on, let's go to the front and I'll email that schedule to you. And we can set up your other one-on-ones," Stella said standing and offering her hand to Olivia to help her get up.

Olivia took her hand standing, "Stella, thanks so much for this. I loved the meditation you taught me and plan to use it tonight when I get ready for bed. And..."

Stella looked at Olivia making her look up, "And, what?"

"And, thanks for believing in me. There's no way I would have even considered doing this triathlon if you hadn't had all this confidence in me."

Stella smiled, "You're welcome." Then she put her arm around her, "I wish you could see the Olivia I see."

Olivia nodded.

"You will. It won't be long and you'll see what I see. And when you do, watch out! All that confidence can be like a magnet. Come on."

They walked to the front and Stella set Olivia up with sessions and the training program.

"Thanks again, Stella,"

"I had a great time tonight too, Olivia. See you tomorrow."

With that Olivia walked to her car feeling strong and happy. She thought about what Stella said all the way home. If she could see what Stella sees? Hmm, maybe she should take a better look at herself.

∽

Frankie drove up to the local animal shelter and saw Grace Gibson's car. She pulled into a parking space next to her and got out. Grace was the counselor that Frankie had been seeing since she and Laura broke up. One of Frankie's clients was a psychiatrist in the same practice and had mentioned counseling in one of her classes, so Frankie gave it a try. She considered the decision to see Grace professionally as one of the best she'd ever made.

She walked in and found Grace in the lobby. "Hey," Frankie said, making her way over.

"Hi, I was just about to get our leashes and see who we could walk first," she said handing a leash to Frankie.

They went to the kennels and one of the shelter workers helped them with the dogs and they made their way out the door.

"Are you sure you don't mind having a session while we walk the dogs," asked Grace.

"I told you, I love this. I don't mind at all."

"Sometimes it can be easier to talk when you're not sitting in an office. That's a beautiful dog you're walking."

"I know, isn't she?" Frankie said as the pitty mix walked obediently next to her.

"She's really well behaved too. Pit bulls have the worst reputation and it isn't fair," said Grace.

"I know, they're not bad dogs at all."

"Well, we have an hour, let's see how many we can give a little walk. So, how have you been since our last session?"

"Things have been busy at the gym but, that's good. I'm a little anxious today though."

"Do you know why you're feeling anxious or is it in general?"

"I know why. There's this new client, Olivia, I told you about her last time."

"I remember. Did something happen?"

"Kind of," Frankie said, remembering their class the night before. "She's taking a strength class I'm teaching and at the first class we do measurements."

Grace listened and let Frankie continue.

"I asked her to let me do her measurements so I could show the class," she said sighing.

"Is there some reason you used her and not someone else?" asked Grace.

"Probably, but I didn't think about it at the time," Frankie said replaying it in her head.

"Are you attracted to her?"

"Yes. I couldn't have said that two days ago but, there is something about her that I've been attracted to since she walked into the gym a month ago. And it isn't just her looks, that's why it's so hard. Because of our conversation about appearance she'd never believe me now."

"Why?"

"She said she's not the type of girl I'd ask out because of her weight which is crazy. And now she's been working out a month, lost weight and if I ask her out now..." said Frankie.

"If you ask her out now that she's lost weight she'll think she was right in the beginning."

"Exactly. And I felt like if I asked her out when she first came in it'd be inappropriate as her trainer."

"Do you think she's interested in you?"

Frankie thought about this while they walked along silently. "I think so. I feel something every time I'm around her and we kind of had a moment the other night. Then she scheduled a one-on-one session with me."

"What happened?"

"It was scheduled for now."

"I'm not following. Now?"

"I forgot to block out my schedule and Stella scheduled her after my last class today but, I had someone else take my class so I could leave early to be here for our appointment."

"I see," said Grace.

"I didn't find out until this morning so it was too late to reschedule."

"Reschedule who? Olivia or our appointment?"

"Both."

"So, you think she's interested in you too?"

"Not now. I know she's going to think I had Stella take her one-on-one so I wouldn't have to."

"Why do you think that? It was a simple mistake."

"I'd been reminding her to schedule the one-on-ones and then I don't show. How would that make you feel?"

Grace chuckled, "I'm the one that asks that question. But, why do you think this is upsetting you?"

Again they walked in silence while Frankie collected her thoughts. "I haven't told anyone at the gym that I'm seeing you. I'm not ashamed or worried about what they would think, I simply want this for me. This is my time."

"Okay."

"I thought about explaining it to Stella and having her tell Olivia, but that seemed like such a bad idea. What a mess."

"I understand what you're saying but, is that why you're upset?"

"No. I haven't thought about another woman and felt what I do when Olivia is around since Laura and I broke up."

"And?"

Frankie sighed and said, "I finally feel something and screw it up within the first couple of days. And now every time I see her, I feel more and more drawn to her, but I'm afraid to do anything about it."

"What are you afraid of?"

"I'm not afraid of rejection, I've had plenty of that. But I don't want her to think I'm one of those shallow people that only cares about looks."

"So what do you do?"

"Here's where you could really help by telling me what to do," said Frankie.

"You know it doesn't work that way. But I will say this, maybe you're not giving Olivia enough credit. What if you told her why you didn't ask her out in the beginning? She could believe you, it is the truth," said Grace.

"I don't know," said Frankie thinking about what Grace said.

"Come on, we have a little time left. Let's take these back and walk a couple more dogs."

Frankie nodded and followed Grace inside to change dogs.

When they were outside again Grace said, "Frankie, are you ever still?"

Frankie looked at her confused, "Still? What do you mean?"

"Well, you teach classes all day, you're training for the triathlon, do you ever simply sit still?"

"Hmm, not really. When I'm busy I don't have time to think."

"I don't think that's necessarily true. You've certainly had plenty of time to think about Olivia and what she thinks of you."

Frankie shrugged but didn't say anything.

"You know this as well as anyone that sometimes you need to rest. Between now and our next session I want you to sit with yourself for a few minutes. You don't have to do it every day, but sit down and let your mind rest. It's been working overtime with all you do and now with Olivia. Let it rest, let your thoughts calm. Then we'll talk about it next time."

"Sit still and let my mind rest. Stella has been after me for years to meditate. Is that what you mean?" Frankie asked.

"Meditation is good, but you don't have to do that. Just sit and relax, read a book, watch TV."

"But exercise is relaxing to me."

"Still, Frankie. Be still, okay. Trust me, try it."

"Okay, got it," Frankie said.

5

Olivia looked up and couldn't believe it was already five o'clock. Where had the day gone? Her phone vibrated and she looked at the screen and could see Sofia's smiling face.

"Hey Sof, how's your day?" she said, answering.

"Not so bad. My students might have actually learned something today," she said chuckling. Sofia was a high school math teacher. Students loved her and she was good at her job. "Hey, do you want me to swing by and pick you up to go pump some iron?" she said growling in a very bad Arnold Schwarzenegger impression.

"Ha ha. No, I'm not near ready to go home yet. I'll have to meet you there, good thing I brought my workout clothes with me. It's been a wild day. I'm looking forward to relieving some of this stress."

"Ok. Veronica texted me and said they are going to meet again after class on Friday if you're interested."

"Veronica? When did you trade numbers?"

"I went by the gym yesterday to pick up my jacket I left there the other night. She was there and asked for my number."

"Uh-huh and what does that mean?" Olivia said a bit suggestively.

"It doesn't mean what you're thinking. She wants to get a group chat going with our class. I'm sure she'll be asking for your number tonight."

"Well dang, I was hoping at least one of us was getting more than good health from the gym," said Olivia.

"I think you could if you'd just give it a try."

"Me?"

"Yeah, you. There's something going on between you and Frankie. I don't know why you won't do something about it."

Olivia sighed, "I kind of tried to do something about it. I scheduled a one-on-one session with her, but she didn't show; she sent Stella instead."

"I'm sure there was a good reason."

"It doesn't matter. I really liked working with Stella, and she's teaching me how to meditate."

"Meditate?"

"Yeah, I hope it'll help me; things here at work have become more and more hectic," Olivia said.

"I'll let you get back to it then. See you at class."

"Bye Sof," Olivia said, then took a deep breath and looked at the plans piling up on her desk. Eventually she knew things would quiet down somewhat when they started the next phase of houses, but until then she was busy and these gym classes meant more and more to her.

She changed at the office and walked into Your Way ready for a good workout. Sofia was already there talking to Veronica and Stacy next to a bench. She walked up and joined the group.

"Hey Olivia, I wanted to get your phone number so I could put you on the group text. I thought it would be fun to meet up after our classes some days."

"Sure," Olivia said, noticing Sofia looking at her and smirking. She took Olivia's phone and put her number in.

Frankie walked up and said, "Olivia, could I talk to you for a minute before class starts?"

"Sure." She walked with Frankie away from the group. "What's up?"

"I wanted to apologize for not being able to do your one-on-one yesterday. I'm so sorry," Frankie said with sadness in her green eyes fidgeting from one foot to the other.

Wow, Frankie really looked like she was sorry. All Olivia wanted to do was take that sadness away. She reached out and put her hand on Frankie's forearm and felt her calm underneath her fingers. "It's okay. Stella explained there was a mix up, don't worry about it."

Frankie slowly smiled and looked into Olivia's soft brown eyes for a moment and then said, "It's not okay. I've been reminding you to do those sessions and when you schedule one, I wasn't there. I want you to know that rarely happens."

"Stella said you cover for each other all the time."

"We do but, I didn't know you had scheduled it. If I'd known I'd have found a way to be there," Frankie said earnestly.

Olivia smiled and nodded her head. "Thanks Frankie, I appreciate that. Everything worked out, I had a great session with Stella."

"I'm glad. If you want, after class we can schedule your other sessions," Frankie said hopefully.

Olivia said, "Um, sorry. After last night's session I scheduled the others with Stella. She's teaching me to meditate."

Frankie's face fell. She recovered quickly, hoping Olivia didn't notice. "Oh, that's great. Stella is wonderful with meditation. She's always trying to get me to meditate. I'm glad it's working for you," Frankie said, rambling a little. She looked around and realized it was time for class to start. "Thanks again for understanding Olivia. I'd better get class started." With that Frankie walked away feeling she'd let Olivia down.

Olivia watched her back as she walked away and couldn't shake the feeling that she had somehow hurt Frankie's feelings. How does this keep happening? She slowly walked over to Sofia and began class.

They partnered up and Frankie led them through a warm up, then explained each movement as the class progressed. Olivia caught Frankie looking at her a couple of times but when their eyes met Frankie looked away.

"What did Frankie want earlier?" Sofia asked as she spotted Olivia on the bench press.

"She apologized for not being here last night for my session."

"Oh, did something happen?"

"Why do you ask that?" Olivia said switching positions with Sofia.

"She looked pretty serious when she walked away."

"I think I hurt her feelings again," Olive intensely whispered.

"How?"

Everyone was finished so Frankie explained the next move before Olivia could answer. Sofia looked at her questioningly. Olivia shook her head and mouthed the word "Later" silently. Sofia nodded and they continued the class.

Frankie walked among the group helping with form, but she never came very close to Olivia and Sofia. Olivia was sure she'd messed up again; Frankie was definitely avoiding her. Frankie started telling everyone about the triathlon the gym was sponsoring.

Olivia said to Sofia, "I'm going to do that."

"What?" Sofia said, turning toward her.

"The triathlon. Stella told me about it yesterday and said she thinks I can do it, so I entered and I'm training for it."

"No shit!" exclaimed Sofia.

"Shh," Olivia said, her eyes widening when a couple of people turned their way including Frankie.

"Okay, that's it for today, let's get in a circle and do a few stretches and we're done," said Frankie leading the group.

When they were through Stacy walked up to Olivia and Sofia and asked, "Are you coming with us Friday night?"

Sofia said, "I think so. It's not like I have a hot date or anything." She paused then added, "Yet."

Olivia laughed, "I'm not sure, probably."

"Good, see you then," Stacy said smiling at Olivia before walking off.

"Hmm, someone is interested," Sofia murmured. "And not in me," she said quietly.

Olivia rolled her eyes and started to leave when from behind Frankie said, "Did I hear you say you're doing the triathlon, Olivia?"

Olivia turned and met Frankie's excited green eyes. She couldn't help but smile and said, "You did hear me say that. Stella talked me into last night."

"That's awesome! Good for you."

"We'll see, I've never done anything like this before."

"That will make it an adventure," Frankie said excitedly. "If you need any help or want to train together, let me know. I'd love to help you."

"I'm sure I'll need help. Stella emailed a training guide, but I'll still need help."

"I ride around here nearly every day. I've got a great place nearby in a new subdivision going up. There's very little traffic." At the mention of the subdivision Olivia was designing Sofia started to interrupt, but a look from Olivia stopped her before she said anything. Frankie continued excitedly, "We run around here, too."

"Stella told me about the Y and swimming."

"Oh good, most of us swim there too," said Frankie. She then realized how animated she'd been and looked at Olivia and Sofia.

"Sorry, I get excited when someone takes on a new adventure like this," she said, a little embarrassed.

"You sure do," said Sofia.

"The feeling when you cross the finish line is unbelievable. I can't wait for you to experience that. I've done this race several times and it still feels awesome," she said her eyes lighting up again. "I'm so happy you're doing this, Olivia."

"I haven't done it yet. But the way you and Stella seem to believe in me makes me think I can."

"Oh, you can! I know it!"

"Hey wait, you have a bike?" asked Sofia.

"Uh yeah, Beth left hers when she moved out."

"Oh. You deserved so much more from that shit storm," said Sofia.

"Sofia!" exclaimed Olivia, her face turning red.

"Sorry, but it's true and you know it!" Sofia turned to Frankie and said, "Talk about a bit—"

"Oh my god Sofia, stop!" Olivia said, interrupting her before she could finish. Olivia was so embarrassed.

Frankie didn't know what to say but she did want to rescue Olivia. "Bad break-up?"

"Yes. Sofia tends to talk too much at times," Olivia said staring daggers at her best friend.

"It's okay. I've been there," Frankie said reassuringly.

"You have? What happened?" asked Sofia.

"Sofia, that's none of your business!" Olivia said.

"It's okay. Mine was the ultimate break-up. She left me for a man," Frankie stated solemnly, shaking her head.

"Oh no! That is the ultimate," said Sofia.

"It gets better, she's marrying him," Frankie said flatly.

"Oh Frankie, I'm so sorry," said Olivia, feeling such compassion she couldn't help but to grab Frankie's elbow.

"It's okay. Actually, that's why I missed our session last night."

"I don't follow," said Olivia.

"When Laura left, I started seeing a counselor. I had an appointment yesterday. I have no idea why I'm telling you this, I haven't told anyone, not even Desi," Frankie said with sadness.

"I'm glad you felt like you could tell us," said Olivia.

"Yeah Frankie, we won't say anything to anyone. I can be outspoken, but that's your business not anyone else's," reassured Sofia.

"Enough sad talk, we should be celebrating your triathlon adventure. Thanks for listening, you two," Frankie said smiling at them both.

"Anytime, Frankie," Olivia said sincerely.

"I've got to get my bag from the dressing room. I'll be right back," Sofia said, leaving them.

"I'm sorry you had to go through that, Frankie. And there's nothing wrong with seeing a counselor. I did after my break-up," Olivia told Frankie, embracing this moment alone.

"You did?"

"I did. Beth made me think there was something wrong with me, that I wasn't good enough. No matter what I did, it wasn't enough. It did a real number on my self-confidence and I buried my feelings in food. That's where the extra weight came from. I think I was trying to eat my way back to happiness. It didn't work," Olivia said chuckling. She looked at Frankie and said, "I've wanted to apologize to you, and this seems like the perfect time."

"Apologize, for what?"

"My idiotic comments about appearance. When I first came here my self-esteem was nonexistent. You told me there was a lot more to Your Way than just losing weight. Of course, you're right. I've wanted to tell you that for a while, but I didn't know how."

"It's okay, Olivia. You don't need to apologize."

"Yes, I do. I obviously have some of my confidence back. And that's because of you and the others. I implied you were all about looks and I know that's not true. I hope you'll forgive me."

"There's nothing to forgive," she said, feeling such relief that Olivia didn't think she was shallow and also feeling pride they had helped her.

"Am I interrupting," said Sofia walking up to them.

Olivia looked at Frankie and smiled, "All good?"

"All good," Frankie said smiling back.

As Olivia and Sofia walked to their cars Sofia said, "Well, that was interesting."

"It sure was," Olivia said, replaying the conversation over.

"Hey, see you tomorrow?" asked Sofia.

"Not sure, I'm doing my first bike ride tomorrow after work."

"You don't expect me to do this triathlon with you, right?"

Olivia chuckled, "No, I don't."

"Good, because there's no way. See ya, OK."

"Bye Sof," Olivia said, getting into her car. On the way home she couldn't help thinking about how dejected Frankie sounded when talking about her break-up. All she wanted to do was take her in her arms and tell her everything would be all right. She was glad to finally apologize for her earlier comments to Frankie and hoped maybe they could if nothing else, become friends. Maybe this triathlon would be a way for them to spend more time together. Olivia's heart started beating faster whenever she thought about the triathlon and training. They believed in her, now all she had to do was believe, too.

~

Frankie found Stella and Desi in the office after her class.

"Hey," Desi said to Frankie. "Good class?"

"Yeah, it was," said Frankie. "Stella, I didn't get a chance to ask you earlier but how did it go with Olivia King last night?"

"Great. I like her, it's been fun watching her change with every class she takes."

"That's good, thanks for covering for me. She said she'd scheduled the rest of her sessions with you," Frankie said, clearly disappointed.

"Hey, I didn't ask her to, Frankie. What's the deal?"

"Nothing," Frankie said looking away from them both.

"Look, I'd let you do them, but she wants to learn to meditate."

"Yeah, she told me," said Frankie.

"Oh no, you like her," exclaimed Stella looking from Frankie to Desi.

"Sure, I like her. I told you the other day she was special," Frankie said shrugging.

"No! I mean you like, like her," said Stella as she stood and forced Frankie to look at her.

"What are we, in middle school?" Frankie said.

"Oh Frankie, it doesn't matter if we're in middle school or grown women; when you get that little feeling in your stomach when someone you like walks in the room, you know what I mean," Stella said, putting her arm around Frankie's neck and pulling her into a side hug. "You're interested in Olivia King aren't you? You all but admitted it the other day."

"Yes, but…" Frankie said.

"But what? Again, I'm glad you're finally interested in someone," said Desi.

"Oh my god, I do feel like I'm in middle school. She apologized to me tonight for those appearance comments she made earlier."

"That's what was stopping you from asking her out, right?" said Stella.

"Yeah, but now I don't know. She said you'd talked her into doing the triathlon."

"I did," said Stella.

"I told her that she could train with us, that I'd be glad to help her," Frankie said, sounding hopeful.

"Good. Now you have a reason to spend time with her outside the gym," Desi said.

"Yeah, we'll see," Frankie said, lost in thought. Olivia did seem to be okay with training together. Stella was right, Frankie's stomach did do a little flip anytime she saw Olivia. Why did this have to be so hard? Fear? Rejection? Was there something else? She knew what she'd be talking to Grace about in her next session.

6

Olivia was glad Friday finally arrived and was looking forward to her class. It had been a long week, but her conversation with Frankie on Wednesday gave her hope that they could at least be friends.

Frankie walked in just in time for class to start so Olivia didn't get a chance to talk to her, but she did smile when their eyes met. What was it about this green eyed, dark haired fitness instructor that captivated Olivia so? Frankie was genuine, that's what Olivia liked so much. She gave encouragement but she also made her feel like she could accomplish anything. Olivia felt like she was growing stronger every day and not just physically, but mentally and emotionally, too.

"How did the bike ride go yesterday," Sofia asked.

"It was like riding a bike," Olivia said, trying to be funny. Sofia looked at her sarcastically. "It was fun. I'm sure when I get on it tomorrow my butt will tell me otherwise. I didn't go too far. I did 5 miles, the race is 10 miles so I think I can do it."

"Good for you. Come on we're at the deadlifts next."

"Sofia, are you liking this? Coming to the gym, working out?"

Sofia stopped and looked at her, "Yeah, I do. I know it's surprising, but I do. I like the people we've met and I feel better. Who knew?"

"Good. I know you came with me for support but I never expected you to join with me. You do know that."

"Of course I know that. You're my best friend OK, but that doesn't mean I'd sweat *just* for you. I'm doing this for me too."

Olivia laughed, "Of course you are."

They made it through the rest of class and had finished stretching when Stacy walked over to them.

"Hey, are you two coming with us?"

Olivia had forgotten they were meeting the group after class. She looked at Sofia with raised eyebrows.

"I don't have a hot date so sure why not," Sofia said chuckling.

"Yeah, I'll go for a little bit," said Olivia. She thought they might as well get to know the group better since they seemed to want her and Sofia to be there.

"Great! I guess I'll see you both there," Stacy said smiling as she walked away.

"I think Stacy has the hots for you," Sofia said to Olivia.

"No, she doesn't. How are you so sure it isn't you she's interested in?" Olivia asked Stacy.

"Because I can tell, it's the way she looks at you," said Sofia.

"And how does she look at me?"

"Who's looking at you?" said Frankie walking up.

"Stacy," said Sofia. "I think she has the hots for Olivia." Olivia felt her cheeks redden as her mouth dropped open. She couldn't believe Sofia said that in front of Frankie.

"Can you blame her?" Frankie said looking at Olivia, feeling a pang of jealousy.

"Exactly," said Sofia. "Hey, a few of us are meeting up at the bar on the corner. Do you want to come with us, Frankie?"

"Uh, I probably shouldn't. I'm not sure you want me there, isn't it an after class thing for the group," Frankie said hesitantly.

"Why wouldn't we want you there? Of course you're welcome," said Olivia.

"Yeah, just because you're the one making us sore and sweaty doesn't mean you can't join," said Sofia chuckling.

"I'll think about it, maybe next time," said Frankie hesitantly.

"There's Desi," Sofia said looking past them. "I need to talk to her real quick then we can go," she said to Olivia and walked off.

"I was wondering if you'd like to go for a bike ride tomorrow?" said Frankie.

Olivia smiled then her face fell, "Oh, I can't tomorrow, I have work. But, what about Sunday?"

"I could do Sunday," Frankie said with a big smile. "Is afternoon all right?"

"Yes, that would be perfect," Olivia said happily.

"Let's meet here, if that's all right, and I'll find us a good route."

"Sounds good. This should be fun," Olivia said, giving Frankie an even bigger smile.

Frankie nodded, looking into those happy brown eyes she nearly lost her breath, "It will."

Sofia joined them, "I'm ready if you are."

"Don't let me keep you. Have fun," said Frankie. "Oh wait, Olivia can I have your cell number to text you about the bike ride?"

"Sure," said Olivia.

"Dang, I don't have my phone with me, it's in the office."

"I have mine. Give me your number and I'll send you a text."

Frankie smiled and gave her the number. Olivia sent her a quick text and said, "Done. You should have a text from me when you get your phone."

"Thanks. I'll see you Sunday, have fun with the group," Frankie said leaving them.

Sofia said, "So, you have a date?"

"No, it's not a date. We're meeting Sunday to train for the triathlon."

"Uh-huh, with any luck you could be riding more than bikes," Sofia said suggestively.

"Ugh, will you stop," said Olivia walking toward the door.

"You say that now but, you know you want to," Sofia said, catching up with her.

Sofia wasn't exactly wrong, Olivia thought. Maybe this bike ride would be the start of at least a friendship with Frankie outside the gym... and from there who knows.

"Come on, let's go. I'm sure they're waiting on us at the bar," said Olivia.

"Hey, I bet you a beer that when we walk in, there will be an empty seat next to Stacy and she'll try to get you to sit there," said Sofia.

"Oh, come on. I'll take that bet. She's not into me," Olivia said shaking her head.

Olivia opened the door to the bar and Veronica waved to them. There were four people already there and two empty seats. And one was next to Stacy. Sofia walked up and sat down leaving the seat next to Stacy for Olivia.

After greeting everyone Olivia said, "Have you ordered yet? I'm going to the bar and get a beer, does anyone need anything?"

"We've already ordered," said Alice.

"What do you want, Sofia?" asked Olivia.

"I'll have a beer," she said smirking at Olivia.

"I'll go with you," Stacy said, getting up.

Olivia smiled and walked to the bar. She ordered and checked with Stacy to see if she wanted anything. Stacy shook her head.

"So, are you enjoying the class?" she asked Olivia.

"Yeah, I like it and pretty much everything at Your Way," she answered without looking at her, keeping her eyes instead on the bartender getting their beers.

"Have you and Sofia been friends for a long time?"

"Uh yeah, since third grade. How old are you in third grade?" she answered.

"Eight or nine I guess," said Stacy.

"Wow, then we've been friends for 25 years. I'd never really thought about it but that's a long time."

"That is. You're thirty-three then? I just wondered since you two always partner up."

Olivia nodded as the bartender set their beers down. She reached for her money when Stacy said, "Here let me get that."

"No, that's not necessary, I've got it."

"Too late," Stacy said, handing the bartender money.

"Well, thanks," she said, taking the beers and backing from the bar with Stacy right behind her. Olivia knew she'd been fooling herself. Stacy was definitely interested. Olivia wasn't attracted to her at all, and now she felt uncomfortable around her. Olivia sighed, sat down and handed Sofia her beer.

"Hey, Stacy bought your beer," she said quietly.

"Thanks Stacy," Sofia said smiling at her. "Veronica has been entertaining us with ER stories. Did you know she was a nurse?"

"I don't guess I did," Olivia said looking across the table at her.

Veronica and Alice took turns telling stories trying to outdo the other. Olivia was having a good time until she felt Stacy put her arm around the back of her chair. She excused herself to the restroom, hoping Stacy wouldn't follow. Once inside, she texted Sofia that is was time to go and that she was right about Stacy and she was uncomfortable. She was hoping Sofia would notice her phone. A few seconds later she got the answer she was waiting for, a thumbs up.

She went back to the table and after a few minutes Sofia said, "Well, Olivia and I have to run. I've got a school thing that we're going to." They said their goodbyes and went to their cars.

"Thanks for doing that, you were right."

"That's okay. You've rescued me more times than I can count. I should've sat next to her, I just couldn't resist making you," Sofia said chuckling.

Olivia smirked at her.

"Let me know how your date goes Sunday," Sofia said.

"It's not a date, but I'll call you when I get back from our ride." With that they both got in their cars and left.

∼

SUNDAY COULDN'T ARRIVE SOON ENOUGH for Frankie. She'd had Olivia on her mind since she left her Friday after class. Yes, she definitely had a crush, but she was really looking forward to spending time with her away from the gym. Even though they would still be technically working out, a Sunday afternoon bike ride would be nice, just the two of them.

"Whatcha doing Frankie?" Desi asked in a sing-song voice.

Frankie looked up and said, "Working on next week's schedule."

Desi nodded, "That's not what it looked like to me."

"What do you mean?"

"Well, it looked to me like you were deep in thought and you had a smile on your face."

Frankie's cheeks started to redden but she didn't respond.

"That smile wouldn't have anything to do with Olivia King, would it?" Desi asked while still singing her words.

Frankie smiled knowing Desi wouldn't believe her if she tried to say different. She said, "It just might. We're going for a bike ride tomorrow."

"Fun. Who all is going?"

"Just the two of us. I offered to help her with her triathlon training."

"I know you did," Desi said suggestively.

"Don't do that. Why do you have to make things creepy?"

"That's not creepy. You just said you'd offered to help. Come on, seriously, I'm happy for you. If nothing else she's taken your mind off Laura and that's a good thing."

"She has. I'd like to get to know her better, you know, besides in the gym."

"Sure, I get it. But, the triathlon does give you a reason to see her."

"Yeah, it does." She hoped they had a good time tomorrow.

"Tell her she's welcome to join the group runs too," said Desi.

"I will."

"Let me know how it goes tomorrow."

"I will," Frankie said with a silly grin.

Olivia lived near the gym so it didn't take her long to ride to Your Way. The gym was open, but they didn't have classes scheduled on Sundays. As she was wondering where she would find Frankie, she walked out the door with her bike. When she saw Olivia coming toward her the biggest smile grew on her face. It made Olivia's heart beat faster. Knowing that she put that smile on Frankie's face felt really good. Olivia knew her face was beaming right back at her.

"Hey, perfect timing," said Frankie. "How's your Sunday?"

"It's getting better. I've been looking forward to this ride all weekend." Olivia hoped she didn't sound desperate. "I just hope I can keep up with you."

"You will. This isn't a race, at least I hope it isn't. I wanted a nice Sunday ride and just so you know, I've been looking forward to this too," Frankie said smiling and putting on her helmet.

"Where to? You're the leader," said Olivia.

"Not today, we can take turns. Are you familiar with this area?"

"Yeah, I don't live too far from here," said Olivia.

"I thought we could ride through these residential areas if that's okay. There shouldn't be much traffic."

"Sounds great, lead the way."

They rode along at a steady pace and at times could ride next to one another and chatted. It was a beautiful spring day in North Texas, very little wind and not too hot. After riding for about half an hour they pulled into a park and rode through to a seating area with several benches.

"Do you want to stop and sit for a minute?" asked Frankie.

"Sure, my butt could use a little break. It's been quite a while since I've ridden. I rode a little the other day but, that's it," Olivia rubbed her aching behind as she dismounted.

They leaned their bikes against a tree and grabbed their water bottles to sit.

"What a beautiful day," said Olivia. "Thanks again for inviting me."

"You're welcome. I'd love to do this anytime."

Olivia smiled and nodded. "Me too," she said shyly.

"So, did you have fun with the strength group Friday night?"

"Yeah, we didn't stay long."

"You don't sit around and talk about your instructor, do you?" Frankie teased.

"You know we do! We talk about how hard she works us and how mean she is," Olivia said, teasing right back. They both laughed "No, we don't talk about you."

"I'm probably not exciting enough, now Desi, I'm sure she'd give you plenty to talk about."

"Why would you say that? You're not exciting?" Olivia said looking her in the eye.

"Not at all. I'm very boring these days. I work and go home, that's about it."

"I don't believe you for a second Frankie Dean. I know there's more to you than just work," Olivia smiled.

Frankie smiled back at her. "Let's see, there is counseling. You know I go to counseling."

Olivia nodded.

"That's about it." Frankie looked up into Olivia's eyes and said, "Honestly, for quite some time I've been afraid to do anything else."

"Afraid?" Olivia said obviously concerned.

"Yeah, I felt like I couldn't trust my own judgement and didn't want to get in another mess like I did with Laura."

"Oh, I get it," said Olivia.

"I didn't tell you and Sofia that this isn't the only time it's happened," Frankie said looking down.

"What! Someone else broke up with you and got married?"

"They didn't get married, but she did leave me for a guy."

"Whoa, what is it with you?"

Frankie shrugged.

Olivia shook her head holding Frankie's eyes, "When is the wedding?"

Frankie looked away and stammered, "Uhhh."

"Come on, I know you know when it is. I'd be concerned if you didn't," Olivia said smiling compassionately.

"Three weeks," Frankie answered.

"Three weeks?" asked Olivia.

"Yeah, a couple of Saturdays from now," Frankie said, releasing a big breath, her shoulders sagging. Of course she knew when it was.

Olivia couldn't stand seeing Frankie sad like this and said, "Well then, would you spend the day with me that Saturday?"

Frankie looked up smiling, "Really?"

"Yes, really. We should find fun things to do to keep your mind off the wedding," Olivia stated.

Hesitating for just a moment, Frankie finally said, "I accept. But it can't be all day, I know I have to work that Saturday until the afternoon."

"Perfect, we can discuss the details later," Olivia said beaming. "You know Frankie, for a long time, all I did was work after Beth left. But you know what helped me?"

"What?" Frankie looked at her seriously.

"I joined this gym and now I can't tell you how much better I feel," Olivia said.

"Oh yeah, a gym?" said Frankie chuckling.

"Yep. I thought I was just going to lose a little weight but was I wrong," Olivia said proudly.

"Stop, you're teasing me," Frankie said.

"I am a little, but I mean it Frankie. You have made me feel better." She held eye contact with Frankie in a burst of confidence.

"I'm glad, you're making me feel better, too."

They both held one another's eyes smiling until Olivia said, "Aren't we supposed to be riding bikes?"

Frankie blinked and said, "I seem to remember something about a triathlon. By the way, Desi said to tell you that you're welcome to run with them. They have all levels so check with her for when they meet."

"Thanks. Come on, I'll even lead part of the way back," said Olivia putting her helmet on and taking her bike from the tree.

"I'm right behind you," said Frankie smiling.

7

The week had started with promise as things were leveling off at work for Olivia. She was meeting Frankie that evening for a bike ride and was looking forward to it. They had fun on Sunday and had chatted after both strength classes on Monday and Wednesday. Olivia liked Frankie and found herself thinking about her during the day. It had been a long time since another woman had occupied her thoughts and she noticed how a silly smile always seemed to play on her lips when Frankie was on her mind.

She left her bike outside the door and walked into Your Way to find Frankie. Stella saw her and waved her over to the front desk.

"Hey Olivia, how's it going?"

"Hi Stella, how are you?"

"I don't think I'm as good as you. That's a nice smile on your face. Would a certain instructor have put it there?"

Olivia blushed, was she that obvious? "I guess the instructor would be you since you're the first one I've seen," Olivia deflected.

"I don't think so, but I'll take it. Are you swimming with me in the morning?"

"Yes ma'am, I'll be there. I think I'm finally getting the hang of all this training. It's not that hard now that I can keep straight which sport is which day. It was very confusing at first."

"I know it is. That's why you have to have a schedule."

"For sure, today is bike day. Frankie and I are going for a ride."

"I'm glad. I wasn't sure she'd forgiven me for doing your one-on-ones."

Olivia looked at Stella confused. "What do you mean?"

Oops, Stella hoped she hadn't just messed up. "Remember when she had me cover for her?"

"Oh right, when we began meditating."

"Yes, she was pretty bummed you decided to do that instead of schedule with her."

Olivia thought back and remembered Frankie looking a little disappointed when she told her about scheduling with Stella.

"Hi ladies," Frankie said walking up behind Olivia. "Would anyone like to go for a bike ride," she said, smiling at Olivia.

Olivia couldn't resist teasing Frankie and said, "Stella was just telling me that she stole me away from you."

Frankie looked at Stella with raised eyebrows, causing her to look, eyes wide, from Frankie to Olivia, not knowing what to say.

Frankie shrugged her shoulders and said, "If you're talking about teaching you to meditate, then yes she did."

Olivia laughed and said, "I wish you could have seen your faces. I've never felt more wanted, two instructors fighting over me." Frankie and Stella both relaxed, laughing with her. "But now you both have me, I swim with Stella and ride with you Frankie," she said looking at them both.

"Then that means your mine right now so let's get riding," Frankie said, getting her helmet and bike from behind the desk.

"Have fun," Stella said as they walked out the door. Thinking there's a romance blossoming there, she couldn't have been happier for them both.

Olivia got on her bike following Frankie out of the parking lot. "Where are we going today?"

"I thought we could go down to the subdivision not far from here. There's no traffic and smooth streets."

"Okay," Olivia said knowing exactly where they were going since she was there most days checking on her house designs.

As they pulled through the entrance, she rode up next to Frankie and said, "You do know that I'm an architect, don't you Frankie?"

"Sure I do. You have no idea how much respect I have for you being able to design buildings. It's amazing."

"Aww, thank you. I happen to be designing this subdivision."

Frankie slammed on her brakes and stopped, eyes locked on Olivia as she kept going. Olivia turned and went back to see what happened.

"What's wrong? Are you okay," asked Olivia.

"You're designing this subdivision. Are you kidding me?" exclaimed Frankie.

Olivia stopped and a little smile crept on her face, "I'm not kidding you."

"Why haven't you told me? That's incredible!"

"I had no idea you were that interested," said Olivia surprised.

"I love walking through these houses and watching them as they go up. I've loved doing that since I was a kid."

"Me too. I guess that's why I became an architect. I never wanted to design buildings, I wanted to design houses and make them unique for each person or family."

"I can't believe it! Do I get a special tour?" Frankie asked excitedly.

"I'd love to give you a tour sometime," Olivia said proudly and also a little embarrassed.

"I'm holding you to that. Can we ride around now and you tell me a few things as we go?"

"Sure."

"I come here almost every day to see what's changed."

"Well, let's go and I'll explain my vision for this area," Olivia said, taking off.

Frankie was in heaven, she was mesmerized as Olivia explained what she hoped each street would look like and each home on it.

As they rode back to Your Way Frankie said, "This may have been the best bike ride ever! I still can't believe you're designing that subdivision," Frankie grinned.

"You've got to stop, you're embarrassing me," said Olivia, her cheeks reddening.

"I don't mean to. It's just so fascinating to me," she said getting off her bike. "You're fascinating, Olivia."

Olivia looked into Frankie's green eyes as they sparkled. Her heart beat faster and it wasn't because they'd been riding. Neither said a word, but Olivia could feel those eyes pulling her closer. She looked down at Frankie's plump lips as she ran her tongue over them and leaned in. She could almost feel her lips on Frankie's when Desi flew out the front door making them jump apart.

"Hey, you two! Olivia, when are you going to come run with us?"

"Uh," Olivia was speechless for a moment trying to gather herself as the moment passed. "Soon. I'll get the schedule tomorrow when I come to class," she said, smiling at Desi.

"Sounds good. Good ride? Where'd you go?"

Frankie had been watching Olivia but turned to Desi, excited all over again. "You're not going to believe this; Olivia is designing the subdivision that I ride in all the time."

"Wow, how about that," exclaimed Desi.

"It's not that big of a deal," said Olivia.

"Yeah it is," Frankie and Desi said in unison.

Olivia laughed, "Well thanks, I appreciate it. But I'd better get going." She turned to Frankie and said, "I'll see you tomorrow in class."

Frankie smiled and said, "Can't wait."

Olivia started to ride away but stopped and said, "Hey Frankie, think about going to the bar after class tomorrow." With that, she waved and rode off.

Frankie watched her go with a smile on her face. Maybe she would go with them this time.

"Hey," said Desi. "Did I interrupt something?"

Frankie continued to watch Olivia until she'd left the parking lot and went down the street. She turned to Desi and said, "Maybe."

Desi smiled and they walked back into the gym.

∽

WHAT A LONG DAY, Olivia didn't think it would ever end. She couldn't get Frankie out of her head. The events of yesterday kept replaying over and over in her mind. She'd catch herself smiling when she thought about Frankie, her face when finding out she was the architect on the housing project had been perfect. Sure, sometimes people would find her profession interesting but, she couldn't remember anyone reacting the way Frankie did. And it felt good.

She got her things together and left her office. There was just enough time to swing by her house and change for class. As she put on her leggings and top she looked in the mirror. She could see the changes in her body, but even better was the change inside. The look in her eyes was one of confidence and if she thought about it there was happiness there too. She smiled at herself in the mirror and nodded her head liking what she saw.

Sofia was waiting for her at their bench, as it had become their starting point for most classes.

"Hi OK, are you as glad as I am that it's Friday?"

"I am. This day couldn't end quickly enough."

"You weren't daydreaming about a certain fitness instructor were you?" teased Sofia.

Olivia started to answer and Sofia said, "Don't even try to deny it because I won't believe it. You should've heard yourself on the phone last night. You sounded rather smitten, my friend."

Olivia shook her head, "Smitten? I think that's a little much. I had a great time and told my best friend. End of story."

"If you say so. Hey, don't forget I'm not going to the bar after class today, I have the school band concert." Then she added, "You could come along if you want."

"No. I may have told Frankie she should join us after class so I'd better show up," Olivia said, hoping Frankie would join them.

"Uh-huh, may have told her," Sofia chuckled.

Class started, ending their conversation. Frankie worked with each set of partners and every time their eyes met they smiled at one another. Olivia was hoping to chat and remind her of the group meet up.

At the end of class as usual Stacy walked over and asked, "Hey, are you two coming to the bar?"

"I can't tonight but, Olivia is," answered Sofia.

"Great, I'll save you a seat," said Stacy walking away.

Olivia looked at Sofia shaking her head.

"Don't sit by her. I won't be able to save you tonight."

Olivia sighed, "You don't have to save me. I hoped she'd get the hint but, I'll say something to her if I have to."

Frankie walked up and said, "Hey, are you free to ride this weekend?"

"Sure. Sunday?"

"Works for me," said Frankie.

Sofia said, "Got to run, kids. Talk to you tomorrow, Olivia."

"Have fun at the concert."

"What concert?" asked Frankie.

"Sofia has a band concert at her school tonight so she can't meet with us at the bar. You should come."

"I might just do that. I have a few things to take care of here but, you never know," Frankie said noncommittally.

"Don't worry, I won't let them talk about you.".

"Thanks. I'll text you about Sunday."

Olivia grabbed her bag and headed for the bar. She hoped Frankie would show up but wasn't counting on it. Veronica and Alice would have plenty of new stories to entertain them. If Frankie didn't show up Olivia, hadn't planned to stay long, especially without Sofia.

She walked into the bar and looked around, not seeing Veronica anywhere. Their usual table was full. Out of the corner of her eye she saw Stacy waving her over to a different table.

"Hi, where is everyone?" Olivia asked, sitting across from Stacy where she could still see the door.

"I'm not sure. Veronica said she couldn't be here tonight and I thought I saw Alice in the parking lot with her girlfriend so she may not be coming either. Looks like it's just you and me," said Stacy.

This is just great thought Olivia. She really didn't want to be with Stacy alone; afraid it would give her the wrong idea.

"Let me get you a beer, I'll be right back," Stacy said, hopping up before Olivia could object.

She thought about texting Sofia but then stopped herself. You're a grown woman, have a beer then leave, she thought. If things get uncomfortable, she'd let Stacy down easy.

Stacy brought her a beer and sat down beside her. "How was your week?"

"Not bad, yours?"

"I always look forward to our class. It's the best way to wind down."

"I know what you mean."

"Hey, since it's just us, would you like to get something to eat or go somewhere else?"

"No, I'm supposed to meet someone here." Olivia didn't know why she said that. She wasn't sure Frankie was coming and she should have told Stacy she wasn't interested.

"Oh. Well, I'll wait with you. I don't want to leave you here alone."

"That's sweet, but I'll be fine." Olivia felt very uncomfortable now. She excused herself and went to the restroom.

∼

Frankie quickly picked up the weight area and went to the office to grab her backpack.

"Where are you running off to in such a hurry," asked Stella.

"My strength group meets at the bar on the corner after class and they've invited me several times so I thought I might stop by tonight."

"Olivia King wouldn't happen to be there, would she?" asked Desi with a hand on her hip.

"Maybe." Frankie said looking from one to the other.

"I thought you didn't feel comfortable asking her out since you're her instructor?" Stella said, her eyebrows raised.

"I know I said that it's not a good idea for us to ask our clients out. But what if a client asks us out?"

"Look Frankie, you're the one that has it in your head about asking clients out. It's not policy. Did someone ask you out?" asked Stella, her voice rising with excitement.

"I told Olivia about Laura and the wedding. She knows it's next Saturday and wanted to take me out to get my mind off it."

"That's so nice. You said yes, didn't you?" Stella said, nodding her head.

"Yeah and I'm looking forward to it."

"I heard her remind you about the meet up yesterday," said Desi.

"So why are you still here? Go!" Stella said, pushing her out the door.

∞

OLIVIA WALKED out of the restroom just as Frankie walked into the bar. She'd never been so happy to see someone in her life. She put her arm through Frankie's and pulled her out of Stacy's line of sight.

"Well, hi," Frankie said startled.

"Hi, I need your help," Olivia said looking at Frankie, her eyes pleading. "I might have told a white lie and said someone was meeting me here tonight."

"That's not a lie. I came here because you invited me if you'll remember."

Olivia let out a breath she didn't realize she was holding and gave Frankie her best smile. She led them over to where Stacy was sitting.

"Hi Frankie, did you finally decide to meet us?"

"Actually, I was here to meet Olivia," Frankie said, reading the situation..

"Oh, that's who you were waiting on," Stacy said to Olivia.

"Yeah, I wasn't sure she was going to come by."

"No problem, I'll leave you to it, have a nice weekend," Stacy said and left.

Olivia turned to Frankie and said, "Thank you. Stacy has been hitting on me nearly every time we come here, but I don't want to hurt her feelings. I didn't know we were going to be the only two tonight or I wouldn't have stayed."

"Why did you?"

"Because I was hoping you'd come by tonight," Olivia said, locking eyes with Frankie.

Frankie smiled and gestured for Olivia to sit, "Then, may I buy you a drink?"

Olivia returned Frankie's smile, "Shouldn't I buy since you rescued me?"

Frankie sat and waved the waitress over. They stayed for both drinks and the conversation never waned. Olivia walked Frankie to her Jeep thanking her again and smiled to herself as she got in her car. Training for this triathlon just became much more fun.

8

Olivia rode her bike into the Your Way parking lot and saw Frankie waiting. Moments from the other night kept running through her mind. She remembered how Frankie's eyes crinkled when she laughed, and that laugh, it was sexy and it woke something inside Olivia she hadn't felt in a very long time. She was looking forward to this ride and especially spending time with Frankie.

"Hey you, are you waiting on someone?" she said playfully.

Frankie chuckled, "I met this beautiful woman in a bar and convinced her to go for a bike ride around the lake today."

"Hmm, you must be a sweet talker, isn't that ride kind of long?"

Frankie laughed, "I thought we could stop for a treat along the way. Have you ever ridden around the lake on a bike?"

"Nope."

"Good. It looks totally different on two wheels. Ready?"

"Oh, you mean I'm the beautiful woman you're waiting for," Olivia teased, placing her hand to her chest for added drama.

Frankie's eyes locked onto Olivia's, thinking she might be the woman she's been waiting for her whole life. "You're the one."

They set off and rode side by side when they could, enjoying easy conversation. The day was beautiful with little wind and the traffic was light around the lake. Frankie was right, the sun reflected off the water's shimmering waves, lazily coming to shore and it was a beautiful sight. Frankie turned off on a little dirt road that ended at the water. Olivia pulled up next to her.

"Ready for a little rest and a snack."

"Sure," Olivia said, taking off her helmet.

"I brought an extra water bottle if you need it," Frankie said while sitting down near the water and stretching her legs out in front of her.

"I'm good," Olivia said, sitting next to her.

"I have trail mix and bananas, help yourself," Frankie said, opening the container of trail mix and setting it between them.

"Thanks. This is a nice little hideaway you have."

"Yeah, I used to come here a lot when I was younger."

"This might be a good place to sneak off with a girlfriend," Olivia said playfully.

Frankie chuckled, "You might be right."

"I hear a story in those words. Come on, spill."

Frankie sat up and faced Olivia, "When I was in high school, I knew I was attracted to girls but that was all, I had never had a girlfriend or anything, until one summer I met a girl that was visiting her grandmother. She was older and in college. We became friends and I was crazy about her."

Olivia smiled urging Frankie to continue.

"The first time she kissed me I thought I was going to die. Needless to say, I fell head over heels in love. We spent a lot of time together until the summer ended and she went back to school. My family and friends had no idea, they just thought we were friends."

"What happened?"

"We stayed in contact and one day she mailed me a card. She would do that sometimes, but this card was full of feelings and how much she missed me. My mother opened it before I got home from school. I still don't know why she did that because she'd never opened my mail before," Frankie said looking off as if reliving it all over again. She took a deep breath and continued.

"When I got home from school my parents were waiting for me. They wanted me to see a counselor and they didn't want me to see her again. I was crushed and confused."

"I'm sure you were," Olivia said compassionately. "What happened?"

"I refused to see a counselor, but I remember feeling like I'd done something wrong."

"What happened with the girl?"

"Occasionally we'd sneak around and see one another when she'd visit her grandmother. I'd get a text when she'd come to town but, other than that we didn't communicate. I was broken hearted, confused, and sixteen years old. That threw me right into the closet until I went to college."

"That's terrible, Frankie! I'm so sorry that happened to you. How is your relationship with your parents now?"

"Now, it's good. I think they came to realize that it wasn't a bad thing to have a lesbian daughter. I got past the anger and hurt, because I knew in their minds that they thought they were doing what was best for me, you know?"

"Yes, but that's still hard. I'm glad you get along with them now. What happened to the girl?"

"I would hear from her occasionally, but I haven't in a long time. Last I heard she was married to a woman and had a bunch of kids."

They sat in silence for a moment. Olivia reached out and took Frankie's hand as they both looked out over the water.

"To this day, sometimes, when I meet someone new, I feel apprehensive if they don't know I'm gay. And that's crazy! I'm not ashamed of who I am, but those wounds run deep and that fear of disappointment will bubble to the surface."

"Disappointment?"

"I have always been close to my parents and never wanted to disappoint them. I went back and forth about whether it's wrong to be gay and what people will think and I never wanted to bring them shame or embarrassment."

Olivia nodded her head and stroked the back of Frankie's hand with her thumb.

Frankie turned to Olivia with a sad smile, "Sorry. I didn't mean to bring you down."

"You didn't. Thanks for sharing that with me."

"I'm surprised I did."

"Why?"

"I haven't told many people about that or talked about it in a long time."

"I'm glad you felt like you could share it with me."

"Me too. Please tell me your coming out was better than mine."

Olivia smiled, "It was. It's just my mom and me and she knew before I did, or she claims she did."

"Well, I'm glad. Coming out is hard no matter how old you are or when you figure it out."

"Wait until you meet my mom, you'll see why that part wasn't so bad. She's easy to talk to and simply a nice person."

"Well, I'd love to meet her and I'd say her daughter is just like her."

Olivia blushed and looked away. "What is it with you, Miss Fitness Instructor? I thought we were supposed to be training?" Olivia said teasing.

"It's you! I seem to forget we're training and not simply enjoying the day. But don't tell Desi and Stella, they'll think I'm losing my tough trainer image."

They both laughed and Olivia said, "Come on, we'd better head back. I have a little work to do when I get home."

"How is the project going?"

"It's progressing, the lots are selling. That's always a good thing."

"I'll have to ride out there this week."

Olivia had a pained look on her face.

"What?"

"It's just that I was going to surprise you Saturday and give you the real tour."

"You were!" Frankie said, obviously excited.

"Yeah, I thought if anything could take your mind off of that evening it'd be those houses."

"You'd be right. Sorry I ruined your surprise."

"You didn't ruin it. I may have a few other surprises tucked away."

Frankie's smile grew, "I can't wait."

∽

OLIVIA WALKED through the door to the pool area and saw Stella sliding off her cover-up. She smiled as Olivia approached.

"Good morning."

"Hi Stella, how was your weekend?"

"My weekend was uneventful, just as I planned."

Olivia chuckled, "Well, good for you."

"How about yours?"

"It was good," Olivia said smiling and thinking back to drinks with Frankie on Friday and their bike ride yesterday. They were getting to know one another better and Olivia found she was looking for ways to see Frankie on days she didn't have class.

"Hmm, that smile wouldn't have to do with anyone I might know, would it?"

Olivia didn't even realize she was smiling. She thought about making something up but it was pointless, Stella knew why she was smiling. "It could be. Do you know... oh, who am I kidding," she said laughing. "Yes, Frankie is why I'm smiling."

"Well, it looks lovely on you. So are you going to tell me about your weekend?"

"Frankie helped me out of a situation Friday night at the bar with another woman. So we stayed and had a couple of drinks and talked."

"A situation?"

Olivia recounted to Stella what happened.

"You know, Stacy isn't the only one I've seen at the gym noticing you, Olivia."

"What?"

"You haven't noticed, I take it."

"Not at all."

"Oh come on, surely you've seen the smiles when you walk by. I have."

Olivia didn't know what to say. She really hadn't noticed anything different. People were friendly when she walked by and she had conversations with some of the people in her class. But this made her wonder, "Stella, do you think these people are noticing me now because I've lost weight?"

Stella studied Olivia for a moment before replying, "What are you really trying to ask me, Olivia?"

"I guess what I mean is, body image and mental health are big issues right now with emphasis on loving your body no matter the size. But isn't the same thing still happening if these people didn't notice me before I lost weight."

Stella took Olivia's hand and led her to a bench by the pool and they both sat. "I can't speak for the people in the gym, but I can tell you what I see. Yes, you've lost weight. We wouldn't be very good at our jobs if you hadn't since that was your goal when you came to us." Stella paused and found Olivia's eyes and continued, "But what I see when you open that door is a happy face with a confident stride. You look friendly, approachable and beautiful. That has nothing to do with your weight."

Olivia thought about what Stella said for a moment. "I didn't feel like a confident beautiful woman when I first came to the gym. But I do now and is that because I've lost weight?"

Stella narrowed her eyes, "Do you really think it's because you've lost weight?"

"Here's what I know, I like coming to class and not because I'm lifting weights. I look forward to seeing you and Frankie and Desi and the people in my class or people I have met while doing other activities. So the change in me isn't because I've lost weight necessarily, but because you've all become my friends."

"But in your mind you still get stuck on body image, don't you?"

"Kind of. I used to think that no one wanted to go out with me because I was overweight, but I'm beginning to see that wasn't necessarily true. I'm sure the vibes I gave off weren't always positive and that's not inviting."

"And the vibes you're giving off now?"

"Well, they're better but ...," Olivia contemplated talking to Stella about Frankie. She still had conflicting thoughts and emotions flying around her head.

Stella quirked an eyebrow, "But?"

"Aren't we supposed to be swimming?"

"Missing a swim isn't going to kill us."

Olivia made up her mind, "When I first came to the gym, Frankie showed me around and I felt something between us. That unnamed tug that drew me to her and I think she felt it too. And I realized how idiotic that was, because look at Frankie, she could have anyone she wanted. She surely wouldn't be interested in someone like me."

"Oh Olivia!"

Olivia put her hand up, stopping Stella, "And then, I signed up for her class and she invited me to ride bikes with her and we've become friends. I know now that was a horrible thing to think about her because she's not like that at all but, that's where I was then."

"And that tug that drew you to her, is it still there?"

A slow smile came to Olivia's face, "Even more so."

"Let me tell you a little secret, in case you weren't sure, Frankie feels it too."

Olivia's smile grew, "We've been riding bikes a couple of times a week since I signed up for the triathlon and getting to know each other better. We're kind of going on a date Saturday."

"Kind of?"

"Yeah, she told me about her ex, Laura. She's getting married Saturday and I told her we'd do something to keep her mind off it."

"That's really nice, Olivia."

"I know that has to hurt even though she says she's past her feelings for Laura. And, I didn't want her to have to go through that day alone."

"You're a good friend. And I'm so glad you've come into our lives," she said, pulling Olivia into a hug.

"I am, too," she said hugging Stella back. "We didn't get much swimming done?"

"I think we gave your heart and head muscle a good workout, don't you," Stella said laughing.

"We sure did. But I'd best get changed, I do still have to go to work."

"I'm not surprised Frankie is drawn to you, she's crazy about that subdivision you're designing."

"I know! That's where I'm taking her Saturday. There should be plenty of distractions to keep her mind off the wedding."

"I think as long as she is with you she won't be thinking about that wedding."

Olivia blushed and smiled.

∼

Frankie pulled into the animal shelter and saw Grace with one of the volunteers leashing two dogs. Since Grace was the only counselor she'd ever been to, she wondered if other counselors had sessions while walking dogs. She liked it and hoped they could continue to have her sessions there.

"There you are! I have an eager Great Dane mix ready to take you on a walk," Grace said, handing the leash to Frankie. "I figured you could handle her since you're a fitness guru."

Frankie took the leash and looked down into the dog's eyes that were at waist level, "What is your name, beautiful?"

"This is Sadie. She should do well on a leash," said the volunteer. "Have fun."

"Let's go. This is Sharon," Grace said referring to the lab mix she started walking. "She and Sadie are buddies."

"What beautiful dogs, I hope they find homes soon."

"But in the meantime, it's good to have friends. How have you been? Have you been sitting still as I suggested last time?"

"I've tried. Before I go to sleep, I turn off the TV, put my tablet and phone on to charge and sit. Thoughts fly through my head, but I try to relax and settle for a few minutes before I get in bed."

"What are the thoughts flying through your head?"

"Sometimes they're about work, or family, or friends."

"Laura?"

"Not really. I would expect her to come up from time to time but, she doesn't."

"The wedding is soon, isn't it?"

"Yep, this Saturday."

"Do you have some anxiety about that?"

"Not really. I'm actually excited."

"Excited? What do you mean?"

"I have a date Saturday night," Frankie said smiling as Olivia's face wandered into her head.

"Good for you. Is this the first since Laura?"

"It is."

"Do you want to talk about it?"

"Isn't that why I see you, to talk about this stuff?" Frankie said sarcastically.

"Not funny. You don't have to talk about anything if you don't want to."

"I was just teasing you. Yes, I want to talk about it. Do you remember in our last session, I told you about a new client that I didn't want to disappoint?"

"I do. What happened with that?"

"Her name is Olivia and we've become friends. She's in one of my classes and she's also doing the triathlon. I asked her to ride bikes with me, so we've been riding a couple of times a week."

"That reminds me, I need to sign up to volunteer for it."

"She's very easy to talk to; I've told her things that I haven't shared with Desi or Stella and that's unusual. Anyway, I told her about Laura and the wedding. She asked me to go out with her Saturday to take my mind off it."

"That's nice of her."

"It is."

"Do you think she asked you out because of the wedding or would she have asked you out anyway?"

"I have asked myself the same question. I hope she would have anyway."

"You told me in our last session that she made you feel again. Do you think this could go somewhere?"

"I hope so. I can feel a connection when I'm with her and think she feels it too. But I want to be careful."

"Because?"

"Because, I can tell she's special and I don't want to screw this up."

"Why would you screw this up?"

"History, Grace. Look at what's happening Saturday."

"But that's not your fault, Frankie. We've talked about it. You had no control over that."

"Didn't I though? I mean Laura said it wasn't anything I did, but that's hard to believe. It takes two."

"Are you telling me you want her back?"

"No. I'm telling you I don't want to mess this up with Olivia. If I made mistakes with Laura I certainly don't want to repeat them with Olivia."

"Frankie, if you go into this with the fear you're going to mess it up, as you say, isn't that exactly what's going to happen? Do you respect Olivia?"

"Of course I do."

"Do you value her opinion?"

"Yes."

"I know you are considerate and kind. So, focus on the good, not on what can go wrong."

Frankie nodded her head thinking about what Grace said.

"For someone that helps people nourish and improve their self-image, you're pretty hard on yourself at times."

Frankie smiled, "I get what you're saying, Grace. I really like her."

"Then she's a lucky woman. Come on let's take Sadie and Sharon back and give some other lucky hounds a walk."

FRANKIE HOPED she wasn't overstepping. Olivia had called to say she couldn't make it for their bike ride today because she was stuck at the work site and would be there for several hours. She saw Olivia's SUV parked at the model home that held the office and pulled in behind her.

Olivia thought she heard the front door open, when she came around the corner she found Frankie standing in the entry holding two drinks. Her face immediately lit up, "Frankie, what are you doing here?"

Frankie walked forward hesitantly but smiling, "I know you said you had to work late but, I thought maybe you could use a pick-me-up. I brought you a smoothie with pineapple and coconut." She extended her hand with the drink.

"Thank you, how thoughtful," she said, taking the smoothie. As she took a drink through the straw her eyes widened. "This is so good. How did you know pineapple and coconut were my favorites?"

Frankie looked down her cheeks reddening, "I may have been paying attention or asked Stella if she knew which your favorite was."

Olivia leaned down capturing Frankie's eyes with her own, "You're really sweet, Frankie. You don't know how much I needed this."

"I don't want to interrupt your work. Enjoy, and I'll see you tomorrow." Frankie smiled but didn't move.

"You are a welcome distraction," she said, taking another sip of her smoothie.

"Well, I'd better go." This time Frankie started toward the door.

"Let me walk you out. I've been stuck in here since lunch."

When they got to Frankie's Jeep she opened the door and got in. Olivia grabbed the window sill and closed the door. Frankie rested her arm on the opened window.

Olivia put her hand on Frankie's forearm, "Thanks again for the smoothie."

"You're welcome," Frankie said as her eyes gleamed a darker shade of green.

Olivia met those eyes with her own turning a deep mahogany, "I'm glad you came by." Her fingers squeezed Frankie's forearm gently.

Frankie smiled and put the Jeep in gear, "I am too." She began to back out, her eyes never leaving Olivia's. When she got to the end of the driveway Olivia gave her a little wave. It took all Frankie had not to jump out of the Jeep, take Olivia in her arms and kiss her.

Olivia watched Frankie drive away. She took a deep breath, trying to calm her racing heart. She was so close to leaning down and kissing Frankie in the Jeep. Saturday couldn't come quickly enough.

∽

Olivia rode her bike up to Your Way just as Sofia was getting out of her car. "Hi stranger."

"Hi to you. Sorry, about this week, I've been busy at work."

"It wouldn't have anything to do with your big date tomorrow, would it?"

"I have been arranging a few things for tomorrow."

"Why are you on your bike today? It's Friday, we drink after class, remember?"

"Yes, I needed to get a ride in and was too busy this week. I even had to cancel on Frankie for our usual ride."

"I guess you can drink and pedal."

"Not tonight, I'm heading home."

"Don't want to fight off Stacy this week?"

"Very funny. Why don't you come home with me and I'll tell you about the big date tomorrow."

"Ooow, that sounds like fun. Besides, I missed you this week OK."

Olivia smiled at Sofia's term of endearment with her initials.

"I missed her, too," said Frankie walking up to the pair.

Olivia turned and was greeted with the most dazzling smile and vibrant green eyes she'd ever seen, "Let me hold the door, you can put your bike in the office."

"Thanks." Olivia went through, followed by Sofia, who gave Frankie a playful smile.

As Olivia came out of the office, Frankie asked them both, "Isn't this your class bar night?"

"It is," Sofia spoke up. "But not for us tonight."

"You're not going? I had a great time last Friday and thought I might go again."

Sofia looked at Olivia and then Frankie, "I don't think it would be as much fun for you tonight. You know there's competition over who gets to sit next to Olivia."

Olivia rolled her eyes at Sofia and shook her head.

"Besides, you'll get her all to yourself tomorrow."

Frankie chuckled, "I sure will and I'm looking forward to it."

Olivia met Frankie's green eyes with her own soft brown ones, "I am too." After a moment she dropped Frankie's gaze, "Aren't we here to lift weights?"

Frankie shook her head, "Something happens when you're around and I forget what I'm doing. Come on!" She grabbed both their hands and led them to the weights, laughter in their wake.

After class Sofia told the regular Friday night group that she and Olivia wouldn't make it. Olivia helped Frankie clean up the weight area.

"Are you riding your bike home? I'd be glad to give you a ride."

"Thanks, but since I missed this week I wanted to get a ride in."

"You're getting serious about this triathlon."

"It's not that far away for a rookie like me."

"You're going to do great."

"So...where should I pick you up tomorrow? I know you have to work."

"I was going to ask you, should I dress casual?"

Olivia smiled thinking this time it's casual but she wouldn't mind seeing Frankie all dressed up. "Yes, this time it's casual. We'll be doing a little walking."

Frankie noticed Olivia said 'this time' and smiled, "Okay, you can pick me up here."

Sofia walked up, "That's one disappointed group that we're not joining them tonight."

"I'm sure they are," said Olivia. "Give me a head start and I'll meet you at the house." Then to Frankie she said, "See you tomorrow."

Frankie smiled as she watched Olivia get her bike.

"Big date tomorrow, huh."

Frankie turned to Sofia, "It is."

"It's not hard to tell, with the way you two look at one another; this is more than friends. I mean, you don't look at me that way," Sofia said chuckling.

"I really like her."

"She likes you too. And I love her," Sofia said looking at Frankie warily.

Frankie frowned, "What are you trying to say?"

"She's a good person, she's had a hard time, and now she's back. I'd like to keep it that way."

Frankie smiled, "Me too."

Sofia searched Frankie's eyes, then nodded, "Okay then, have a good time tomorrow."

9

Olivia walked into Your Way, a little nervous. She wasn't sure what to wear and ended up in black jeans that she felt good in, and a vee neck tee shirt that was slightly fitted. She realized as she changed clothes several times, that she and Frankie had only seen one another in work-out clothes. It was no secret that she wanted to impress.

When she walked into the office, Stella and Frankie's heads both turned; one look at Frankie's face and Olivia knew she'd chosen the right outfit. She smiled with a hint of a smirk and then noticed that Frankie was wearing jeans that showed her muscles and curves with a light green button down that made her eyes appear like dark emeralds. Her sleeves were rolled up showing off her tanned and muscled forearms.

"My god, you two are gorgeous," exclaimed Stella.

Frankie found her voice, "I agree. Olivia you are beautiful."

"Thank you, both. I thought you looked good in work-out clothes but, wow, you should wear jeans more often," Olivia said, the smirk vanishing and her eyes darkening.

Stella chuckled, "I don't think I've ever seen you in anything but spandex or a swimsuit, Olivia. And I don't get to see Frankie in jeans very often."

Olivia's eyes had been locked on Frankie's since she walked into the office. Shaking her head she said, "Are you ready to go?"

Frankie nodded, "Lead the way." She walked toward Olivia.

"See you, Stella."

"Have fun, you two." Stella had her fingers crossed, a little luck couldn't hurt.

Olivia drove them to the model home and they went inside. "I thought it might be fun for you to design your own house. We can start with floor plans and kind of go from there. Or does that sound terrible?"

"This may be the best date ever," Frankie said, her face beaming.

Olivia chuckled, "Come this way and we can get started."

She showed her several floor plans and different sizes. Some were two stories, others were single floors; some were on the small side, others were sprawling.

"I have a question. Am I choosing what I'd like to build, like a dream home in my perfect little world or one that would fit me now?"

"That's entirely up to you but, if it were me, I'd go perfect world. Why not? It's all for fun."

"Sometimes I have a hard time imagining a perfect world and not being practical."

"There's nothing wrong with practical, but tonight is for fun. Let me help you design your dream."

Frankie looked up from the plans, catching Olivia's gaze. "Are you my dream, Olivia King?" she said quietly.

A slow smile reached Olivia's eyes, "We'll see." She dropped Frankie's eyes and reached for the designs, "Now, answer a few questions and we'll narrow this down."

Frankie did as Olivia said and they came up with two plans she liked.

"We happen to have both of these in construction so I can show you what they actually look like. Want to see?"

"Heck yeah, let's go."

Olivia was happy Frankie seemed to be enjoying herself. She wasn't sure when she'd come up with the idea and could've taken Frankie out for dinner. But she wanted to do something different and make it special.

They walked through the garage and Olivia opened the door to the driveway. In the light Frankie could see a golf cart.

"Hop in, we'll take a spin around the area and to your houses," Olivia said climbing behind the wheel.

"How fun. Olivia, this gets better and better."

"I'm glad you're having a good time," she said steering onto the street.

"A very good time. This is so much fun."

Olivia pulled into the first house plan that Frankie chose. "This one is framed in and you can get an idea of what the rooms look like but, the walls aren't sheet rocked yet."

"Olivia, do you have homes already going up for all those plans we looked at?"

"No, not all of them."

"Then, how did you know I'd pick ones that were built?"

Olivia paused and smiled, "I just had a feeling. Maybe one of them is one I'd pick too. Come on, let me show you."

They walked through the home with Olivia explaining what each room was and helping Frankie to picture the layout with completed walls, flooring, and even furniture.

"You're really good at this. I can see the picture you're painting with your words," Frankie said in awe.

Olivia blushed and chuckled, "I'm glad. I'm kind of passionate about this, as you can see."

"Is this the one you liked?"

"Actually, it's the next one. Are you ready to move on? We can stay if you want."

"No, we can go. I really like this house though; I can't imagine the next one being better."

"I didn't say it was better, just that it's the one I like. I like this one, too. I like parts of all of them," Olivia said sweeping her hand gesturing toward the street as they got in the golf cart.

Frankie looked around, "Olivia King's kingdom."

"My kingdom," Olivia said laughing. "Not hardly."

"Why not? It is your vision, isn't it?"

"Well, the house designs themselves and trying to place them where they don't all look alike is my vision, you could say."

"I do and it's beautiful," Frankie said, gazing at Olivia's profile as she drove them to the next house.

Olivia glanced over locking eyes with Frankie as they pulled into the driveway.

"This one is farther along so you'll be able to see the whole concept better."

They walked through the front door into an open concept living and kitchen area. There were large windows bringing in the last light of the day.

"Oh wow, Olivia. I see why you like this."

"It's so bright and open. Having the sheet rock up makes a difference too."

"I like how you can see through to the back window and door into the back yard. Does it have a patio?"

"Yeah, we can go through and see it before I show you the rest."

They walked through the backdoor onto the patio where a small table was set up with chairs. There were two ice chests, place settings, and glasses.

Frankie turned to Olivia and with surprise in her voice said, "What's all this?"

"I did invite you on a date and to me that means dinner," Olivia said smiling. The surprise on Frankie's face sent a warmth through Olivia.

Frankie took Olivia's hand, "You are something. First, you ask me out to help me forget the wedding. Then you take me to one of my favorite places, build me a house and now dinner. Thank you, Olivia, no one has made me feel this special."

When Frankie took Olivia's hand, electricity shot through her body. "You are special, Frankie. Surely you've felt that before."

"This is wonderful."

"Is it working? Has this taken your mind off the wedding? I didn't want to ask and bring it up, but…"

Frankie squeezed her hand, "Yes, it's working."

"Good. Let's sit and eat. I brought beer or wine, your choice?"

"How about wine?"

"Wine it is." Olivia poured them each a glass and made Frankie sit while she placed salads out for them both. "Since you do own a gym, I thought I'd better bring something healthy, but save room for dessert."

"Shall we toast," Frankie said, raising her glass. Olivia followed suit and smiled. "To new friends and adventures." They clinked glasses and sipped.

Frankie chuckled as they began to eat. "You know, I hope this isn't the only time we do this."

"Me either."

"But you've kind of set the bar so high, there's no way I'll be able to top it."

"You're the one that did that." Olivia said, causing Frankie to look at her questioningly. "You've taken me on so many beautiful bike rides. And what makes them special is that I would've never done that myself, Frankie."

"Were they dates?"

"Maybe not at first, but Thursday when we went to the lake. You made that special, didn't you?"

"I tried to."

"It was. I didn't want to go home."

"I've wanted to ask you out since the day you walked into the gym," Frankie admitted.

Olivia looked up and narrowed her eyes, "Really? The first time?"

"Yes, but after our conversation in the dressing room, I didn't think you would go out with me."

Olivia looked down sighing, "I didn't think you would be interested in me. Let me apologize again for that conversation because I know you are not like that. But the first day?"

Frankie nodded, "Olivia, I have been drawn to you since that first day. I haven't felt that in such a long time; it scared me. My confidence in my own judgement is pretty low."

"I know exactly what you mean. You saw me, my confidence was gone, too."

They both stared at one another, eyes sparkling.

"But I seem to have found mine again."

"I can trust my judgement again."

Neither said a word, both caught up in the moment.

"Ready for dessert?"

"Yes, please."

Olivia reached into the cooler and brought out two pieces of key lime pie. Frankie's eyes lit up.

"Is that key lime pie?"

Olivia nodded as she cleared their salad plates and set the pie down.

"It's my favorite!" Frankie studied Olivia for a moment then asked, "Did you know?"

Olivia smiled and looked down, "I might have paid attention or asked Stella."

Frankie laughed and Olivia joined her. As they ate the pie Frankie thought it might be the sweetest she'd ever tasted. She looked at Olivia and then around the back yard. "You know, my counselor is trying to get me to be still."

"Be still?"

"Yes, she thinks I'm on the go all the time with classes, the business,and working out, and that I don't ever stop and be still."

"From what I see, she's right."

"I can't decide if she thinks I need to calm the thoughts running through my head or if she thinks I'm running by not slowing down."

"Hmm, what do you think?"

"Before I started seeing her, I would agree, I didn't slow down because I didn't want to think about the pain of Laura leaving and what my future looked like after that."

"If you don't mind me asking, did you see a future with Laura?"

"I never looked ahead as far as us getting married. I really didn't look ahead at all. I mean we were, or I was, comfortable in what we had. But maybe that's a mistake I made by not talking about the future. Anyway, I'm in a better place now. When I'm still it's to calm all the thoughts running around my head and just resting."

"You know, that sounds a little like meditation."

"Oh no you don't. You're not trying to get me to meditate like Stella, are you?"

Olivia chuckled holding her hands up, "No. Stella told me that wasn't your thing. But, it certainly has helped me. When things are crazy at work, like they've been for a while now, it helps ease stress."

Frankie narrowed her eyes, "Between the two of you, I don't stand a chance."

Olivia laughed again, "Ready to see the rest of the house?"

"Yes and thank you."

"For what, not making you meditate?"

"No, for all of this, the meal, the pie, and especially you."

"You're welcome. Come on."

They went back in the house and as they went down the hall Olivia asked, "In both houses you chose three bedrooms. Any particular reason?"

"Well, you said to dream, so in my dream I'd share the master bedroom with my wife and need an extra bedroom or two for kids. I know it's getting a little late for me but, I can still dream."

"It's not too late for you!"

"Maybe. Do you want kids someday?"

Olivia smiled, "I've thought about it and yeah, I hope so someday."

She showed her the two extra bedrooms and a bathroom. "Here is the master suite and this is why I like this house. The room is big, but it also has great closets and a nice bathroom."

"Oh wow, you're right and French doors that open to a little patio." Frankie looked around the room and then walked into the bathroom. "These closets are huge and that shower."

"I know, isn't it great?"

"I've always wanted a shower like this." Frankie could feel her face heating up as an image of she and Olivia in that shower flashed in her mind.

Olivia noticed Frankie shake her head, "Are you alright?"

Frankie smiled, her eyes brow raised, "Some of those thoughts running through my mind."

That made Olivia blush and chuckle.

Frankie took a deep breath and walked back into the bedroom asking over her shoulder, "What would this look like if it were your bedroom?"

Olivia followed her, still smiling, "Um... let's see, I would probably put the bed here and I'd put a rocking chair looking out the French doors."

"A rocking chair?"

"Yeah, I have a thing for rocking chairs. When I was a little girl I had one and I've been rocking ever since. I've always had one."

"How about that," Frankie said, fascinated. She walked over to the doors opening them and looked out into the night. "Is it okay?"

"Sure," Olivia answered walking over to stand next to her, their shoulders brushing.

"It's so quiet."

"And still."

Frankie turned to her, their bodies close. "But my mind isn't still." She looked into Olivia's eyes, slowly bringing her hand up and running her thumb along Olivia's jaw. She cupped the back of her head as she leaned in and brought their lips together in a soft kiss. Frankie's heart raced but at the same time she felt like she was home. An incredible feeling of contentment filled her as a fire began to build in her soul. Olivia sank into the kiss and slightly parted her lips asking for more as her hands, now on Frankie's hips, pulled her closer. Frankie obliged and Olivia slipped her tongue inside and melted against her. The world fell away as Olivia thought this was the best first kiss ever. After several moments they pulled back, both breathing hard.

Frankie looked into Olivia's deep brown eyes, "I can see the reflection of the moon in your beautiful eyes."

"The moon?"

Frankie had a hard time tearing herself away but she looked out the doorway, Olivia following her gaze and saw the beautiful full moon shining down.

"Would you like to go for a walk in the moonlight?"

"I'd love to. Let me close these doors and grab the coolers."

"I'll help."

They made quick work of loading the coolers in the golf cart and closing up the house.

"This looks like a safe neighborhood," Frankie said playfully.

"I'm sure you'd protect me."

"I would. Shall we?"

Olivia nodded as they walked down the driveway to the street. There were a few streetlights that illuminated their way but, it was quiet and secluded.

Frankie took her hand as they walked side-by-side down the empty street, a comfortable silence between them.

"This may be better than that bike ride to the lake," Frankie said, looking sideways at Olivia.

"How so?"

"It's hard to hold hands on a bicycle."

Olivia chuckled, "That it is."

Frankie slowed and faced Olivia, "And it's hard to stop and do this." She grabbed Olivia's other hand and brought their lips together for a kiss. Olivia moaned and reached up taking Frankie's face in her hands and deepened the kiss.

Olivia put her forehead on Frankie's as their lips parted, "I didn't think this night could get any more romantic but, Frankie Dean, you're making me swoon." They both released a contented sigh.

"We'd better make our way back to the golf cart and the office, your tour isn't quite complete."

"Are you kidding me? I don't think I could take much more, I'm floating as it is."

They pulled the golf cart into the garage where they'd started and walked into the house. The plans were laid out on the kitchen table.

Olivia walked over with the two plans Frankie had chosen, "So, which one did you like better?"

"The last one, for sure."

"Are you're sure it was the house and not the key lime pie?"

Frankie laughed, "The key lime pie was a bonus, but I liked it best, especially the bedroom and those French doors. And what happened at those French doors and the neighborhood and…"

"I think I get it," Olivia laughed. She took the plans, signed them, and put them in a large envelope with Frankie's name on it. She handed it to Frankie.

"I get to keep them?"

"They're all yours, signed by the architect. If you ever decide you want to build that house you'll be ready."

Frankie looked at her skeptically, "Really? That's too much Olivia. These are expensive, I've looked before."

"You didn't know the architect before."

"Thank you."

"My pleasure. We'd better load up. I think I have a long bike ride tomorrow with a relentless trainer."

"You do, and your trainer can't wait."

10

After being dropped off at the gym, Frankie jumped in her Jeep and couldn't stop smiling all the way home. She could feel Olivia's lips on hers and remembered that absolute peace when Olivia pulled her close, like she was home. She had never felt like that before and wanted to again.

When she pulled into her driveway she noticed a car parked in front of her house. She thought that was a little odd but figured someone was visiting across the street. When she got out of her Jeep and walked to her front door someone was sitting on her front porch.

"Hey Frankie,"

"Holy shit," Frankie exclaimed, peering through the darkness. "Laura? Is that you? You scared me to death!"

"Sorry, I didn't mean to scare you."

"What are you doing here? I thought you got married tonight."

"Could we go in and talk for a minute."

Frankie unlocked the door and held it open for Laura. She turned on the light, "Have a seat."

"Thanks," Laura said, sitting heavily on the couch, letting out a big sigh.Frankie could see that Laura was upset, her forehead was creased and she wasn't wearing makeup but had been crying. Her chocolate brown hair was pulled into a messy bun on top of her head with tendrils framing her face.

"What happened? Did he do something?" Frankie felt protective of Laura even with all the history between them.

"I couldn't go through with it." After taking a deep breath she looked up with tears in her eyes.

"Oh Laura," Frankie said and sat down next to her. She wanted to put her arm around her or take her hand but decided not to.

Through tears she said, "I know you're going to hate me."

Frankie did grab her hand then and said, "I don't hate you. I couldn't."

"You will when I tell you what happened."

Frankie squeezed her hand and encouraged her.

"As the wedding got closer and closer, I felt more and more unsure, but I thought it was just nerves. At the rehearsal last night, standing at the altar and looking at everyone I thought I was going to be sick. Nothing has ever felt so wrong in my life. While getting ready at the church this evening, all I could think about was you."

"Me!" Frankie said surprised.

Laura turned to Frankie wiping the tears from her face. "Yes, you! I've made a horrible mistake Frankie. I should never have left you! And I'm going to spend the rest of my life making it up to you."

Frankie released Laura's hand and got up, pacing around the room. She couldn't believe her ears. Months ago she would have rejoiced at hearing those words but now, so many things had changed.

"Would you like something to drink? I'm getting a beer," she said, walking through the living room to the kitchen. She ran her fingers through her hair and looked at the ceiling. What was happening? Was this some kind of joke? Was she having a dream? She reached into the refrigerator and pulled out two bottles of beer.

When she walked back into the living room Laura had her head in her hands. Frankie stood there, her heart breaking for Laura, but she was confused. She sat back down and handed Laura the beer.

She took a long drink then set it on the table in front of the couch and turned to Frankie. "I can't imagine what is going through your head right now, but please give me a chance, Frankie. I don't expect to walk back into your life and pick up where we left off."

Frankie found her voice, "Where we left off was you leaving me." She didn't want to make things worse for Laura but, her heart hadn't healed completely.

"I know, I know." Tears sprang to Laura's eyes again. She took Frankie's beer and sat it on the table and took both her hands. "I am so sorry I hurt you. If there was any way I could go back, I would. It breaks my heart that I hurt you."

Frankie looked at Laura knowing what she said was true, but that still didn't mend her broken heart. Her date with Olivia felt like a lifetime ago. Olivia! What about Olivia? She cleared her throat, "Laura, I know you're sorry, you've told me that already. And I forgave you." Frankie stood up, trying to put some distance between them. "But, this is a lot for one night. You have to be emotionally drained, what with calling off the wedding and coming here."

"I had to tell you myself, Frankie. You had to know. I came here straight from the church."

"From the church? You've been sitting out there for hours?"

"Yes. I had to see you." Laura stood and went to Frankie. "Please, hear me out. Please give me a chance. Please give us a chance."

Frankie was overwhelmed and couldn't think. After several moments she swallowed took a deep breath, "Laura, you've got to give me time to process this; I need time to think."

"Of course," she said instantly, taking Frankie's hand. "We have nothing but time. We can work through this no matter how long it takes."

Frankie released a breath she didn't realize she'd been holding.

"I don't want to leave you tonight. I'm afraid?"

"What? Afraid?"

"I'm afraid I won't see you again. I'm afraid you'll make up your mind and won't talk to me, not hear me out."

Frankie smiled at Laura kindly, "I wouldn't do that. Of course I want to hear what you have to say. Just not right now. Okay?"

"Okay. I'll go. But Frankie, I never stopped loving you. When you start processing all of this please remember that. I love you."

She walked Laura out to her car. "I'll call you tomorrow."

"However long it takes, Frankie." She started her car and pulled away from the curb.

Frankie had never been more confused in her life.

∽

After dropping Frankie at her car, Olivia called Sofia.

"How was it?"

Olivia laughed, "Hello to you too."

"Come on. You've just gone on a date for the first time in forever. A date that you planned, so we don't have time for hellos," Sofia said, laughing.

"Well," Olivia said, drawing the word out. "It was wonderful! We had the best time!"

"Yay! I'm not surprised. You two fit, you've got that thing about you."

"What?"

"You know, when you see two people together and they just fit. I don't know how else to describe it."

Olivia thought about this. She did feel comfortable around Frankie and loved being with her.

"Hmm, we fit. I like that."

"So tell me, did she like the house thing?"

"She did. The food was good. She was surprised by the pie. And we took a walk in the moonlight."

"And, what else happened?"

"Oh Sofia, it was so romantic," Olivia gushed. "We walked along hand in hand, it was perfect."

"And?"

"And that's all I'm going to tell you. I can't wait to see her tomorrow."

"Tomorrow?"

"Yeah, it's our bike ride day."

"I'm so happy for you. No one deserves to be happy more than you."

"Aw, thanks Sof."

"Are we still on for dinner tomorrow?"

"Yep, I'll text you when I get home."

"Sweet dreams."

"I'm pretty sure they will be," she said, disconnecting the call. Her thoughts took her right back to that bedroom, the French doors, and that kiss. She could feel Frankie's lips on hers, those soft, delicious lips. Tomorrow couldn't come soon enough.

∾

FRANKIE COULD SEE Olivia sitting on the bench in the park waiting for her exactly where they'd planned to meet. She was looking at her phone. Her golden hair, shining in the sun, was in a low ponytail so it would fit in her helmet. She took her breath away and then her stomach dropped. How was she going to tell Olivia about Laura? And what would she do? Would she run from all the baggage Frankie suddenly carried like the weight in their class?

She had barely slept last night. There were so many thoughts running through her head. Laura showing up on her doorstep caused a flood of memories to come rushing back. And when she did doze off, she woke to Olivia's beautiful face and remembered those luscious lips on hers and how her heart melted when their tongues met.

Olivia looked up as if she felt Frankie there before she saw her. And when she did, the smile that appeared on her face was breathtaking. As Frankie got closer, Olivia's face turned from joy to concern.

"Hey, are you alright?"

"Do I look that bad?" Frankie said, leaning her bike against a tree. She sat down next to Olivia.

Olivia watched her for a moment. "You look tired. Is something wrong?"

"I didn't sleep much last night."

Olivia's eyebrows raised her face full of concern. "What happened? Were you sick?"

"No, not exactly. But before I explain, I want to tell you thank you again for such a wonderful time last night." Frankie looked at Olivia earnestly.

Olivia was happy that Frankie had a good time, but her stomach fell; something didn't feel right. "I'm glad you had a good time. I did too."

Frankie took a deep breath and held Olivia's eyes. "When I got home last night, Laura was sitting on my front porch."

Olivia's face fell, "Laura? I thought she got married last night."

"It seems she couldn't go through with it. She had been having doubts and when she got to the church she realized she was making a mistake."

"Wow. That must have been so hard for her."

"Yeah, she was really upset."

"Why did she show up on your doorstep though?" Olivia was beginning to get a really bad feeling about this. And her compassion for Laura was waning. When Frankie looked away Olivia's heart sank.

"She said it was a mistake ever leaving me." Frankie found Olivia's eyes again, her face falling as her stomach dropped. The last thing she wanted to do was hurt Olivia.

"Whoa."

"Yeah, I was obviously surprised and totally caught off guard."

"What did you do?" Olivia asked tentatively.

"I didn't know what to do, it was all so confusing."

Olivia could see the pain on Frankie's face. "I'm sure it was."

"I listened to her for a minute while she calmed down, but I told her I needed time to process everything she said."

"What all did she say or am I overstepping?"

"No," Frankie said, reaching for Olivia's hand. "You're not overstepping. I still can't believe it." Frankie took a deep breath and continued, "She said she was going to spend the rest of her life making it up to me and asked me to please give her a chance. Give us a chance."

Conflicting emotions ran through Olivia. She felt compassion for Laura, but she was also mad at her for putting Frankie through this. And Frankie? They were just getting started. Or was it over before it really began? She was in love with Laura not that long ago. They sat in silence as these feelings continued their assault through Olivia's heart and mind.

Olivia had to know. She sat up straighter, "What did you decide to do?"

"Nothing."

Relief washed over Olivia for a moment, "Nothing?"

"Not last night. That's when I told her I needed some time." Frankie felt weary. She still had to call Laura and they had to talk at some point.

"Have you decided what you're going to do?" Olivia asked weakly.

"I told her I'd call her today. I promised to hear her out, but it was too much last night."

"That's why you had so much to think about last night."

"Yeah, at one point I thought of you and Stella."

"What?"

"There was so much flying in and out of my head and I remembered you both saying meditation can calm your mind. I was sorry I never let you show me how."

"Oh Frankie, I'm sorry you're having such a hard time." Olivia stroked the back of Frankie's hand with her thumb.

Frankie looked into Olivia's velvety brown eyes with tears in her own, "I don't know what to do. I feel like I've got to at least listen to what she has to say."

Olivia's eyes began to dampen as her heart ached for Frankie, "Of course you do. What can I do to help?"

Frankie shook her head. "Would you mind if we didn't ride today?"

"Not at all."

"Thanks. I don't think I have the energy."

"Understood." Olivia had never been in a situation like this. She wanted to comfort Frankie, but she also wanted her. She didn't want to bash Laura, but she hurt Frankie and therefore needed a little bashing.

"Could we just sit here a minute? Oh man, Olivia. Am I making you uncomfortable? After a wonderful night, I show up talking about an ex. Why aren't you running away."

Olivia chuckled, surprised that she could. "I'm not running because I'm on my bike. We did have a wonderful night, but Frankie I'm your friend and whatever you need, I'm here. So, I'd love to sit here and hold your hand. Okay?"

"I really need that."

"Done." Olivia sat back and took Frankie's hand. People meandered through the park, birds sang, and kids played. Frankie's breathing calmed and she laid her head on Olivia's shoulder. Olivia smiled to herself and leaned her head on Frankie's. They stayed like that for a few minutes until Frankie sat up.

"I'd better go."

Olivia nodded.

Frankie leaned over and kissed her cheek. "I'll see you tomorrow in class?"

Olivia smiled, "I'll be there. And Frankie, if you need anything…"

"Thanks."

She watched Frankie ride away. Olivia couldn't believe how wonderful her life was an hour ago and how unsettled it felt now. Frankie wasn't the only one that didn't feel like riding, so Olivia pedaled home. As soon as she got there she pulled out her phone and texted Sofia.

Olivia: Feel like doing some day drinking?
Sofia: What happened to your bike ride?
Olivia: Can you come over?
Sofia: Be there in 30.

. . .

One thing Olivia loved about Sofia was that when she really needed her, she'd drop what she was doing and be there. Just like now. While she waited for Sofia, she changed clothes and got a beer, then sat in her metal rocker on the patio. The rhythmic movement could sometimes ease her troubled mind, but not today. Last night with Frankie had been almost perfect. She could sense the strengthening of this cord that pulled them together. They had been seeing each other several times a week for several weeks and building a friendship and yet, there was that tug… to be more. They had finally taken that step and now what?

"Hey, where are you?" Sofia called.

"Out back, grab you a beer."

Olivia heard the refrigerator door open and close and the hiss when Sofia opened her beer. She heard her open the cabinet door to get a coozie and then step on the porch.

"What a beautiful day," she said sitting in a chair next to Olivia and taking a drink of her beer.

Olivia smiled, Sofia was rarely subtle but she knew just how to act with Olivia. "Yeah it is."

"So, why are you not riding your bike with Frankie?"

Olivia sighed, "After such a perfect date last night, today couldn't have been much worse."

"Uh, I believe you said it was the most romantic night of your life. So what changed?"

Olivia looked at Sofia, "Laura called off the wedding. She was waiting on Frankie's porch last night when she got home."

"Oh my god, you're kidding!"

"Nope, and it gets better. She said she made a terrible mistake and wants Frankie back."

"Too bad! I hope Frankie sent her on down the road."

Olivia looked at Sofia, shaking her head, "You know Frankie isn't going to do that. She was crying and upset. I guess she came from the church and was waiting on her."

"So what did she do?"

"Nothing. She's supposed to call her today so they can talk." Olivia looked out over her yard and rocked harder.

"Nothing?"

"That's what she said. Frankie looked so tired, she didn't get much sleep and I know she's confused. She said she didn't know what to do."

"Hmm."

"Yeah. I guess she's going to hear her out and, I don't know, maybe they'll get back together?"

"Wow. I don't know Olivia, it's been awhile and she seemed over her, you know?"

"That's what she told me but, she was in love with her, remember. And you don't just fall out of love."

"I know that, but time passes and you move on. That's what Frankie's done."

"Maybe. But she was forced to move on, Sof. She wasn't the one that broke up."

"Yeah," Sofia sighed. "What are you going to do?"

"What can I do? I told her I was here for her, but I'm not really the one she should be talking to about this. She did say she had a wonderful time last night."

"That's something," Sofia paused. "Look Olivia, I know Frankie is a nice person and has a big heart, but she said she was never going to be someone's first again. Remember?"

"Yes, I remember. But I don't think that matters now," Olivia sighed. "She did say she'd see me tomorrow."

"Good. This is really unbelievable, isn't it?"

"That's the way things go for me. I finally work my way back from feeling like I'm not good enough and find someone that's wonderful! Only for the ex that she was in love with to come back." Olivia finished her beer and stood, "Do you want another?"

"So that's it, you just let Frankie go back to this woman that broke her heart and will again?"

"Let her? It's not up to me, Sof."

"You could give her a better option."

"What?"

"You know Frankie felt how wonderful last night was, too. So show her there's a better woman for her and it's you."

Olivia thought about what Sofia said and went in to get them both another beer. She handed one to Sofia, "I don't know, she said she didn't know what to do and I don't want to add to the pressure she already feels. But part of me feels like this was the beginning of forever." She turned to Sofia, "Please don't make fun of me. I know all we've shared is a kiss, but that kiss... it was like a promise of everything to come."

"Olivia, are you falling for Frankie?"

"I already have," she said with a sad smile.

11

Frankie watched Grace walk into the restaurant with relief. She hoped talking to Grace would help her make sense of the whirlwind that had suddenly become her life.

"Thanks for making time for me today."

"Glad I could. I have to say, it seems that we meet anywhere but the office."

"It works though."

"And that's what matters."

Their waitress took their drink order and gave them a few minutes to peruse the menu. Grace watched Frankie over the top of her menu, her anxiety visible.

"Are you not hungry? You may be looking at that menu, but you're not seeing it."

"No, I'm not. And before you ask, I haven't had much sleep either."

"Want to tell me what's going on?"

The waitress came back over bringing their drinks and took their orders. When she left, Frankie took a deep breath. "I had the best date with Olivia Saturday night."

"Oh, that's right. Good for you!"

"When I got home, Laura was there. She couldn't go through with the wedding, left the church, drove straight to my house, and waited until I got home."

"Why did she call it off?"

"According to her, she began having terrible feelings that she was making a horrible mistake. All she could think about was me and these feelings built until she couldn't go through with it."

"How did that make you feel."

"Confused, angry, happy."

"Understandable. Let's start with the happy."

"I used to dream that she would show up one day and tell me she still loved me and was wrong to leave."

"So did that dream come true?"

"Not really. Part of me wanted to grab her and hold her, but that quickly turned to anger."

"Go on."

"You can't mess with people's hearts like that, but then again I know now that's not what she was doing."

"What do you mean?"

"I didn't talk everything through with her that night because it had all just happened. I didn't want to say something I would regret or couldn't take back."

"That was smart."

"I have learned a few things from you and our sessions. I met her the next day and listened."

The waitress brought their food and they waited until she walked away.

"Hold on just a sec. You said you were happy, angry and confused. What was the confusion."

"I had just been on this romantic date with Olivia and that's all I was thinking about. Then I look up and there's Laura. There were a lot of emotions running through me."

"Do you want to tell me about this date?"

Frankie's eyes glazed over as she went back to Saturday night, she remembered their moonlight walk, how Olivia's hand fit so perfectly in hers. And that kiss... her cheeks reddened just thinking about it.

"I've told you how I feel drawn to Olivia, and when we see one another it's usually in class or on bike rides and other people are around. But Saturday night it was just us and we didn't have to fight that pull. We could sink into, embrace it. Like I said, it was very romantic and...," Frankie didn't finish as she searched for the words.

"And?"

"It's hard to explain but, you know that feeling when you're exactly where you're supposed to be? You could feel peace, comfort, excitement, or all those rolled into one. Saturday night I felt like Olivia King was the woman I was supposed to be with," she paused. "Maybe forever."

Grace nodded her head, "How was your talk with Laura?"

Frankie sighed, "She said everything I wanted to hear, if it had been months ago. But now? I could see her heart breaking because she didn't want to hurt me, but she did. She knows that and wants me to give her a chance, give *us* a chance. When she says it like that it makes all these good memories flood back. She said she will earn my trust back." Frankie stopped and took a deep breath.

Grace waited, giving Frankie a moment.

Then she continued, "She said she didn't want me to make any kind of decision right now. She's texted me a couple of times, but she hasn't been pushy."

"And what about Olivia?"

"I saw Olivia on Sunday and told her about Laura showing up on my porch. And I told her she wanted me back."

"How did she react?"

"As a good friend would; she said she was there for me, but I can't really talk about this with her, now can I?"

"So, what now?"

"That's what you're supposed to help me figure out."

"You know where to look."

"I know, in my heart. One minute I think about how good it was with Laura and how happy we were. Then the next minute, I think what it could be like with Olivia. Next, I ask myself if I could ever trust Laura again. Does she mean it this time? Because she did before. Then all I can see is Olivia's face and feel her hand in mine. It's like that, back and forth, back and forth. I'm exhausted."

"Maybe you need to step back from all of this, let the emotions calm somewhat and then take a fresh look."

"I have class with Olivia tonight and feel like I owe her something. An explanation. And we ride bikes tomorrow."

"An explanation? What would you say to her?"

"That's just it, I don't know."

"And what about Laura, how did you leave that?"

"She said she'd give me some time."

"You haven't eaten much. My advice is to get some rest, eat what you can, and try to step back and take a breath. You'll figure this out Frankie, but you don't have to do it today."

Frankie nodded and released another deep breath.

∼

OLIVIA HAD BEEN THINKING about Frankie all day and couldn't wait to see her. This was the last week for their weight-lifting class. She wasn't concerned because she knew she'd still see Frankie during their bike rides and when she came to workout at Your Way. But Laura's proclamation that she wanted Frankie back had changed everything. Olivia was unsure where that left her and Frankie and that made her want to talk to Frankie even more.

She was working at the site, and when the developer came in with her boss, she knew it wouldn't be good news. They had asked for several changes on one of the plans and she had been working on it all day.

After their brief meeting, Olivia needed to stay and wait for the prospective buyers to come see the changes. There was no way she'd make class, so she called Sofia.

"Hey, I'm going to miss class tonight."

"What? You never miss class. What's up?"

"I have to work, no way to get out of it."

"Okay, I'll let Frankie know."

"Thanks. I'll text her too. I really wanted to talk to her tonight and see how she's doing."

"I know. I'll text you when class is done."

"Okay, thanks. I'd better go."

Olivia sighed and thought about what she wanted to say to Frankie.

Olivia: Hey, I have to miss class, can't get away from work.

Frankie: Oh no! I was hoping we could talk.

Olivia: How are you doing?

Frankie: Better.

Olivia: Good. Are we still riding tomorrow?

Frankie: I hope so.

Olivia: Me too. I'll try to text tonight when I'm finished.

Frankie: ok

Olivia stared at her phone. She wants to talk to me, and she wants to ride tomorrow. Hopefully, that's a good thing. Olivia shook her head; Frankie wasn't the only one that was confused. Should she hope Frankie doesn't go back to Laura? What if that's where Frankie belongs? *Stop, Olivia, you know what you felt.*

Olivia walked the prospective buyers through the changes they wanted and showed them how some would work and how others wouldn't. She guided them to make changes that worked better than what they originally planned and would still be within the guidelines for the subdivision.

When the buyers left, Olivia's boss, Elizabeth McMillian, turned and studied her for a moment. "That was impressive Olivia. You led them right to where we needed them to be, but they also got what they wanted. Well done."

"Thanks Elizabeth. After figuring out what it was they really wanted, it was just a matter of showing them a better way as far as the design was concerned."

"Yes, but when I talked to them earlier, they were adamant about keeping things how they wanted, or they were walking. You diffused that situation, gained their trust, and designed their dream home."

Olivia liked Elizabeth, but she was firm in what she expected and very tough. This was high praise coming from her and made having to stay late unexpectedly easier to take. "Isn't that what I'm supposed to do?"

Elizabeth chuckled, "It is, but thanks for staying late, good job."

Olivia gathered her things and noticed a text from Sofia. When she got in her car and left the office, she called her.

"Hey, just saw your text."

"Hi, just getting off?"

"Yeah, long evening, but my boss actually thanked me."

"Wow, maybe she's finally seeing how good you are."

"Maybe, how was class?"

"It was strange without you there and Frankie was quiet."

"Quiet?"

"Yeah, I could tell she had a lot on her mind. She didn't interact as much with the group."

"I texted her earlier and thought I would again when I get home. I don't really know what to say. 'Hey Frankie, going back to your ex? Or can you still feel that kiss too?' I mean."

"Well, she'd be crazy to go back to her when she could have you."

"Thanks, but you might be a little biased."

"I don't think so. She can trust you."

"She said we were still riding bikes tomorrow so that's a good thing."

"You deserve to be happy Olivia. And if Frankie's the one to do that then great, but you don't deserve any back and forth with her and the ex."

"I know Sofia, but I want to be her friend, too. You didn't see her, she was so upset."

"You've got a big heart Olivia and so does Frankie, but please be careful."

"I will. I'll talk to you tomorrow."

Olivia thought about what Sofia had said. She didn't know where things were between her and Frankie without talking to her, so she was trying not to think too far ahead. They'd get a chance to talk tomorrow on the bikes.

As Olivia walked into the house her phone pinged, it was from Frankie.

Frankie: Hey, are you through working?
Olivia: Just got home. How was class?
Frankie: Not the same without you.
Olivia: Aw, wish I could've been there.
Frankie: Sorry, but I can't ride tomorrow. I have to cover one-on-ones all evening.

Olivia was disappointed, but she knew that was part of Frankie's job and she tried not to read more into it. She didn't want to add to Frankie's problems.

Olivia: No problem. I'll do a ride on my own. I've got to keep training for that triathlon.
Frankie: Thanks for understanding. Could we talk after class Wednesday, maybe go somewhere?
Olivia: Sure, I'd like that.
Frankie: Ok, see you then.

~

Frankie walked into the office after teaching the early morning spin class.

"Where's Stella, I thought she was here early today," she asked Desi.

"She'll be here in a little while; this is her swim morning. How was spin?"

"Good class, it was full."

"So, are you going to talk to me about Laura or hold it all inside? You stayed busy yesterday, is that your plan again today?"

Frankie sighed, "You were gone Sunday or we would've talked then."

Desi looked at her with an 'are you kidding me' expression.

Frankie took a deep breath, "I'm so confused. I still can't believe she showed up on my porch."

"Have you talked to her since?"

"Yes, she said she isn't going to push me, but she plans to make this up to me."

"Damn. Do you believe her?"

"Yes, but that doesn't mean I can trust her though, does it? And then there's Olivia."

"What if there wasn't an Olivia. Would you give Laura another chance?"

"I don't know. It would take time for me to trust her again."

"And Olivia?"

"I'm torn, Desi. There's something about Olivia. I'm comfortable with her in an unexpected, unpredictable, exciting way. When I know I'm going to see her, I can't wait to see what happens next. But then I think of Laura and what we used to have. You remember, we were really good together."

"I do, until she came home and told you she'd been sleeping with a man."

Frankie let out a breath, "I guess that tells me what you think I should do."

"Frankie, I want you to be happy. I do remember how happy you were with Laura, but she broke your heart and I don't want that to happen again."

"I don't either, Desi. But the same thing could happen with Olivia." Frankie took a deep breath, "Look, I haven't told you this, but after Laura left, I was having a really hard time."

"I remember. I was worried about you."

"Well, I started seeing a counselor then."

"You did? Good for you!"

"You don't think I'm weak or crazy?"

"Of course not! You didn't think that did you?"

"I was a little embarrassed about it, that's why I didn't tell any of you. But Olivia knows."

"You told Olivia but not me?"

"Don't get upset, it came out one day. That's what I mean about being comfortable with her."

"So, have you seen your counselor since all this happened?"

"Yeah, she suggested I step back so the emotions can calm some."

"That sounds like good advice. You know Laura is going to wait, but what about Olivia?"

"I don't know. She's so understanding, but this is a bit much. She hasn't run from me yet, but I wouldn't blame her if she did. It seems like a lot to ask. We've only had one real date."

"And? Your face looks like it was good."

"It was so much better than good," Frankie said, smiling and remembering their kiss.

"Maybe that's your answer."

"It should be, but I'm apprehensive because Laura was very convincing."

"So, what's next?"

"I'll see Olivia tomorrow after class."

"Good luck. No matter what, I'm here for you."

"Thanks Des."

∼

OLIVIA SLICED THROUGH THE POOL, allowing the underwater silence to envelop and soothe her weary mind. It felt good to use her arms and legs after missing her Sunday bike ride as well as her strength class last night. She loved the quiet of the pool. The sounds above water of voices or splashes from other people swimming could be left behind by simply putting your head under the water. Though she had to work her muscles to stay afloat there was also a calmness and peacefulness similar to when she meditated.

At the end of the pool she stopped, checking the time, she'd gotten there early today and was finished with her workout when she noticed Stella walking toward her.

"Good morning."

"Hi Stella."

"You're early this morning."

"Yeah, I'm already finished." Olivia made her way out of the pool.

Stella handed her a towel. "How are you doing?"

"I'm okay, well not really."

"Quite a shock about Laura calling off the wedding?"

"Is it? I don't know anything about her except she hurt Frankie when they broke up."

"She's not a bad person; I think she doesn't know what she wants or maybe she does now. Who knows? I wasn't surprised when she broke up with Frankie in the first place."

"Really? Frankie told me she never looked ahead when they were together. That their relationship was comfortable, but she didn't think about the future."

"Hmm," Stella said thoughtfully. "What about you?"

"What about me? I've been asking the same question. Did Frankie say anything to you about our date?" Olivia smiled, thinking back on their incredible evening.

Stella returned the smile, "She said it was one of the best dates she'd ever had."

"Same for me. But she obviously has a lot to think about now."

"I guess she does. Frankie isn't one to make hurried decisions when they involve people. She sometimes thinks about the other people's feelings before considering her own and that's not always a good thing. What I'm trying to say is, don't give up on her because she may take some time with this."

"You know, I don't want to add any additional pressure on her, but I'm torn. There's something between us and I'd like to see where it could go. But Laura wants her back."

"I'm going to jump out there and say this Olivia. Frankie would be crazy not to see what you two can build together, but as I said she'll take her time, that's just the person she is. You're worth so much more than you give yourself credit for and I think you're beginning to see that."

"I do. I need to sit down with Frankie before I do anything though."

"Just know that I'm here for you anytime."

"Thanks Stella, but I understand Frankie is your friend."

"You're my friend too," she said hugging Olivia to her.

∽

OLIVIA COULDN'T WAIT to get to class, not that she necessarily wanted to lift weights, but because she'd finally see Frankie. She felt like it had been so long since they'd seen one another, and it had only been two days. Sofia waved as she walked up, but she didn't see Frankie anywhere.

"It's great to see you too," Sofia said as Olivia looked around for Frankie.

Olivia faced Sofia then, "Sorry Sof, it's good to see you too."

"I haven't seen Frankie, and I got here early to walk on the treadmill."

"I'm sure she'll be here; we're finally talking after class tonight."

"I hope she's as smart as I think she is."

Olivia smiled and then her face fell when Desi walked in.

"Hey everyone, Frankie was called away unexpectedly, so I'll be your instructor for the evening. I apologize she's not here, but I assure you it'll be a good workout. I teach this same class in the mornings so, if you're ready let's warm up and get to it."

Olivia noticed Desi looking at her as they warmed up and wondered what could've happened. She went through the motions for the rest of the class and was glad when they finished. When she took her phone out of her bag she had a text from Frankie.

Frankie: Hey, I'm so sorry I can't meet you tonight. Family emergency. I'll text you soon.

Olivia had a bad feeling in her stomach. She believed Frankie and hoped her family was okay, but she couldn't help feeling that maybe they weren't meant to talk, much less to be together.

12

Frankie shook her head as she thought back over the last few days. She had been trying to talk to Olivia and every time they planned something one of them had to cancel. Her Mom's fender bender was the latest reason she had to cancel. It had been almost a week since their date and so much had changed. Their last weight training class was tonight and she hoped nothing would happen between now and then so they could finally talk after class.

Olivia could hardly believe when she walked into Your Way and Frankie was there. When their eyes met both their faces lit up. Frankie walked toward her, "I'm so glad to see you, finally."

"I am too. We haven't had the best luck this week. How is your Mom?"

"She's fine. It damaged the car, not her luckily."

"That's good."

"It's your last class tonight, are you glad?"

"I'm ready to do something different, but, I kind of like the instructor, so maybe I'll have to see what she's teaching next." Olivia couldn't believe with everything going on with Frankie that they slipped so easily back into their rhythm.

"Hmm, we do offer personal training," Frankie quipped.

"I'll keep that in mind."

"Come on, the class is waiting."

They made their way to the weight area where the class waited.

"Here we are at the end of your six-week weight training program. Do you feel stronger? We're going to go through the same measurements we did back on the first day, remember? And we'll look back at where you started on the different lifts and where you are now. This is one of my favorite days in this program." Frankie's excitement was contagious.

"Am I going to measure you this time?" Sofia asked Olivia.

"Very funny. Yes, you're measuring me. We know how to do it now."

They took turns measuring and ohs and ahs could be heard throughout the room as their measurements had changed over the course of the program. Everyone had increased their weight lifted and a feeling of accomplishment was seen in everyone's faces.

"Let's celebrate, everybody," said Veronica. "Are we done Frankie?"

"That's it for tonight. Thank you all for taking the class, I'm proud of every one of you. Let me know if you need help choosing another class or this one will be offered again soon; we take a little break. If you want to keep lifting on your own, you have the basics and can continue. I'm here to help though, just because class is over doesn't mean I won't help you when you need it. Just ask."

"Frankie, you're welcome to come with us."

"Thank you, but you all deserve this without me tagging along."

Everyone thanked Frankie and started to leave for the bar.

Stacy walked over to Olivia and Sofia, "Hey, are you coming tonight?"

Sophia looked at Olivia, "I'll be there, but Olivia can't make it tonight."

"Aw, that's too bad. I'll see you around the gym Olivia."

"Have fun Stacy." She turned to Sofia, "Are you going?"

"Yeah, Veronica and Alice will be a hoot tonight. Call me later," Sofia said, winking and walking away.

Olivia saw Frankie waiting. "Let me grab my stuff and we can go." They walked to the office and while Frankie gathered her things she said, "Do you want to get a drink or go somewhere?"

"It doesn't matter to me, wherever you want to go is fine." Olivia looked at the class schedule outside the office while she waited. The front door opened and a beautiful woman walked up as Frankie walked out.

"Hey," she said, kissing Frankie on the cheek.

"Laura, what are you doing here?"

"I thought I'd surprise you and see if you wanted to grab a drink. You're through for the night, aren't you?"

Olivia watched the scene play out and felt her stomach fall. She recognized Laura from the first day she came in Your Way. This was the woman that pulled Frankie away from her and Sofia during their tour. She was stunning, her dark hair was long, rich, and full. It gleamed in the overhead lights. Her legs were long and she had curves in the right places. You could see her love for Frankie shining in her eyes.

Frankie looked at Olivia and said, "I can't Laura." Laura noticed Olivia then and Frankie said, "Laura this is Olivia King, Olivia this is Laura Phillips."

"Hi," Olivia said, extending her hand.

Laura shook it and smiled.

"Okay. I'll see you tomorrow then, it was nice to meet you Olivia."

"You too Laura."

As she walked away, Frankie looked at Olivia, "Sorry, that was awkward."

"No big deal, where do you want to go?"

"How about the lake?"

"Where we went before?"

"Is that all right?"

"That'd be great."

"Maybe we can catch the sunset. Ready?"

Olivia looked into Frankie's eyes, unable to read her. "I am."

Frankie drove them in her Jeep and pulled up near the water. She grabbed a blanket from the back and spread it near the water.

"This is beautiful."

Frankie sat down and let out a deep breath. "I've been here a couple of times the last week, to think."

Olivia sat crossed legged next to Frankie but facing her. "I know you're having a hard time and I'm sorry this is happening to you."

"The last thing I want to do is hurt anyone and I'm afraid that's what I'm going to do."

"Frankie," Olivia took her hand and couldn't believe what she was about to say. "I hate seeing you like this. I think I should back away so you can see if you have anything left with Laura. By the way, she's stunning and I could see how much she loves you."

"Is that what you want? To back away."

"No, but if I did then maybe it would be easier."

Frankie held onto Olivia's hand, looking in her eyes not saying anything.

Olivia looked down, "Besides, the class is over, so we won't see one another then."

"What about our bike rides. Do you not want to ride with me anymore?"

Olivia looked up, "Of course I want to ride with you." She reached up and cupped the side of Frankie's face, "But I don't want us to get down the road and you ask, 'what if' about Laura. You know that could happen and everyone would be hurt."

Frankie had tears in her eyes. "I hear what you're saying and if it's the best thing to do why does it hurt?"

Olivia looked at Frankie with a sad smile, "Look, work is getting crazy again and I'm training for the triathlon. Let's try to ride one day on the weekend like we've been doing."

Frankie looked panicked, "You're still coming to the gym, aren't you?"

"Yes, I'm still going to lift two days a week. But Frankie, won't that make it hard, seeing one another?"

"I don't care. I have to see you and know you're okay."

"You will. I'm still doing yoga with Stella, too." Olivia paused then added, "And Frankie, I'm your friend. If you need me, I'm here."

Frankie nodded, "I'm here for you too. Don't hesitate if you need me Olivia."

Olivia sat next to Frankie straightening her legs and looking out over the water. She held Frankie's hand with both of hers and put her head on her shoulder. They stayed like that as the sun set. Frankie drove them back and pulled up next to Olivia's car and rolled her window down.

Olivia walked around the car and was reminded of the day Frankie brought her the smoothie. When she backed out of the driveway that day, Olivia had wished she'd kissed her. This time she looked down into Frankie's eyes and leaned over, she gently placed her lips on hers. The soft kiss begged to be deepened, but Olivia pulled away, instantly missing the feel of Frankie's lips.

Frankie grabbed Olivia's hand, stopping her from walking away. She placed her lips on the back of Olivia's hand and then pulled it to her cheek closing her eyes. She let out a breath she'd been holding and said, "Text me when you want to ride this weekend."

Olivia said softly, "Okay." Then she got in her car and drove away, her heart breaking.

∽

It rained all weekend so Olivia did not get to ride with Frankie. She laughed at the twist of fate that kept them apart all week and seemed to continue. There was a hole in her heart from her last conversation with Frankie. She'd had no intention of backing away from Frankie unless she had asked her to. But while talking to her, it became apparent that was what she needed to do. Olivia was good at hiding things from herself, she'd known she was falling for Frankie, but told herself she was being silly. The loss and pain she felt all weekend was anything but silly. She wasn't sure, but she didn't think she felt this bad when Beth left and they'd lived together.

She'd always heard you don't choose who you fall in love with, but she'd chosen Frankie. If anything, she tried to talk herself out of it using her awful self-image belief when she first came to Your Way. But slowly, her confidence began to return and that awakened her spirit thanks to Stella and Sofia and even her job. But mostly Frankie was responsible because she made her feel good enough again. And the most amazing part to Olivia was that she didn't really say anything, it was just how Frankie made her feel.

Now as she got ready for work, she looked in the mirror and said aloud, "What were you thinking? Why would you walk away from what could've been your happily ever after?" She continued to stare and tears once again pooled in her eyes. Deep down she believed this was the right thing to do, but would she be the one asking "what if" someday? She shook her head, "God, I hope not."

She had to work at the site today and normally she loved it, but today all she could think about was Frankie. As she drove by the house they looked through, she could still see them on the porch having dinner and feel the kiss they shared on the patio. She felt Frankie's hand in hers as they walked the neighborhood and remembered the stillness of the night and the smell of the sweet night air.

Shaking herself from the memories, she noticed her boss' car in the driveway. Olivia wasn't expecting her to be here, this was odd. When she went in the house, the site manager and Elizabeth were in conversation.

"Good morning, Olivia," Elizabeth said as she closed the door.

"Good morning. I didn't know you were going to be here today."

"I wanted to talk to you and didn't want to drag you away when I knew you needed to be here today to meet clients."

"Oh, okay."

"Brian said we could use his office because he's going to one of the new constructions this morning."

"I'll leave you to it. Olivia, I'll be back later to talk changes with you."

"Great," Olivia said half-heartedly.

"They're not bad this time, I promise. See you, Elizabeth." Brian left and they went into the office.

"How was your weekend?" Elizabeth asked.

"Uh, it wasn't the best," she said truthfully.

"I'm sorry. The rain kind of messed it up for a lot of people I think." Elizabeth walked to the couch and sat down.

Olivia nodded, taking a seat on the chair opposite her.

"I've been so pleased with the work you're doing Olivia. And the way you handled those anxious clients the other day was impressive."

"Thanks, sometimes that's part of the process."

"It is, but you handled it better than most. You're aware that we're developing another subdivision very similar to this one in the Houston area?"

"I am."

"Well, they are experiencing some of the same problems that have come up here."

"Really?"

"Yes, and the architect's approach isn't, let's say, as gracious as yours."

Olivia didn't know why Elizabeth would be sharing this so she patiently waited.

"What I'm getting at is that I'd like you to go down there and work with them and show them how you're doing it here."

Olivia was surprised. She rarely traveled for work in the middle of a project. "If I do that, what about issues that arise here? Because you know there will be more."

"I know and I'll take care of them."

Olivia studied Elizabeth, she didn't really deal with clients so this was unusual for her. "You'll take care of them? I didn't think you did that anymore."

"You're right, I don't, but this is a special case."

"Special?"

"Yes, to be honest Olivia, the Houston deal is falling apart, and I know you can save it."

Olivia's eyebrows shot up her forehead. "Save it?"

"Don't look so surprised. You are great at what you do and yes, you can save it. I should've sent you down there a month ago, but I gave them a chance to straighten things out and they didn't."

"So when would I leave?"

"I want you to get things lined out here this week and then be there next Monday."

"Wow, do you have any idea how long you want me down there?"

"Hopefully, I can keep things going here so you won't have to worry about that. I want you to focus on Houston. So, two weeks, maybe more."

Olivia let the idea run through her, maybe two weeks away wouldn't be such a bad idea right now. She loved this project but surely it would be okay for two weeks. And the faith Elizabeth had in her was a bit daunting but also encouraging.

"Why don't you think about it and let me know later."

Olivia shook her head, "No, if you need me to go, I will. I'm just not sure about saving the project as you said."

Elizabeth smiled, "Thanks Olivia, I know you can do this."

Olivia smiled back, "Okay then, I'll get things together and go over it with you at the end of the week."

"Sounds good," Elizabeth said, getting up.

∽

"Do you want me to hang around and help you close tonight?"

"No Des, I got it, you go on home."

"You know, I can't decide if Laura calling off this wedding was a good thing or a bad thing."

"What do you mean?"

"You were really sad when she broke up with you but now, I think you're worse. Shouldn't you be happy? Aren't you working things out?"

"I don't know what I'm doing. Laura and I went out Saturday night. It was strange. I mean, there was awkwardness at first but that passed somewhat. She was trying so hard to make sure I was having a good time. It all felt forced."

"Forced by you or her?"

"By me. She didn't do anything wrong, I just have a lot to get past,

I guess."

"Can you? Get past it?"

"I don't know. I think that's what we're trying to find out?"

"Do you want to get past it?"

"What?"

"Maybe you don't want to. Maybe you have moved on or want to move on with Olivia."

Frankie sighed. Just the mention of Olivia's name made her heart speed up. She missed her this weekend. They texted a couple of times to ride but couldn't because of the rain.

"Did you talk to Olivia earlier?"

"Is she here?"

"You didn't see her come in? I think she's in the gym playing volleyball."

"Playing volleyball? Maybe she's doing that since our class is over."

"I think she was playing with Veronica and her group."

Frankie thought about this, Veronica was in the group that met after their strength class. Olivia said Stacy used to hit on her but she never mentioned Veronica. Why did she feel a pang of jealousy?

"Are you okay?"

Desi's question brought Frankie out of her thoughts. "Yeah, why?"

"Your face is getting red." Desi said thinking she was mad or, "Hey, are you jealous?"

"What!" Frankie tried to defend herself.

Desi smiled putting up her hands, "Calm down, I didn't mean anything by it."

Frankie looked away and got up from her desk, "I'm going to pick up towels and straighten up before I close. See you tomorrow."

Desi watched her go, thinking Olivia King might be the one Frankie couldn't get past on her way back to Laura.

Frankie cleaned up the weight area and picked up a few towels from the treadmills. The workout room was picked up but she wiped down the spin bikes so they would be ready for class in the morning. She walked through the dressing rooms and picked up a few more towels and put them in the hamper to be added to the first load of laundry tomorrow.

As she walked into the gym, the familiar sound of shoes squeaking on the floor met her along with the pungent odor of sweat mixed with shouts, cries, and laughter. This was her favorite place in Your Way. The assault on her senses usually led to fun and happiness either with a basketball or volleyball.

On the near end of the gym a small group was shooting baskets and on the far end a volleyball game was in progress. Her eyes immediately found Olivia. The ball came to her and she easily set it to Veronica to slam for a point. They high fived as the ball found the floor. The smile on Olivia's face lit up the gym, but when she saw Frankie it grew even brighter and she waved. As Frankie returned the wave Veronica grabbed Olivia around the waist pulling her back into the game. There went that pang of jealousy again.

Frankie gathered stray balls laying on the floor and put them in the racks. The basketball group finished up, adding their balls and left the gym. She walked to the end of the gym to make sure the other door was locked as the volleyball game ended. Olivia walked over to the stands with her team to get her bag and looked around until she spotted Frankie walking toward her.

Veronica put her arm around Olivia's neck, "Thanks for filling in, you were great!"

Olivia turned to her, "It was fun! I didn't know how much I'd missed playing until we started."

"You are welcome anytime, I'll text you our schedule. Next game is Thursday."

"Ok."

"Hey Frankie, when are you going to play with us again?" Veronica said, seeing her walk up.

"Let me know when you need a sub."

"I think we've found us a ringer," she said, putting her arm around Olivia again, making Frankie uncomfortable.

"Not hardly, but it was fun."

The group said their goodbyes and started out of the gym.

Olivia turned to Frankie, "Have you got a minute?"

"Always for you."

Olivia smiled. "I'm going to be out of town on work for a couple of weeks. I'm not sure why, but I thought you should know."

"Oh," Frankie said. "Out of town, where are you going?"

"Houston. There's a project very similar to the one here that's having trouble."

Frankie nodded her head, "So they're sending you down there to straighten them out."

Olivia looked at Frankie, chuckling at her choice of words. "I guess you could say that."

"How long? A couple of weeks?"

"I hope that's all it will take. I don't usually travel for work so this is unusual."

Frankie looked at Olivia earnestly and quietly said, "I'll miss you. I've missed you."

This was harder than she thought, "I'll miss you too." She swallowed hard, then forced a smile, lightening the moment, "Keep an eye on the subdivision for me. My boss is supposed to be looking after things, but I don't know if I can trust her."

This made Frankie smile, "I will. What about the triathlon and your training?"

"I'm staying at a place with a good fitness center so I can keep training. I won't be doing anything else but working so I should have plenty of time."

"When do you leave?"

"I have this week to get everything ready here, then I'll be there Monday."

"Will you have time for a ride this week?"

They started walking to the front of the building, "You'll have to let me see, at this point I may have to work short rides in during the day."

"I'll see you again before you leave, won't I?"

"Frankie...maybe this will be good. I won't be around and you'll have time with Laura."

Frankie looked away shaking her head. "Please come by before you leave."

"I will. I have a volleyball game Thursday. I'll find you." She opened the front door, stepping out. Frankie watched her walk to her car. When she got in Frankie waved with a sad smile on her face. If it hurts so bad to see her leave, how can this be the right thing to do? Frankie shook her head sadly.

∼

Olivia sat on her patio with Sofia, sharing a bottle of wine. She couldn't believe it was already Friday. This week at work had been challenging, getting everything ready for Elizabeth to take over while she was gone. She couldn't help thinking this was some kind of test; Elizabeth hadn't said anything, but they were having dinner Saturday night, so hopefully she would get the information then.

"Why the serious look?"

"I was just thinking about this whole trip. I think there's something Elizabeth isn't telling me."

"Like what?"

"That's just it, I don't know."

"Maybe she's going to give you your own project, finally."

"I don't know about that. Maybe she'll tell me tomorrow night. We're supposed to have dinner."

"So, are you seeing Frankie before you leave?"

"No. I saw her last night after my volleyball game. Hey, you should play. I remember how good you were when you played on that team with the girl you were trying to date. What was her name?"

"It doesn't matter, she was more interested in the coach."

Olivia laughed, "Oh yeah, I remember that now. But still, when I get back, I'll tell Veronica. It'll be fun."

"Yeah, yeah, I'll think about it. So, what happened with Frankie?"

Olivia sighed, "It's so strange, she was actually sad I was leaving.

And I already miss her."

"It's not strange. You two don't see it. You're in love."

"What! Love? She's getting back with her ex."

"No she's not. I'm not sure you've done the right thing here, Olivia. It's obvious she's into you and I know how you feel."

"But—"

Sofia interrupted her, "I know, I know, you have to give her a chance to see if there's anything left with the ex. But does that mean you aren't willing to fight for her?"

"Not at all. I'm trying to keep us both from getting hurt."

"And how's that going? Looks to me like both of you are hurting."

Olivia topped off their glasses and didn't say anything.

"Have you talked to Stella?"

"About?"

"Duh, about Frankie."

"No. Stella is one of her best friends, Sof. I'm not going to ask her about Frankie. Besides, what would I ask her?"

"I just thought she might know if Frankie and Laura have been going out. How it's going."

"I'm sure they have been. I don't want to know."

"Look Olivia, if you insist on this 'give them time' thing, then you should go to Houston and forget all about this. Have some fun."

"Have some fun? I'm going for work."

"Yeah, but you can't work the entire time. You have to eat. Check out the hotel bar. There will be other people there that might not want to eat alone, just like you."

"I'll be fine. I'm not going to try to pick someone up in a bar! are you kidding me?"

"I'm not saying hook up with them. I *do* know you! Maybe someone you work with can show you around. All I'm saying is, use this time to relax a little and forget about all this here."

"It's not such a bad idea to try and forget about this, but I don't know if I can."

"Just try."

Olivia nodded and smiled. Sofia was a good friend.

13

Frankie agreed to go to dinner with Laura Saturday night and picked her up at her apartment. Since Laura had called off the wedding, they had been on one date that week, but they met at the restaurant. Things weren't quite as awkward, and Laura kept the conversation going during the drive. They had lived together for almost a year after all, and Frankie could tell Laura was nervous, too.

When they were seated, Laura smiled and asked Frankie, "Do you remember this place?"

Frankie met her smile, "I do."

"That was the night you asked me to move in with you."

"I remember." Frankie noticed two women walk behind Laura as they were seated across the room. She could feel the heat rush to her face as she immediately recognized one of the women as Olivia. The other woman looked to be Frankie's age and walked with confidence and grace. When she turned, Frankie saw how beautiful she was.

"Is something wrong?" Laura asked as she glanced behind her. "Do you know them?"

"Uh, yes. One of them is a member of the gym."

"Oh. People look different when they're not wearing workout clothes, don't they?"

Frankie couldn't keep her eyes off Olivia, "Yes, they do." She watched as the other woman ordered, pausing to ask Olivia something. And Olivia nodded her head. Frankie was brought back when she heard her name.

"Frankie?"

She looked at Laura and hadn't noticed the waiter standing at the table. "I'm sorry?"

"What would you like to drink?"

They ordered drinks and Frankie looked down at her menu trying not to look at Olivia. So many questions were going through her brain. Who could the woman be? Was Olivia on a date?

"Frankie, are you all right?"

"Yes, sorry."

"You've been distracted since those women came in. Is something going on?"

"No. I was surprised to see my client, that's all." That's all? That didn't come close to how Frankie was feeling. How could Olivia be on a date? But why wouldn't she be? Frankie was doing the same thing. She had to let it go. She was there with Laura and that was where her focus should be.

The waiter brought their drinks and Frankie noticed a bottle of wine delivered to Olivia's table. It had to be a date; Frankie felt herself getting jealous and knew she had no right.

"Babe, do you know what you want to eat?"

Frankie pulled her eyes away from Olivia's table and looked at Laura, hearing what she called her. "I'm not sure," she said looking down at the menu. "What about you?"

Laura looked at the waiter, "Give us a couple of minutes, please." The waiter left and Laura reached across the table and gently touched Frankie's hand. "Talk to me Frankie. What's going on? I can tell something is off. If we're going to make this work, you have to talk to me. I know you don't want to hurt my feelings, but I have to know where you are so we can work on it, together."

Frankie sighed. Laura was right. If they had a chance Frankie needed to try. "Would you mind if we got out of here? I know this place is special, but let's find someplace else to start over."

Laura smiled, "That's fine with me. I'm sorry, I thought you liked this place." She reached in her purse.

"Let me get this," Frankie said, putting money on the table. "Come on," she said holding out her hand.

Laura got up and took her hand, "Lead the way."

∽

Movement caught Olivia's eye. She saw a couple leaving. Was that Frankie and Laura? She couldn't be sure; they were too far away.

"Do you like the wine," Elizabeth said following Olivia's stare across the room.

Olivia brought her attention back, "I do."

"Did you know them?"

"No. I thought it was someone I know but, it wasn't."

"I wanted to have dinner with you as a way of thanking you for taking this trip. I know you don't usually travel and stay with a project to the end, but this is important."

"I'm glad to do it."

"I also wanted to tell you that I've seen a change in you."

Olivia looked puzzled, "A change?"

"Yes. You've always been excellent in your designs and responsibilities, but something has changed. You seem more confident; not afraid to step up and give your opinion. Which is usually on point."

Olivia's cheeks reddened with the praise, "Thank you."

"I'm not trying to make you uncomfortable, Olivia I just wanted you to know that I've noticed. I know I expect a lot, and I'm pleased with your work."

"Thanks Elizabeth. But you didn't have to take me to dinner."

"I wanted to. So tell me, what's changed? I'm not trying to pry into your personal life, but we professional women have to stick together."

Olivia couldn't believe her ears, she had no idea Elizabeth

thought of her as anything but an employee; someone she supervised. She considered her words as she took a drink of the exquisite wine. "This may sound a bit ironic but, I think my work has improved because I'm not focused on just work all the time."

Elizabeth smiled nodding her head, "That makes sense. So, what else have you been spending your time on then?"

Olivia considered how to answer but decided to be honest, "I joined a gym, and I've made several commitments that have become, quite surprisingly, wonderful."

"Tell me more," Elizabeth said, interested.

"Well, I completed a strength program that gave me a boost of courage every time I went. I could see my fitness improve that also improved my attitude. It's still unbelievable to me."

"Unbelievable? What do you mean?"

"I'm not one to commit to things outside my comfort zone. And not only did I take the class, but I signed up to do a triathlon," she said, shaking her head.

"A triathlon? That's impressive. So, you've been training?"

"Yes. Actually, I bring my bike to the site sometimes and ride there or run after work. It's a great place with no traffic, so it's safe."

"And that's what's given you this new attitude?"

"Not only that, I've made friends there too."

"What made you decide to join?"

"Ego, vanity."

"What? You're not like that."

"I didn't like the way I looked or felt, and I was tired of just working. It sounds so vain now, but it was more than that. My self-image was terrible."

"You hid it well and your work never suffered."

"Yeah, but if I've learned anything it's that work isn't everything," she said cringing. "I know you may not feel that way."

"Oh, but I do. When I was your age, I almost lost my wife."

Olivia knew Elizabeth was married, but she didn't talk about her family very often. "Lost her?"

"I was working all the time and we wanted to start a family. She finally sat me down one day and told me, in no uncertain terms, that she was not going to raise our kids by herself."

"Wow, I'd like to have seen that." Olivia jumped, "Oh no, I said that out loud, didn't I?"

Elizabeth laughed, "I know it's hard for you to imagine, but I haven't always been quite so demanding. I'm that way because if I expect exceptional work that's usually what I'll get. That leads to fewer problems and more time for me with my family."

Olivia nodded, thinking about what she'd said.

"See, I'm selfish. I love my wife and kids and that's where I'm happiest. So, if I get you to do the hard work then mine is a breeze," she said, chuckling.

"I know that's not entirely true," Olivia said skeptically.

"Back to this triathlon. Will you be able to train in Houston?"

"Yes, I've already checked out the hotel's fitness amenities and the surrounding area. So, I'll be working and working out," she said with a little laugh.

"I don't expect you to work all the time Olivia. Remember balance. Houston has some fine restaurants you should try. I'll send you a list."

"Thanks."

"Now, would you like to see why I don't work all the time?" she said, taking her phone out."

Olivia smiled kindly, "Of course I would."

Elizabeth caught herself, "I don't mean to bore you with pictures of my family."

"You're not. I really would like to see them."

Elizabeth scrolled through several pictures with obvious pride as she told Olivia who each one was. "Do you want kids, someday?"

She smiled, "I do."

"I never dreamed they'd bring me this much joy. Okay, I do need to go over a few things about the project. Back to business."

They finished their meal as Elizabeth went over a few things for the Houston project. Olivia had such a good time and she was surprised at how forthcoming her boss was.

On the way home she kept thinking back to the couple that she saw leaving. It looked like Frankie and Laura, but she wasn't sure. It made her sad thinking about them on a date, which was foolish. Of course they would be dating. A streak of jealousy shot through her thinking of Laura kissing those lips that had claimed her own. Was Sofia right, should she fight for Frankie?

∼

Olivia's Uber pulled into the driveway of the model home that housed the office. She had planned to go by the hotel before coming to the site, but the airline didn't seem to care about her plen.

She walked into the office with her bags and was immediately greeted by a tall, striking woman who lightened her load.

"Hi, I'm Lucy Baxter. Let me help you."

"Thanks, I'm Olivia King."

"Nice to meet you, Olivia and I'm glad you're here. Right this way to your office."

Olivia followed her into a room much like her office at her own site. Lucy had short auburn hair and bright green eyes. She walked with an assuredness that reminded her of a young Desi.

"I'm your assistant while you're here. Wes, the project manager is with the site manager at one of the houses. He'll be back later."

Olivia noticed a frustrating tone when she mentioned Wes. "Thanks Lucy, it's nice to meet you, too."

"Let me know if you need anything. Elizabeth said I work for you."

Olivia raised her eyebrows, "Okay?"

"Elizabeth is a force. I'd like to pick your brain about her sometime while you're here."

Olivia chuckled, "Oh, so you're after Elizabeth's job."

Lucy shook her head laughing, "Not at all. I might just have a little crush on her."

"Oh!" Olivia joined her laughter, "I get it, she's pretty awesome, but demanding... and married."

"Oh, I know. And you're the Rockstar she's sent to save us."

"Rockstar!" Olivia said, astonished.

"Totally, you're here to save us."

Olivia narrowed her eyes, "Does Wes know this?"

"He knows that your project is doing much better than this one and is very similar. Elizabeth explained that you were going to show him what has worked up there in hopes that it will work here."

"Good, I didn't want to step on any toes."

"You're not. Are you staying at The Abbott?"

"I am."

"I'm there too. I haven't been here very long and I'm still house hunting. Did you rent a car?"

"No. The plane was late. How can a 45-flight be so late? Anyway, I didn't want to take the time."

"You can ride with me if you want."

"Thanks Lucy. That'd be great."

The rest of the day passed quickly with Olivia familiarizing herself with the subdivision. Lucy drove them to the hotel and helped her with her bags.

"They have a good bar here. It's not too crowded or too loud. Why don't you meet me after you get settled in, say 20 minutes?"

"A drink does sound good after this day. Ok, see you then."

Olivia found a stool at the bar and was trying to decide what to order while the bartender waited on another customer.

"Long day?"

Olivia looked next to her at a woman dressed in a business suit, with dark brown hair that barely touched her shoulders. She had a friendly face and sat on the stool next to her.

"Is it that obvious? But yes."

"Then let me buy you a drink."

"You don't have to do that."

"Please, I'd like to."

"Ok. Wine."

She gave the bartender their order and turned to Olivia extending her hand, "Hi, I'm Jenna Seda."

Olivia took her hand, "Olivia King, nice to meet you."

"Let me guess, travel plus work has made this a long day?"

"It has, do I look that bad?"

"Not at all. I'm going to say you came from the Dallas area."

"Wow, I did. How'd you know?"

"It couldn't have been a long flight if you worked today too. What do you do?"

"I'm an architect. You?"

"Cyber security for a financial institution here. I'm on loan."

"That's kind of what I'm doing too."

"I'm sure you came in to save a project."

"That's pretty close, but I don't want to talk or think about work."

"Deal." Jenna looked thoughtful as she studied Olivia. "Let's play a game, I ask you a question then it's your turn."

Olivia took a moment to consider, "Okay."

"Me first. Tell me something you are proud of that you've done lately."

"Wow, that's an interesting first question." Olivia thought about what she was proud of and work was off limits. "I am not in any way an athlete, but I'm training for a triathlon."

"A triathlon! That's a big deal! What made you do that?"

"Oh no, it's my turn. What are you proud of lately?"

"I am proud… that I bought you a drink and introduced myself first because that is way out of my comfort zone."

"Really! You give off a very self-assured vibe. What made you do that?"

"Hey, I see you've met Jenna," Lucy said sitting on the other side of Olivia.

"I have."

"I knew it! You're the savior Lucy's been talking about."

"I don't know about that, but I'm here to help. No work talk, remember," Olivia said smiling.

"What are you drinking? I'll buy a round."

"Oh no, one's enough for me tonight."

"Aw, come on."

"No really, I'll be asleep after this one as soon as I get to my room."

"Ok, there's always tomorrow."

"Thanks."

"What time do you want to leave in the morning? I'm usually the first to the site around eight-thirty."

"No one comes in earlier?"

"Nope."

"You can get a lot done when no one else is around."

Lucy nodded, "Ok. Seven-thirty?"

"Just because I go early doesn't mean you have to."

"I want to learn from you, Olivia."

"Okay, seven-thirty is fine." Turning to Jenna, "Thank you for the drink."

"You're very welcome. I hope to see you again soon."

Olivia noticed that Jenna had a nice smile, "Me too."

While Olivia unpacked, her thoughts wandered to Frankie. She wondered if Sofia was right and she should fight for Frankie. But she felt like she was doing the right thing by giving her the space to be sure. And then there's Jenna. She wasn't sure, but Jenna seemed interested and Olivia had to admit that it felt good. This could all wait for another day. She was tired and had a job that needed her focus.

∽

Frankie stared at the computer screen, going over next week's schedule. She sighed and rubbed her eyes.

"Something wrong?"

"Oh, hey Stella. No, I'm fine."

Stella looked at her with a questioning glance.

"Actually, I'm confused. That's me, Francesca Confused Dean. It's my new middle name," she said pointing to herself.

"Okay, what's got you confused?"

"Women, me, love."

"Whoa, that's quite a list."

"Yeah," she said, clearly frustrated and sighing again. "I don't know what I'm doing."

"Haven't you been going out with Laura, reconnecting?"

"Yes, but one minute it feels like before and then it doesn't. Time is a mysterious lady."

"How so?"

"At times I feel like that maybe I did get over Laura and moved on. It's hard because when I look at her, I still feel the hurt she caused by leaving."

"I don't mean to overstep, but have you two, uh…?" she trailed off.

"No. It's too soon for that. I did kiss her the other night," she paused. "And I thought of Olivia."

"Yikes."

"I know. I saw her the other night when I was out with Laura."

"What happened?"

"Nothing. I think she was on a date, at least that's what it looked like to me."

"A date? That doesn't sound right Frankie."

"What do you mean? Why would she sit around and wait on me? She's an amazing person; I'm sure there are tons of women that want to take her out."

"What did you do?"

"I was so distracted, I asked Laura if she would mind going somewhere else."

"I see. Did Olivia see you?"

"I don't think so. I wonder how she's doing. Have you talked to her?" Frankie shook her head, "You don't have to answer that, I know you're her friend."

"Frankie, I'm also your friend! You're one of my best friends!"

She smiled, "Thanks Stella, I didn't want you to betray a confidence."

"We've texted a few times. I wanted to see how her training is going. She was concerned about it when she left. She sure is committed to that triathlon."

"I know. I'm so proud of her."

"Yeah, me too. All we talked about was training and her job. Frankie, let me give you something to think about. When Laura broke up with you, did you ever think about what could've been? What your life would look like if she hadn't? And have you thought about what your life would be like with Olivia?"

"Hmm."

"Don't answer me. Just give it some thought, maybe it will help your confusion."

"Okay."

14

Olivia walked into the hotel bar and found her friends at a table.

"We made it to the weekend!" said Jenna.

Olivia sat down and blew out a breath, "I wasn't sure we'd make it Lucy, but we did"

Lucy laughed, "I hope you don't mind but I ordered for you."

"I don't mind at all."

"I'd say it's been a good week. You're turning things around at work."

"We are getting there. With Wes on board now I think it may work out."

"Your ideas are so good! And the way you talk with the clients is incredible. You make them feel heard."

"You know Lucy, you do the same thing. I saw you with that couple yesterday."

"Thanks. I'm learning from you."

"I know we don't like to talk work at our happy hours, but you can do what I'm doing, Lucy."

"What? That's what Wes is doing."

"I know, but keep up the good work and I'll be telling Elizabeth about the excellent assistant here. Your designs and changes are just as good as mine."

Lucy sat back, obviously surprised, "Thanks Olivia, I really appreciate that."

Olivia smiled, "Ok, enough work talk. How are you Jenna?"

"I'm glad it's Friday, too. What are your weekend plans? Are you two working?"

Olivia frowned at Lucy, "I need to go in for a little while tomorrow."

"I know, I do too."

"And I have a bike ride and run after that."

"Let's go to dinner tomorrow night then," said Jenna.

"You two go, I'm house hunting after work. My realtor has lined up a couple of prospects for me."

"How exciting! How about you Olivia, dinner?"

"Sure. Couldn't you meet us after you look?" she asked Lucy.

"We'll see, but you two should go."

∼

Olivia walked into the lobby and spotted Jenna waiting on her. She smiled as she walked toward her.

"Hey, you look beautiful."

"Thanks," Olivia got the impression this might be a date. "You look good yourself."

"I got us a car because I want to drink more than one glass of wine tonight. How about you?"

"That does sound good."

They were quiet in the car. It wasn't awkward, more of a comfortable silence.

"Where are we going?" asked Olivia.

"There's a nice restaurant not far from here I've been wanting to try, but I didn't want to go by myself."

"I know what you mean."

The car pulled into the parking lot and they went in. Olivia felt Jenna's hand softly on her back as they were seated.

"How was your ride today?"

"It was good. I borrowed a bike from one of the workers at the site. It was so nice to get outside. I've been using the exercise bike in the fitness center and it just isn't the same."

The waiter walked up to take their drink order.

"Would you mind splitting a bottle of wine?" said Jenna.

Olivia considered, raising her eyebrows, "Okay, that sounds fine."

Jenna placed the order and looked at Olivia, "You have the softest brown eyes tonight."

This surprised Olivia, "Tonight?"

"Yes, I think it's because you're relaxed. That mind of yours is usually on that subdivision and your eyes are more intense. Tonight they're soft."

"Well, thank you. I don't think anyone has ever told me that."

"So, who is missing you back home?"

"If you mean someone special, I doubt anyone. Maybe my best friend."

"What do you mean, you doubt it?"

Olivia considered her situation with Frankie. Jenna had been nothing but kind to her all week and interested in how her project was going.

"I didn't mean to make you uncomfortable," she said.

"You didn't. I'm in the middle of a... I don't know what to call it. I was sort of seeing this woman but her ex has come back in the picture."

"Sort of?"

"We've been out several times, but only on one real date, I guess. Anyway, her ex was getting married and called off the wedding at the last minute because she wanted her back."

"Wow, that is a situation."

"I decided to back away so she could see if there was anything left with ex. I didn't want either one of us to get hurt later down the road if she still had unresolved feelings for her."

"Hmm, from what I know of you, Olivia and I'm not trying to be, well... she'd be crazy to let you get away."

Olivia smiled, "Thanks for saying that."

Their waiter came back with the wine and they ordered their meals.

"What about you? Who's waiting on you?"

"No one. My wife died a year ago."

"Oh my gosh, Jenna. I'm so sorry."

"It's okay. I never thought I'd be a widow at thirty-five, but here I am. Anyway, I'm working through the grief."

"That must be so difficult. Do you mind if I ask what happened?"

"Not at all. It was an accident - a car wreck. But we've established that no one is waiting for me and probably no one for you, so let's drink another glass of wine and enjoy this good food."

Olivia grabbed the wine and filled both their glasses. Their food came and the meal was delicious, and so was the conversation. Jenna was easy to talk to and they had a lot in common.

When they returned to the hotel Jenna said, "What about a night cap?"

"May as well, but I'm already a little tipsy."

"Me too," Jenna said laughing.

They went to the bar and Olivia looked around, "I don't see Lucy. I wonder if she found a house."

"I hope so, she's tired of living in this hotel."

"Do you get tired of it? Traveling and hotels?"

"I hadn't because it made things easier at home. But I'm feeling stronger and may try to cut back some. So, what are you doing tomorrow? More training?"

"All I have to do is get in a twenty-minute swim then I may sit by the pool all afternoon."

"That sounds inviting."

"Why don't you join me."

"Let me know when you're through with your swim and I'll come down."

They finished their drinks and walked to the elevators. When they got in Jenna hit the button for Olivia's floor. Jenna was on the floor below her.

"Aren't you stopping at your floor?"

"No. I asked you to dinner so I'm walking you home like a proper person should."

"Aww, that's nice, but I think I can make it." The elevator doors opened on Olivia's floor.

"After you," Jenna said holding her hand over the door.

Olivia fished her phone out of her purse and found the app to open her door.

"Thanks for a nice evening, Olivia." She leaned over and kissed Olivia's cheek.

"Thank you, Jenna. It was fun."

They looked into one another's eyes and Jenna leaned in again, placing her lips lightly on Olivia's. She backed away, "I'll see you tomorrow at the pool." Then she walked back to the elevator.

Olivia walked into her room wondering what just happened. She was tipsy, but she didn't see that coming.

∽

ONE THING OLIVIA loved about swimming was the quiet. As she stroked across the pool, she had to concentrate on turning her head to get a breath, but she could also think. And all she could think about was Jenna. They had a wonderful evening with dinner and drinks, and when Jenna walked her to her room, she thought it was nice. The kiss on the cheek was sweet, but the brief kiss on the lips - though soft and inviting - was also questioning.

She chuckled to herself, Sofia would tell her to go for it. Olivia had never been the one-night-stand kind of girl, but Sofia would say it's an out-of-town-for-work fling. For god's sake have a little fun. But she knew she wouldn't. Because of Frankie. Deep down, she felt like her connection with Frankie was stronger than what Frankie and Laura had. She liked Jenna, and if her heart didn't belong to Frankie, then she would've kissed her back.

She touched the end of the pool and brought her head up wiping the water from her eyes. A pair of feet were right in front of her, and they belonged to a very shapely pair of legs. She looked up into Jenna's smiling face. She had on a one-piece swimsuit that hugged her curves and the vee in her top showed off her cleavage and the tops of her perfectly round breasts. Her shoulders were strong and tanned and she had her hair up in a messy bun. Olivia's heart may belong to Frankie, but she could appreciate a beautiful woman.

"Are you finished? I didn't want to interrupt your workout, but I couldn't stay inside one more minute and waste this beautiful day."

"Just done."

"Mind if I join you?"

"Not at all, the water is great."

Jenna slowly walked down the stairs into the pool knowing exactly what she was doing.

Olivia smiled, shaking her head slightly, "You look very nice."

Jenna looked at her feigning shyness, "Thanks. How'd you sleep?"

Still smiling. "Not bad, you?" Olivia said playing along.

Jenna tilted her head, "I woke up in the middle of a very good dream."

"Hmm, want to share?"

She leveled her sparkling blue eyes at Olivia as they darkened slightly, "I would let you guess, but I'm sure you have a pretty good idea."

Olivia chuckled, "Jenna, are you trying to seduce me?"

Again, she tilted her head, "Is it working?"

This time Olivia's smile grew and she covered her face, "If I didn't have someone back home, yes, it's working and it probably wouldn't be long until we ended up in one of our rooms for the rest of the day."

"Now that would be amazing."

"It would, but you know, the girl back home."

Jenna looked at her questioningly, "But is there really someone back home?"

"Yeah, there is. And I've fallen for her. You are one beautiful, sexy woman Jenna and I wouldn't be able to resist otherwise."

"Thanks Olivia, I haven't had an inkling about being with someone else until I met you. Maybe it's time."

"Wow, that's quite a compliment."

"I may not stop trying, I still have a few days before you leave."

"You are doing wonders for my self-image."

"What? You don't love yourself?"

"I like myself a lot more now than I did a few months ago. That's how I met Frankie, the girl back home. Well, I shouldn't say girl, she's quite a woman."

"So how did you two meet?"

"I had gained weight and was out of shape. This gym was running a special and I went for a tour and she's one of the owners. I didn't think there was any way she'd ever be interested in me because I was stuck on my appearance and how it made me feel."

"She'd be crazy not to be interested in you!"

"Well, as I began to take classes, of course I lost weight, but the biggest change has been inside and how I feel about myself. I've taken on challenges I wouldn't even have thought about doing before and it's shown me my own self-worth. I'd lost sight of that."

"Oh Olivia, I haven't known you long but it's obvious you are a very talented woman. And before you say anything, I mean that as hopefully your friend, not someone that wants to spend the afternoon in your room. However incredible that would be."

Olivia chuckled, "Thanks Jenna, I hope we're friends too."

"We need to make a deal."

"A deal? What kind of deal?"

"If something happens when you get back home and that woman, Frankie, is an idiot. Promise me you'll give this a chance," Jenna said pointing back and forth between them.

Olivia smirked at her and narrowed her eyes, "If something like that happened, I'd be an idiot not to take you up on that deal." She swam over and extended her hand. They shook on it.

"What are two shaking on?" said Lucy putting her things down and jumping in the pool, splashing them both.

"Hey, watch where you're jumping!"

"It's a swimming pool, you're supposed to get wet."

They all laughed.

"So, what's with the handshake?"

"A little negotiating for later in the week. Did you find a house?" asked Jenna.

"I think so," she said bobbing up and down in the water.

"Tell us about it," said Olivia.

"I'll do you one better. After our swim I'll take you to it, it's not far."

"Can we get in?"

"Yeah, the realtor is having an open house today. Now, I want to know about your date last night."

"Date!" Olivia and Jenna both said surprised.

"Oh come on. Two beautiful women, dressed up, nice restaurant, it's a date."

"How do you know we were dressed up?" asked Olivia.

"I may have seen you leave the hotel."

"Where were you?" asked Jenna.

"I may have been in the parking lot coming back to the hotel."

"Why didn't you say anything?"

"Like I said, you were dressed up, smiling, and I didn't want to be a third wheel."

Olivia and Jenna exchanged a look.

"Uh huh, so how was it?"

Olivia looked at Jenna then Lucy and said, "We had a lovely time."

"Aw, I'm so glad. You two are perfect for one another."

Jenna chuckled, "Not exactly."

"What? Why?"

"There's a lucky someone waiting back home for Olivia."

"Really. How did I not know that? She can't be very special if you've been here a week and haven't mentioned her," Lucy said pinning Olivia with a look.

Jenna jumped in, "It's complicated, Lucy. Give the woman a break. You are working for her, remember."

"Sorry, you're right, Jenna. That was out of line Olivia. I apologize."

"No problem Lucy. I wasn't aware that matchmaker was on your resume."

"It's not, that was all the two of you. I simply stepped back."

"Okay, enough. Let's go see this house of yours."

"Meet in the lobby in half an hour," said Lucy.

15

Frankie watched Grace get out of her car and walked to meet her, handing her a leash with a cute little terrier attached.

"This is Octavia. Who comes up with these names?"

"Well, I think it's perfect," Grace said, bending down to pet the dog's head. "And who do you have?"

"This is Virginia. Apparently these two were brought in close together and became friends."

"They're little cuties. Maybe you should adopt them."

"You know, if my life wasn't so messed up right now, I might consider it."

"So, what's so messed up, as you call it?"

"I feel like I'm paying you to talk about my love life. That's what brought me to you and now that's what's messed up."

"Don't you think it's a little more than that? You've got friends you can talk to about your love life with, but I'm pretty sure you don't talk about your feelings."

"I don't, I talk about my confusion."

"How are things going with Laura?"

"We've been on a couple of dates and met for drinks."

"How did it go?"

"Not bad I guess, it was awkward at first, but it's better now."

"And Olivia? Have you seen her?"

"She's been out of town working. But I did see her before she left."

"How did that go?"

"It's hard because I have feelings for her." She paused then, "But, the night I was on a date with Laura I saw Olivia in the same restaurant. What are the odds that would happen?"

"Really. Did you talk to her?"

"No. It looked like she was on a date. I guess backing away means she's dating other people."

"Hmm, from what you've told me about her, that doesn't sound like something she would do ."

"Why wouldn't she though? I was so distracted we left the restaurant before Laura knew what was happening."

"Let's go back to Laura and when you two were together. Now don't take this the wrong way, but what do you think made her leave?"

"She wanted a man."

"But that's not true because she wants you back. What was happening in your relationship that made her unhappy or think about someone else."

They walked for a bit while Frankie thought about this. "I don't really know."

"Surely you two talked when she told you about the affair."

"We did, but it was about him. And within a month they were getting married."

"Do you think she wanted to marry you?"

"We never talked about it."

"Did you make future plans or talk about what your relationship looked like down the road?"

"Not really."

"Why do you think that is? If she was so quick to marry this guy, do you think she didn't feel secure in her relationship with you?"

They turned around and headed back to the shelter as Frankie considered Grace's question.

"Now that I think back, she did drop hints sometimes about wanting kids, but we never talked about having kids together."

"Why not? You were with her over a year and you lived together. Could you not see your relationship lasting? Because if you didn't, maybe Laura picked up on that and didn't think you saw her in your future."

"You could be right. I was secure in our relationship, but I never thought about marrying her or us having kids... I need to talk to Laura."

"I think you do because if you don't know why she left then how can you not repeat the same thing again?"

"I thought she felt secure too, but obviously she didn't. I'll talk to her."

"Now, let's talk about Olivia for a moment. Have you seen a future with her?"

"Yes."

"That was a quick answer."

"I know. I've been thinking about that and even before we went on an actual date, I could imagine us together."

They walked along in silence.

Frankie stopped. "I'll talk to Laura, but I think I know what happened and what I need to do."

"Do we need to get a couple more dogs and walk them?"

"Nope. I need to talk to Laura."

"Okay. Let me know if you need to talk."

"I will."

∼

Frankie heard a knock at her door. She came out of the kitchen with a beer and set it on the table before opening the door.

"Hi," said Laura.

"Hi, thanks for coming over."

"Sure, you said you wanted to talk and I'm here."

"Would you like something to drink? I'm having a beer."

"Beer sounds good," she said, sitting on the couch.

"I like how you've changed things up in here."

"Oh, thanks," she said, handing Laura a beer and sitting on the other end of the couch.

After they both drank Frankie said, "Laura, do you remember us ever talking about the future or kids when we were together?"

"Well, I did. But you never wanted to have that conversation."

"What do you mean?"

"Frankie, every time I would bring up kids or talk about marriage, you'd change the subject or we'd get interrupted and never finish the conversation."

Frankie shook her head as she said this, "Laura, I didn't even know I was doing it."

"What? I thought you didn't want to get married, and I wasn't sure about kids."

Frankie swallowed, "Did you want to get married?"

Laura took a deep breath, "Yes, I do want to get married someday, but I know you don't want to and that's okay."

"It's not okay if that's what you want. And I never said I didn't want to get married."

"Frankie, what's going on? Do you want to get married now?"

"No. I've been thinking, and there had to be some reason in our relationship that you wanted out. Is it because we never talked about the future?"

"Honestly Frankie, I messed up, too. I wanted you to fight for me, but when you didn't, I figured you didn't really want to be with me."

Frankie sat back on the couch, "I'm sorry if I made you feel like you couldn't talk to me. And I'm sorry that I didn't talk to you."

"It's okay, at least we're talking now."

Frankie sat up and took Laura's hand, "Yeah, but...,"

"It's too late. Isn't it?"

"I don't know if it's too late. I loved you Laura, and when you left, I was devastated. I think we just weren't meant for forever and you figured that out before I did."

"But I love you, Frankie. And we could have a good life together."

"Yeah, but don't you want more than good?"

Laura smiled sadly, "It's that client, isn't it?"

Frankie furrowed her brow, "What?"

"That you want to have a great life with, not good?"

Frankie didn't answer.

"I'm not blind, Frankie. You couldn't take your eyes off her at the restaurant."

"I'm sorry. I tried. That's why I wanted to leave."

"What made you try this then?" Laura said pointing between the two of them.

"I wanted to be sure. I did love you."

Laura sighed, "I love you, Frankie." They sat for a moment before Laura got up, "Thanks for the beer."

Frankie walked her to the door and Laura turned to face her, "I'm sorry I hurt you Frankie. All I want is for you to be happy." She kissed her on the cheek and walked out the door.

∼

Frankie thought about her conversation with Laura all night. When Desi came into the office the next morning, she told her what Laura said.

"Am I hard to talk to, Des? Am I oblivious to other people? I mean how could I not see this when we were together?"

"No, you're not hard to talk to. Sounds to me like she may have wanted you to bring it up first, and when you didn't, she dropped a few hints."

"And I didn't notice."

"Maybe you didn't want to notice."

"What?"

"You said yourself you never did see a forever with her, so maybe you avoided those hints because you didn't want to hurt her."

"It makes me a terrible person for not noticing."

"No it doesn't Frankie."

"I don't want to do that though, Des. I want to be honest, and I wasn't."

"How were you not honest?"

"By not talking about it, that's not good."

"Look, you were both insecure in the relationship, but didn't want it to end. You can see that now, but you couldn't when you were in it. You were uneasy because Laura had never been with a woman before. And Laura wanted a whole lot more than you wanted at the time. Neither one of you communicated very well."

"How do I keep that from happening again?"

"Well, you know now. I don't think you'll do that again. Relationships are hard, Frankie. Look at us, we're both single at forty-four. Personally, I think you have to be brave in a relationship and tell the other person your needs. And at the same time you have to want to hear theirs and work together to find the balance that makes you both thrive."

Frankie looked at her dumbfounded, "Where did that come from? Dang, Des!"

"I'm not just a pretty face," she said, smirking. Then added, "and body."

Frankie chuckled, "You are both." Then she studied Desi, "Did you see this happening? Why didn't you say anything?"

Desi sighed, "I didn't know all of that was happening, but I could tell she wasn't the one for you."

"How could you tell?"

"I just knew, you're my best friend. I'm not saying you didn't love her Frankie, because you did. But if you remember, you were helping her through a hard time and she needed a friend. You became a friend with benefits."

"Ugh, that sounds bad!"

"No it doesn't. You were there for one another when you both needed it. I'm sorry it ended with both you hurt, but it's life Frankie. We live, love, and learn."

Frankie sat there contemplating what Desi had said when Stella walked in.

"Morning, you two." She looked at them both, "What's going on?"

"Real talk with Desi. Did you know she could be a counselor?"

Stella's eyebrows raised and she laughed, "I knew she had talents."

Desi slightly bowed her head, "Why thank you, Stel."

Frankie caught Stella up on what they had been talking about and Desi's observations.

"So, you know what you need to do now," said Desi.

"And what would that be?"

"Come on Frankie don't play dumb. You know exactly what you want to do." Desi looked at her, head nodding, coaxing her. "Are you going to make me say it? Go get Olivia."

Frankie looked from Desi to Stella, sighing.

"I think what Desi is trying to say in her eloquent way is that you felt a connection with Olivia. Now that you have ended things with Laura and know it's over, you might want to explore this connection."

Desi tilted her head, smiling at Stella and then looked at Frankie, "Yeah, that's what I said."

Frankie said softly, "I hope I'm not too late."

"What? Isn't she away working?"

"Yeah, but I saw her in a restaurant before she left on a date with a very beautiful woman."

"I told you that I doubted it was a date, Frankie," said Stella.

"But the more I thought about it, that woman was sophisticated and she ordered for them. Olivia was obviously enjoying herself."

"Oh my god, are you sure you haven't been obsessing about it and maybe reading a little too much into it. You tend to do that, my friend," said Desi.

"She'll be back in a couple of days. Talk to her"

"I don't want to mess this up."

Stella and Desi looked at one another then at Frankie, "We won't let you."

16

The week had flown by for Olivia. She, Lucy, and Wes had made headway and now the project was back on track. She knew Elizabeth would be pleased. It had been a tough two weeks, but she was proud of the work they'd done and what they'd accomplished.

It was her last night at the hotel; her flight left the following afternoon. She would miss her evening drinks with Jenna and Lucy. Most of the times her drinks were water or an occasional wine; the conversation and friendship is what she would miss. They were meeting in the lobby to go to dinner. Jenna insisted on sending her back home with a night she wouldn't forget. She flirted with her at times and Olivia had to admit she liked the attention, but she could hardly wait to get home and see Frankie. She wasn't sure their connection was as strong as she had told Jenna. Was she being hopeful? Foolish? These questions entered her mind daily and the answer changed just as often.

Two weeks away had been long enough. She'd given Frankie time with Laura, but now she was coming home and was determined to show Frankie that they should see where this could go. One more night and she'd be home, where she belonged. Or did she? The thought had crossed her mind while working on this project that maybe it was time to push for her own and create the subdivision that lived in her head.

When she walked off the elevator Jenna was waiting with a beautiful smile and a single red rose. She shyly dipped her head, then handed it to Olivia.

"I know this is cheesy, but I wanted you to have it. You look incredible."

Olivia took the flower and inhaled it's sweet scent, "You look stunning, Jenna. Thank you for the rose, but mostly thank you for making me feel amazing."

"You are amazing and I hope when you leave here you'll remember that. Shall we?"

"Where's Lucy?"

"She's meeting us at the restaurant and she's bringing someone with her."

"She is?"

"I think she's met someone and kept it quiet."

"She hasn't said a word to me."

"She hasn't really to me either, but I noticed her texting a lot lately and she's gone up early the last few nights."

"I thought I was working her too hard," Olivia said with a giggle.

"Here's our car," Jenna said holding the door open for her.

They made it to the restaurant and didn't have to wait for their table. The waiter gave them menus and left them to wait for Lucy.

"I thought you'd take a flight out tonight."

"I wasn't sure we'd be finished and that way I'd have the morning to tie up loose ends."

"Well, I'm glad. I wanted one more chance to seduce you."

Olivia laughed playfully, "See Jenna, that's what I like about you. Straight to the point so there will be no misunderstandings. Maybe I need to be more like that."

"I'm not usually like this. I don't know what you've done to me, but you've woken me up and I know our time together is short, so I'm making the most of it."

"I'm glad I could do that. Hmm, there comes Lucy, we can continue this later. Okay?"

Jenna nodded, "Can't wait."

"Hey y'all," Lucy said walking up. "This is Audrey. Audrey, this is Olivia and Jenna."

"Hi Audrey, nice to meet you."

"Hi Audrey. You two have a seat."

"Thanks," Audrey said looking around. "I've always wanted to come here."

"Glad you could join us." Jenna continued, "We're saying goodbye to our new, yet very good friend Olivia."

"That's what Lucy told me. She said she's learned so much from you."

"Aww, that's nice. We did make a good team. I'll miss these two," she said looking from Lucy to Jenna.

"Isn't it funny how quickly you get to know one another when you're staying at the same hotel," said Lucy. "I mean I saw more of you than Jenna since we work together, but I feel like I've known you two forever."

"I know, I feel the same," added Jenna.

"Now, when is the triathlon? We're coming up to cheer you on," said Lucy.

"What! You don't need to do that. I'll tell you all about it when I finish."

"Don't you want us there?" asked Jenna.

"Of course it'd be nice to have you cheering, but that's a long way to come for a race."

"No it's not, we're kind of your coaches now. If it wasn't for us do you really think you'd have gone for those swims, bikes, and runs? Knowing we'd be waiting with a drink after your workout had to be motivation," Lucy said, laughing.

"You know it was! Those happy hours were the highlight of my day, that's why I worked out so early in the morning," she replied laughing.

The rest of the meal was spent in easy conversation and laughter.

Lucy left with Audrey and promised to see Olivia before she left tomorrow.

On the ride back to the hotel, Jenna said, "We have to have one more drink together."

"I'd be hurt if we didn't." This brought a huge smile to Jenna's face.

They got out of the car and walked into the lobby. Jenna turned to Olivia, "I have a very nice bottle of wine in my room."

Olivia smiled, "Glasses?"

"I have those too."

"Let's go."

The ride up in the elevator was quiet. As they walked down the hall Olivia said, "You're not trying to get me drunk, are you?"

"Oh Olivia, I wouldn't do that. If anything ever happened between us I'd want for you to be sure with no reservations or influence."

"Influence? You'd be the influence, Jenna."

She unlocked the door and they went in. Jenna opened the wine and poured them both a glass. Olivia sat at the table and took a drink. "Oow, this is good."

"I thought you'd like it."

"Are you and Lucy really coming up for the triathlon?"

"We want to."

"If you do, y'all have to stay with me."

"Will Frankie mind?"

Olivia smirked, "I don't think she will have moved in by then."

"So, what is your plan when you get back?"

Olivia smiled, "You know Jenna, you actually helped me with this."

"I did?"

"Yeah, you've shown me my worth. As you said, Frankie would be crazy not to be with me."

"It's the truth!"

Olivia chuckled, "I don't know why, but I really do think our connection is strong enough to at least see what's next. Don't get me wrong, I've been in love before, but there is a force between us. I've never felt anything like it. Sometimes I have doubts that maybe I dreamed it"

"What you described sounds a lot like what my wife and I had. You think about them most of the time and when you're not, something pulls your thoughts right back to them. She would surprise me at work sometimes and it was like some Spidey sense, I knew she was there before I saw her." Jenna released a big sigh.

"I don't mean to make you sad."

"Oh, I'm not sad. I miss her all the time and I know it'll always be that way. But I also know there is love out there for me. And she is orchestrating it from wherever she is."

"So, she sent me to you?"

"Yes."

"What do you mean?"

"Before I saw you sitting on that bar stool, I hadn't looked at another woman. It's not like I didn't try! I would see a beautiful woman and nothing. But then there you were and something moved inside me. So yes, she sent you to show me that there is someone out there for me."

"What's your wife's name?"

"Amber."

"Maybe Amber knew you needed a friend, and that's me. I can't imagine leaving here and not staying in touch, Jenna."

"Me neither. That's why you'll see me in two weeks. I'll be the one cheering your name from different places on the course. Lucy and I have researched how to be a fan at a triathlon."

"No you haven't!"

"You know Lucy, right? The queen of research."

"Well, that's true." Olivia sipped her wine, looking off in the distance.

"What are you thinking?"

She let out a breath, "When Elizabeth asked me, which really means told me that I was coming down here I wasn't very happy about it. I never dreamed I would make two incredible friends. This has been the best work trip ever."

"I could make it a lot better," Jenna said suggestively.

Olivia laughed, "I know you could. I can't believe I'm turning you down. It gets harder and harder because it would be an honor to be your first since your wife. I mean, it would be your first, right?"

This made Jenna laugh, "Yes, you'd be the first!"

Olivia finished her wine and stood, "Thank you for dinner and wine but mostly, the conversation. I'll see you tomorrow before I leave."

Jenna stood, "I'd better. Come on, I'll walk you to your room."

"You don't have to do that."

"I know, but I want to."

They walked to the elevator and rode up to Olivia's floor in silence. As they walked toward Olivia's room, she put her hand in Jenna's. She unlocked her door and turned to Jenna, "Thanks again for the party. I'll miss you."

"I'll miss you, too. With you and Lucy both leaving I guess I'll be drinking in my room."

"You might miss out on someone in the bar."

"Doubt it." Jenna reached up and cupped one side of Olivia's face gently. She ran her thumb over Olivia's cheek, gazing in her eyes with desire. They stayed like this a moment until Jenna leaned in pressing her lips to Olivia's firmly. Olivia put her hand behind Jenna's neck and pulled her in closer and kissed her back.

Without their lips parting, Olivia pulled her in the room and closed the door. When the kiss ended, they stood staring at one another, panting.

"Olivia," Jenna said softly.

She put her arms around Jenna's waist and pulled her close. "I think we've talked enough."

"Are you sure?"

Olivia answered by crashing their lips together. They both moaned. Olivia parted her lips and licked across Jenna's, enticing them to open. Jenna obliged and when their tongues met, she let out a deep groan. Olivia invaded her mouth with sweet surrender. She slowly trailed her hand down Jenna's thigh to the hem of her dress.

Jenna's hands were lost in Olivia's hair, pulling their mouths even closer.

Olivia began to pull Jenna's dress up and up until she raised her arms so she could finish taking it off. Jenna reached down, mirroring her moves pulling Olivia's dress over her head. Olivia gently guided Jenna to the bed, her eyes filled with lust and need. When Jenna's legs touched the bed she sat down, Olivia stepped between her legs and reached behind her, expertly unclasping Jenna's bra.

"It's been a long time for me too," she said, softy tossing the bra to the floor. She reached back and undid her own and throwing it to the side.

Jenna looked up at her, "You are so beautiful." She put her hands on Olivia's hips and pulled her closer. She inhaled deeply as she kissed between Olivia's breasts and turned her head to slowly laze her tongue around her nipple. Olivia gasped, digging her fingers into Jenna's shoulders. She sucked the nipple into her mouth and Olivia moaned, throwing her head back.

"God Jenna, that feels so good," she said breathlessly.

Jenna slowly made her way to Olivia's other breast, giving it the same attention.

"Scoot up the bed," Olivia said, pushing Jenna's shoulders back. She did, their eyes locked. Olivia slowly lowered her panties, kicking them away. She crawled up the bed between Jenna's legs and gently put her fingers inside her panties. Jenna raised her hips slightly so she could pull them off.

Olivia looked down at Jenna's glistening sex. She met her eyes with a sexy smile and leaned down, her hands on either side of her and kissed her deeply, easing down until their breasts touched. With a groan Jenna grabbed her and held her close, their tongues dancing.

"You're such a good kisser," Olivia panted. "But I've got other places to taste." She kissed down Jenna's neck and across her collarbone to the base of her neck. She licked and nipped as Jenna writhed beneath her.

"Good god Olivia, you're killing me."

Olivia smiled against Jenna's chest and slowly kissed her way down to her breast, and licked and bit and then sucked it into her mouth. Jenna groaned louder. Olivia went to the other side and did the same while she tweaked the first with her fingers. Jenna's hands were buried in Olivia's hair, keeping her close. Olivia kissed her way across Jenna's stomach and down. She could smell what she wanted to taste and breathed in. It had been so long since she'd smelled an aroused woman and she had missed it.

Her hands were on Jenna's stomach as she dipped her tongue between her lips. Jenna bucked and Olivia held her down gently and began to slowly lick through her folds, then down to her opening and back up again and around her clit. Jenna fisted the comforter with both her hands as Olivia continued to drive her wild.

Olivia took her right hand and stroked Jenna's raised thigh as she briefly stuck her tongue inside. Jenna's leg fell open wider and Olivia slid her hand down and replaced her tongue with one finger slowly pushing inside.

"Fuck," she groaned breathlessly.

Olivia's tongue swirled around her swollen clit while she added another finger and slowly moved in and out. Jenna matched her rhythm with her hips. When Olivia increased her pace, Jenna grabbed Olivia's head with one hand keeping it in place and squeezing the comforter even harder with her other hand. Olivia could tell she was close and went in deep, curling her fingers and sucking her clit into her mouth. Jenna stiffened, raised up and fell back on the bed panting.

"Fuck Olivia," she said, still panting, laying spread-eagle on the bed.

Olivia smiled and laid down next to her chuckling, "I think that's what we just did."

She propped on one elbow and laid her hand on Jenna's stomach.

Jenna cracked one eye open, "I knew you were incredible, but dear god!"

"Thanks?" They both giggled.

Jenna put her hand on Olivia's intertwining their fingers. She looked into Olivia's eyes, trying to see what she was thinking.

"What are you thinking? Do I want to know?"

She smiled, "I'm thinking about kissing you again."

"Then do it."

Olivia leaned down and kissed her softly. Jenna deepened the kiss and pushed Olivia onto her back.

Their eyes met, "I want you, Jenna."

That's all she needed to hear. Olivia blocked out everything but Jenna. It felt so good to be wanted and she let Jenna show her with her hands and mouth.

They lay there spent after another round. They'd pulled the comforter down and gotten into the bed. Olivia twirled a tendril of Jenna's hair as she lay on her chest.

Jenna sighed, "This is so nice."

"It is."

"You're not having second thoughts?"

"What? No! Could you not tell how much I wanted you?"

Jenna sat up and leaned against the pillows next to Olivia. "Yes, I could tell. But I also know you have someone back home."

Olivia sighed, "Honestly, I don't know that." She turned to Jenna and took her hand, "You've been honest with me since I've known you." They both laughed. "Even though that hasn't been long, you made it clear how you felt about me. When your self-image and worth are low like mine were, it's hard to think someone wants you, but you did. And sure, you told me, but I could see it in the way you looked at me and in how you treated me. You were sincere about it, not creepy, for lack of a better word. Feeling desired like that, it felt so good, Jenna. And I haven't felt that in a very long time."

"I get that. When you pulled me in this room during that kiss, and then you looked at me…I almost came right then and there." They both laughed. "The desire in your eyes, Olivia. Whew, I get hot again just thinking about it. But we both know that's not everything. There's no reason you can't go home tomorrow and get Frankie. Just know that she's not the only one that wants you."

Olivia smiled appreciating what Jenna said, "I don't really want to talk about home right now." She tilted her head, intertwining their fingers, "What was that you said about wanting..."

Jenna smiled, moving in front of Olivia and pulling her down in the bed, she yelped and giggled.

She hovered over Olivia, pinning her hands by her head with a sexy smile, "You are intoxicating."

Olivia smirked, "Want another drink?" And drink Jenna did.

Later, she woke to Olivia staring at her and smiling. She remembered falling asleep with Olivia in her arms, her head on her chest. It brought back sweet memories of how Amber used to fall asleep the same way.

"Have I worn out my welcome?"

Olivia looked puzzled, "No, why?"

"What time is it? I thought you might be kicking me out."

"I'm not kicking you out."

"Why aren't you sleeping?"

"I had to go to the bathroom."

"Mmm," she snuggled up to Olivia. "Are you going to tell Lucy?"

"I don't know. She may be able to tell by the looks on our faces. Do you not want her to know?"

"No, I mean it doesn't matter to me."

"Why does it feel like you're trying to protect me?"

"Maybe I am."

"I don't need protecting, Jenn. What's the deal?"

Jenna sighed, "This has meant everything to me, Olivia. I can't explain to you how lost I was and I didn't think I'd ever feel anything again. I don't want you to be sorry this happened and for it to mean so much to me. So, no one ever needs to know."

Olivia sat up and straddled Jenna as she leaned against the pillows and headboard. "Jenna, I'm not sorry. I won't be sorry. I have no regrets. This means just as much to me, although in a different way. It's been a long time since I've felt this wanted." She smoothed Jenna's hair back with her hands and gently kissed her cheek. She paused gazing softly into her eyes and barely touched her lips to

Jenna's. "If anything, I'm sorry it took me so long. Just imagine all the fun we could've been having," she said smiling.

A smile grew on Jenna's face until she grabbed Olivia and kissed her hard. "Should we make up for lost time?"

Olivia returned her smile as Jenna sat up, rolling her on her back again.

17

Olivia walked out of the airport terminal and started down the sidewalk. She found Sofia four cars down. She threw her bag in the back and got in.

"You didn't have to pick me up."

"I know I didn't, I wanted to. I missed you."

"We talked nearly every day."

"Yep, but it's Saturday and I needed a drink. There's a cute little bar I've wanted to stop at. It's on the way to your place. You up for it?"

"I'd rather get a six-pack of beer and sit on my patio."

Sofia looked sideways at Olivia and studied her for a moment. "You look different. Did something happen you need to tell me about?"

Olivia looked out the side window not replying.

"How was the work trip?"

"Best work trip ever," Olivia said, turning to look at Sofia.

"Beer and the patio it is. I want to hear all about it."

Olivia chuckled, "Get me home!"

Traffic was light; they stopped to get beer and were sitting on Olivia's patio within the hour.

"You look tired."

"I am a little."

"I know you didn't work the entire time or you wouldn't have had those happy hours."

"No, you could say I was up late last night."

"Don't be cryptic, you know what will happen if you make me guess."

Olivia chuckled, "Sometimes those guesses are quite entertaining. But you remember the friends I made, Jenna and Lucy."

"I do. Your happy hour buddies."

"Right. They took me out for a nice dinner last night since I was leaving today."

"That's nice. Did you stay out late partying?"

"Not exactly. Do you remember me telling you about how Jenna liked to flirt with me?"

"Of course I do. I believe I told you to flirt back and go for it."

"You may have said something like that."

"I did tell you to have a good time while you were gone. So?"

"So, Lucy met us with a date and left with her. When Jenna and I got back to the hotel, she had a good bottle of wine in her room."

"Did you get drunk?"

"No. We just talked and she walked me back to my room, and..."

"And?"

"Did I tell you she was a widow?"

"You did and you told me she was smart, interesting, and hot, too."

"I didn't say hot!"

"You may have not said hot but, you let me know she was."

Olivia took a deep breath, and the words tumbled out "She had such want in her eyes for me, Sofia! And then she kissed me and I pulled her into my room and she spent the night."

Sofia's eyebrows flew up her forehead. She jumped up and did a little dance. "I'm so fucking proud of you!"

Olivia laughed and joined her in the dance.

They sat back down and Olivia grabbed her beer and drank deeply.

"Look at you, Olivia King! Tell me everything!"

"I will not. All I'll say is it was… incredible."

"Well, how did you leave things? And what about Frankie?"

"Who knows about Frankie, she and Laura are probably ready to move back in together," she sighed.

"What makes you say that?"

"I haven't heard a word from her since I told her goodbye the day before I left for Houston."

"I'm kind of surprised."

"Have you seen her?"

"Yeah, I've seen her at the gym. I played a couple of volleyball games with Veronica's team."

"Now I'm proud of you!"

"It was fun, but back to Frankie. I saw Laura come in a couple of times. Frankie didn't seem like she was crazy glad to see her. Actually, Frankie looked kind of sad."

"Maybe they aren't back together, yet."

"When you left here you were pretty confident in the connection you two share; I think you may have said you've fallen for her."

"I think I was trying to make myself believe it. I do feel connected to her, but I may be wrong about how she feels for me."

"Is that what made you pull Jenna into your room?"

"Sof, the way she wanted me, it felt so good. She was open about it and respectful because I told her about Frankie. We were both going through dormant feelings being reignited."

"What does that mean?"

"She hadn't looked at another woman since her wife died. And you know how low I was after Beth left and that lasted for months until I met Frankie. So, when I saw that want in her eyes and it was for me, I was flattered. But in my head, there was this back and forth about Frankie. And I imagined her with Laura."

"Are you saying you made a mistake? Because you didn't, OK. You backed off so Frankie could be sure. That doesn't mean you wait around."

"I wonder if Frankie will see it that way."

"It doesn't matter how she sees it. You didn't do anything wrong. You had sex with a woman that was into you and you were into her. That's it."

Olivia took a deep breath and then drank the rest of her beer.

"How did you leave things? I mean are you going to see her again?"

"I am. She and Lucy are coming for the race."

"The triathlon?"

"Yes, they claim to be my coaches now and they're coming up that weekend to see me race. So, you'll get to meet them."

"How cool is that. But?"

"Just so you know, I didn't make a mistake. I don't regret it and I'd do it again given the circumstances. I think it was something we both needed. I'm not in love with her. I do have feelings for her as a friend, and our chemistry is off the charts in bed." Olivia giggled.

"Who are you and what have you done with my best friend."

Olivia chuckled, "This has been a transformative few months for me, Sof. Work has been crazy but good, and these past two weeks of leading that project was incredible. I never thought I'd like doing that; I've always liked being in my little box doing the changes to make every home someone's dream home. But I loved being over the whole thing. I know it was because Lucy is so good, but we were quite the team."

"You know I don't think Elizabeth gives you the credit you deserve."

"It's like I've found myself again. I never liked being that sad girl; depressed, out of shape, only good at her job. When we joined Your Way, those people and classes slowly brought me back. I feel good about myself again and feel like I have something to offer, you know."

"So are you going to turn into a fitness freak?"

"Not at all. I love working out and it's helped me feel better, but the difference is inside me."

"What's next then?"

"I'm looking forward to riding my own bike tomorrow. I think I'll ride over to the subdivision and see if Elizabeth had any problems.

"I'm glad you're back. I loved that other Olivia, but this is the one I love the most."

"I'll drink to that! I'll get us another beer."

∽

Olivia couldn't believe how good it felt to be back on her own bike. Using the exercise bike at the hotel and borrowing the bike from the site had kept her fitness level up, but being on her bike and flying through the empty streets of the subdivision really gave her joy. She laughed to herself at this thought, *who gets joy from riding a bike?* apparently she did.

To the random person driving through the area not much had changed, but Olivia could see progress that had been made in just the two weeks she was gone. She was proud of the work in Houston, but this was still her baby. Back to making people's dream homes *not* look like the neighbor's next door. Being away gave her a few new ideas that she wanted to apply here.

Riding along in her own little world, she heard her name called out. Turning to look behind her, she saw Elizabeth drive alongside her.

"Hey, making sure I didn't screw anything up while you were gone?"

Olivia laughed, "Maybe. What are you doing here on a Sunday? I thought one of the perks of being the big boss was weekends off."

Elizabeth laughed, "Usually, but I left a set of plans here I need for the office tomorrow and came by to get them. Would you have a minute to come by the model now?"

"Sure, I'll follow you."

Elizabeth pulled into the driveway and got out of her car, waiting for Olivia to ride up. She leaned her bike against the garage as Elizabeth approached her. Olivia looked up when she noticed a bike rider zoom past. It looked like Frankie. Olivia called to her but she kept going; it felt strange.

"Did you know her?"

"Yeah, well I think so. That looked like Frankie, we ride bikes together a couple of times a week. Must not have been or surely she would've stopped."

"Do you want to go after her?"

Olivia looked in the direction the bike rider went. "No, it couldn't have been her." She turned her attention on Elizabeth, "What'd you need to show me?"

"Come on in."

~

Frankie had been at Your Way catching up on the schedule for next week. She'd ridden her bike there and planned to go for a ride in the subdivision before heading home. Thinking of the subdivision made her wonder if Olivia was back yet.

She was looking forward to seeing her. All Frankie wanted to do was explain to Olivia that things were over with Laura for good and then she wanted to take her in her arms and kiss her like her life depended on it. Because it did. Olivia was who she didn't know she was waiting on all this time.

She hopped on her bike and headed to the subdivision; her thoughts on the last time she was there with Olivia. This led her right by the house where she'd surprised her with dinner on the patio. That may have been the best first date Frankie had ever had. She hoped Olivia would come to the gym tomorrow, but if she didn't, she planned to call her and ask her out on a real date. Just the thought of seeing Olivia again brought a smile to her face.

In the distance she noticed a car coming towards her. This was odd because there was rarely any traffic here, especially not on Sunday. The car pulled into the model home where the office was located. That's when she noticed a bike rider behind the car. Frankie slowed down and the woman that got out of the car was the same one she saw with Olivia at the restaurant. And then she saw Olivia! She was back and meeting up with this woman again. Frankie didn't know what to do, she panicked; she sped up and rode by, hoping they wouldn't notice her. She thought she heard Olivia call her name, but she kept going.

So many emotions were running through her head. Desi and Stella were wrong, Olivia was on a date with that woman and seeing her again as soon as she got back from Houston. How could Olivia forget about her so quickly? She thought Olivia felt that connection between them, too. It took so long for them to finally connect and stop fighting it and then Laura had shown up. Did Olivia give up? Was it not worth giving them a chance? Frankie couldn't believe she was asking these questions much less the answers. She realized this was hypocritical but, her feelings for Olivia were blinding.

∾

OLIVIA WALKED into the pool area hoping for a relaxing swim in order to get her mind off Frankie. She hadn't slept well last night. The more she thought about it, she was sure that was Frankie that rode by at the subdivision office. She started to text her last night but stopped because the idea that she was with Laura was too much for her to handle. Maybe that's why she didn't stop, maybe she and Laura were back together. The idea of that made her toss and turn. Once again, had she messed up by backing away from Frankie?

She took her cover-up and shoes off and was about to get in the pool when Stella walked in. When she spotted Olivia, she hurried to her and wrapped her in a hug.

"I'm so glad to see you!"

Olivia chuckled, hugging her back, "I'm glad to see you too! I've missed our swims and therapy sessions."

Stella held her at arm's length, "Therapy sessions, I thought we were being friends."

"We are, it's just that sometimes I needed your perspective."

"You needed perspective while you were gone?"

"I probably could've used it, but I know I need it now."

"What's up? You look tired."

"I am tired, I didn't sleep much last night."

"Because?"

"I was riding my bike at the subdivision yesterday. My boss pulled in and wanted to show me a set of plans, so I was in the driveway when I thought I saw Frankie ride by on her bike. I called out to her, but she kept going. I guess she's back with Laura, but I thought she would've at least stopped. I haven't heard a thing from her since I left. I don't know what I expected, but I thought she might let me know if they got back together or what." When she finished, she took a deep breath and sighed.

Stella took a minute to process all that Olivia said. "First, she is not back with Laura. They've ended it for sure this time."

Olivia looked at her astonished, "They aren't together! Then why wouldn't she stop? Why didn't she want to see me?"

Stella thought about what Olivia described and then it came to her. "Olivia, was your boss in the driveway, too?"

"Yes."

"Can you describe her for me?"

Olivia looked at her skeptically, "Okay, she's older than me and I would describe her as very put together. She's very confident and you can tell she's in charge. Why?"

"One more question, do you go out with her sometimes?"

"No! She's married and has kids!"

"I don't mean like that; do you have work dinners?"

"Oh, uh yeah, we've done that a couple of times."

"I think I know what's happened. Why don't you sit down a minute."

Olivia sat down, her heart racing and a sick feeling building in her stomach.

"Did you have dinner with your boss before you left for Houston?"

"Yes."

"Frankie saw you."

"What? I don't understand."

"While you were having dinner with your boss, Frankie and Laura were there."

"I thought I saw them, but they were leaving. I figured I was mistaken. What does that have to do with this?"

"Frankie thought you were on a date."

"On a date!" Olivia got up and paced, thinking back to that night.

"How could I be on a date. I'd just told her goodbye; that doesn't make sense. I don't want to date anyone." As the words came out of her mouth she thought of Jenna. She didn't want to date Jenna either but, they'd certainly fallen into bed together.

"That's exactly what Desi and I both told her. You wouldn't be going on a date so soon after Laura showed back up."

"But what about yesterday? Why wouldn't she stop? And why didn't she text me the entire time I was gone." Olivia felt tears spring to her eyes. She just now realized how much it had hurt that Frankie hadn't gotten in touch with her while she was gone.

"If she saw your boss, I'm sure she thought you were there with her again."

A tear rolled down her cheek, "But why wouldn't she just ask me? Why didn't she text me something while I was gone?"

"Now that, I don't know. She did ask me if I'd heard from you. And I know she was looking forward to you coming home."

"She has a funny way of showing it.

"Come here," Stella took Olivia in her arms. "You two need to sit down and talk. This is all a misunderstanding."

"I can't believe Frankie would think I'd do that, though. Is that what she thinks of me?"

"No! She's had a pretty hard time too, Olivia."

"I know that. That was the whole reason that I backed away - to make it a little easier for her. But sometimes I feel like I shouldn't have done that. And then all these crazy ideas fly through my head. I swear, I'm thirty-three years old; I'm supposed to be an adult and act like one, but I feel more like I'm back in high school."

Stella laughed, "Oh honey, it doesn't matter how old you are, love is complicated and makes us feel foolish at times."

Olivia laughed too, "It sure does." After a moment she turned to Stella, "What do I do now?"

"Swim. I'll see Frankie this morning and tell her what an idiot she is."

"That still doesn't answer why I didn't hear from her while I was gone."

"You can ask her when you talk. Promise me right now that you will talk to her."

Olivia nodded, "I will."

"Good. I'll get the same promise from her. Now, go relax and swim. I'll call you later."

"What about you? Aren't you going to swim?"

"No. I'm going to go find Frankie right now!"

Olivia chuckled, but felt a little bad for Frankie because Stella meant business.

"You two need to communicate if this relationship is ever going to go anywhere. This should be a good example of what happens when you don't. You've got to talk to each other."

"I know, you're right. I won't let it happen again."

Stella smiled and walked away wondering what would've happened if she hadn't figured this out. She hoped they would have eventually talked before too much damage had been done. Communication was the key to any relationship. We all know this. Why is it so hard sometimes?

∽

STELLA WALKED into the office to find Frankie and Desi both at their computers answering emails.

"Less than two weeks till the triathlon and we're still getting entries. That's great and all, but I sure hope these people have been training," said Frankie.

Stella stood with her hands on her hips staring at Frankie. She finally looked up, "What?"

"What is wrong with you?" she said, clearly frustrated and angry.

"What do you mean?"

"You saw Olivia yesterday and just rode on by?"

"You and Desi were wrong, that was a date. I saw her again yesterday with the same woman!" she said defensively.

"So you kept going?"

She sighed, frustrated. "I didn't know what to do. I saw her and then I saw that woman and I panicked."

"Again, so you just rode on by!"

"Yes, I rode on by. I was hurt and embarrassed."

"Oh Frankie, my dear, sweet, idiotic friend."

"What happened, Stella? How do you know this?" asked Desi.

"Because I swam this morning with Olivia. She is very confused and hurt because she didn't hear from you the entire time she was gone, and when she saw you yesterday she called out for you, but you kept going."

"She's hurt? Why is she hurt, she's the one that has already started dating someone else."

"The woman you saw her with both times was her boss. She was not on a date; it was a business dinner. And she ran into her yesterday while she was riding. She didn't say this, but I'm going to guess that maybe she was riding in that area in hopes of running into you!"

"Her boss? Oh my god!" she said, putting her head in her hands.

"What are you going to do now?" asked Desi.

"I'll tell you what she's going to do. She's going to call Olivia and they are going to sit down and have a conversation," She looked at Frankie severely, "Got it?"

"Yes Stella, I'll call her now."

"Wait just a second, why didn't you text her while she was away?" asked Desi.

"I don't know. I wasn't sure she wanted to hear from me. It was bad enough that she had to back away, and I didn't want to throw Laura in her face."

"What a fucking mess," said Desi.

"Yeah, but I think we may have made it worse by not talking," she said, looking at Stella.

"Let's hope you two can work it out. You're both my friends and I think you would be good together if you communicate."

"I get it, Stel. Thanks. If you'll excuse me, I'm going to call her now."

Five minutes later Frankie walked back into the office.

"We're meeting when she gets off work this evening at the subdivision. Would one of you please cover my 5:30 class?"

"I'd be happy to," said Desi.

"Do me a favor, Frankie," said Stella, putting her arm around Frankie's shoulders. "Be honest and don't be scared to tell Olivia what was going through your head at the time. All of this really messed you up, but she'll understand."

"I hope so."

18

Frankie saw Olivia's car in the driveway at the model house office and pulled in behind her. She didn't think she'd ever been this nervous. She had been an idiot, and she hoped Olivia would give her a chance not only to explain, but would figure this out with her.

As she raised her hand to knock on the door it opened. Olivia stood before her and Frankie lost her breath. They both smiled a little shyly.

"Hey," Olivia said quietly. "Come on in."

"Thanks"

"Let's sit over here," she said, leading them to the couch.

They both sat, next to one another but not touching. Neither said anything as they looked into one another's eyes.

"I'm trying to find the best way to start. So, here goes. After we said goodbye, I was lost. That evening I went to dinner with Laura. When we were seated, I looked up and you were sitting across the room from me with a beautiful woman - who I only now know was your boss." Olivia nodded and let her continue. "Here is what I saw: you with a sophisticated woman that was the total opposite of me." Olivia started to speak, but Frankie held up her hand, "Please let me continue." Olivia nodded. Frankie went on, "This beautiful woman appeared to be ordering for you both. You laughed a few times and I almost got sick. I couldn't keep my eyes off you, so I asked Laura if we could leave without telling her why."

"I saw you, too. I wasn't sure, you and Laura were leaving. I was trying to not think about you and concentrate on my job, so I thought I was seeing things."

"I told Desi and Stella what I saw and they told me I was crazy that you wouldn't be on a date the day you told me goodbye."

"But you thought I was. You thought I would do that."

"No, I didn't, but the way my mind was working that's what I saw. When I told them about it, I could hear how stupid it sounded. I think I told myself that because I couldn't blame you. Who would want to wait around to see if someone was going to get back with their ex?" she said, her voice getting higher.

Olivia smiled, "I would because I'm the one that suggested it. And now, I don't think that was what I should've done."

"You don't?"

"No! What good did that do? It showed you that I wasn't willing to fight for us. No wonder you thought I was on a date," she said, sighing.

Frankie scooted closer to Olivia and took her hand, their knees touching. "I'm sorry I didn't text you while you were gone."

Olivia looked up into her eyes, "Why didn't you?"

Frankie shook her head, "I didn't think you'd want to hear from me. You'd backed away and I didn't want to make it harder on you, and instead I hurt you. I'm so sorry, Olivia. That's the last thing I ever wanted to do."

Olivia gave her a small smile. "I could've contacted you, too. But I was afraid."

"Afraid of what?"

"I was afraid you'd text me back and tell me you'd worked things out with Laura."

Frankie nodded. "I knew within the first couple of days it wasn't going to work. I don't love her anymore. But I also realize I had to take some of the blame. If she had been happy, she wouldn't have turned to that guy. So, after several sessions with Grace and talking to Laura I now see my mistakes."

Olivia asked the question with her eyes.

"I never talked about the future with her. She would bring it up and I'd change the subject without even knowing I was doing it. She was insecure about our relationship because of that. I told you I never saw us together long term, which would've been fine if I'd talked to her about it. I seem to be bad at talking because with you I jumped to conclusions instead of simply asking you about your boss." She squeezed Olivia's hand. "I'm not doing that anymore."

Olivia looked puzzled, "What does that mean?"

"I want another chance with you. I know what I feel when I'm with you and I hope you still feel it too, because you did once. When you opened that door our connection pulled me to you and I don't ever want it to stop. I see my future with you, Olivia. I saw it when we rode bikes together. I saw it when you were in class. I saw it and felt it the night you kissed me right down the street. I don't mean to overwhelm you, but I want you to know for sure and not have to wonder how I feel."

Olivia looked into Frankie's eyes; she had heard all she needed to hear. It took everything she had not to jump into Frankie's arms and kiss her when she first opened the door. And now she knew Frankie felt as she did, even though they hadn't yet said the word.

"Frankie, I...," Olivia took Frankie's face in her hands and pulled her close. She stopped and looked in her green eyes as they darkened, then she looked down at her lips and captured them with hers. The kiss was soft, but full of yearning. Olivia parted her lips and touched her tongue to Frankie's, and she immediately opened them. When their tongues met Olivia lost her breath. They deepened the kiss and explored one another's mouths, making up for the time lost over the last few weeks. All the kisses that should have been kissed were wrapped up in this one life-changing moment.

They finally stopped to breathe, looking deeply into one another's eyes.

"I have something to ask you," Frankie said.

"Okay?"

"Would you please go out with me on a proper date?"

Olivia's smile was immense then playful, "Proper, huh?"

"Yes. There is no way I'll be able to top the date you took me on, but I would like the opportunity to try. Will you go out with me?"

Olivia chuckled, "Yes, I will. When?"

"How is your work week?"

Olivia sighed, "Busy, getting back from being gone."

Frankie nodded, "How about Friday?"

Olivia nodded, "Friday will be great."

"I'll let you know the details later. Now, if it's okay with you, I would like to stop talking." She pulled Olivia close, her lips hovering over Olivia's as she stared into her velvety brown eyes. She brought their lips together firmly and took Olivia's mouth possessively with her own.

They were holding one another close, enjoying the kiss when the door opened. Startled, they pulled apart.

"Whoops."

Olivia bowed her head, smiling, then looked up, "Elizabeth, I'd like you to meet Frankie. Frankie, this is my boss, Elizabeth." She had laughter in her eyes as she watched the recognition on Frankie's face.

Frankie hopped up and extended her hand, "Nice to meet you."

Elizabeth smirked, taking her hand, "Nice to meet you." She wanted to mention something about the bike drive-by yesterday, but didn't because she knew Frankie was important to Olivia.

"I didn't know you were coming by this evening, Elizabeth," Olivia said standing.

"Obviously. Sorry to interrupt. I needed to grab a set of plans and hoped to discuss something with you if you were still here."

"I'll go so you can finish work," Frankie said, turning to Olivia.

"I'll walk you out. Be right with you, Elizabeth."

She walked Frankie to her car, "I'll call you when I get home."

"I can't wait," Frankie said kissing her lightly and opening her Jeep door.

Olivia wrapped her hand around Frankie's neck pulling her in and brought their lips together in a crushing kiss. Breathless, she said, "Okay, you'd better go before she comes looking for me."

Frankie got in her car still smiling. She started the car and began backing out, her eyes never leaving Olivia's. With a small wave she drove off.

Olivia took a deep breath trying to calm her heart before going back inside with a grin plastered across her face.

∽

THE NEXT DAY Elizabeth picked up her office phone, "Hello?"

"Elizabeth, this is Frankie Dean, Olivia's friend. We met last night."

"Right. That was some kiss I walked in on," she said, teasing.

Frankie's cheeks turned red as she cleared her throat. "Uh, yes well."

"It's okay Frankie, I'm teasing. What can I do for you?"

"I know this sounds crazy, but I'm taking Olivia out on a date Friday. That subdivision is a special place to us both and I had an idea, but I need your help."

Elizabeth considered this for a moment. It had been a long time since she'd been part of something fun like this and if anyone deserved it, it was Olivia. "Why don't you tell me what you have in mind."

∽

SOFIA LOOKED up into the stands and saw Frankie watching their volleyball game. "Looks like you have a cheering squad," she said to Olivia.

She looked up and smiled at Frankie, "I sure do."

"You're looking kind of lovestruck there, OK."

Olivia chuckled, "Maybe I am."

Veronica served the ball and they turned their focus back to the game. They won the point and the game.

Frankie came out of the stands and walked up to them, "Good game. Sofia, I didn't know you had such a wicked serve."

"Thanks."

Frankie winked at Olivia and kissed her on the cheek.

"Oh no you don't. I'm worth more than a peck on the cheek."

Frankie brought her lips to Olivia's for a quick sweet kiss. "Better?"

"Better," she said smiling.

"I'm not even going to tease you two about that. I'm happy you're together and now all is right with the world."

They all laughed. "I don't know about the world, but all is right in my little piece of it now," said Olivia.

"Mine too. I've got to gather these balls so I can lock up."

"I'm going to help. Sof, I'll see you tomorrow."

"Have fun," Sofia said, walking away.

They gathered the balls and made sure the doors were locked.

"Thanks for helping," Frankie said as they walked to the dressing room.

"I have my reasons," Olivia said, walking in and looking around. The room was empty and she turned around and put her arms around Frankie's neck. She pulled her in and brought their lips together. Frankie deepened the kiss and backed Olivia up to the wall. She flipped them around taking Frankie's hands and pinning them to the wall.

"I'm not going to make love to you for the first time in a dressing room," she said, looking at her seductively.

"I do own a gym so it could be appropriate."

"I didn't say it wasn't going to happen, just not the first time."

Frankie answered by nodding.

"That doesn't mean I'm through with you though," she said, claiming her lips again. Frankie moaned when Olivia put her thigh between her legs.

After a moment, Olivia stepped back, "We'd better go before I finish what I didn't really mean to start."

Frankie smiled, looking from one of her hands to the other still pinned to the wall and raised her eyebrows.

Olivia smirked, letting her go, "I can't wait for our date Friday."

"Me too," she said, putting the towels in the hamper.

"You haven't told me where we're going."

"It's a surprise," she said as they walked out of the dressing room and into the office.

"You have to at least tell me what to wear."

"Look at you two," Desi said, walking up and bringing them both in for a hug. "This makes my heart so happy."

"Thanks, Des."

"See you tomorrow," she said walking out.

"I had no idea so many people wanted us together," said Olivia.

"Me neither. Hey, you never did tell me how work went in Houston. Is everything ok?"

"Oh, that's right, we never did talk about that. We had more pressing things to get to. But Frankie, I never thought I'd like being in charge, and you know what? I did! I loved it."

Frankie chuckled, "I'm sure you were a natural."

"After getting everyone on board, I was able to try some things that I couldn't here. They worked, so now I can do them here, too."

"Congrats! I'm not surprised, you are so talented."

"Thanks, but I had such a good team. My assistant Lucy is so good. She's creative and works well with clients."

"Sounds a lot like you."

"I can't wait for you to meet her."

"I'd like to but, isn't she in Houston?"

"She is, but she's coming here for the race."

"Really!"

"Yes. We both stayed at the same hotel. She hadn't found a house yet. Well, she did while I was there. Anyway, she and I and another woman staying there, Jenna, would meet for happy hour after work."

"Sounds like fun."

"Lucy and Jenna would make sure I got my workouts in after I told them about the triathlon. So, now they think they're my coaches. They are both coming up next weekend to watch me race. Can you believe that?"

"I can. You are quite mesmerizing. Who wouldn't want to cheer you on?"

"You'll love them both."

"Do they know what was going on between us?"

"Yes. I wasn't the most fun person to be around when I got there. I tried to focus on work and forget about what was going on here. But they could tell."

"I see. So, does that mean they're going to kill me?" Frankie said hesitantly.

Olivia laughed, "No. They know it was a tough situation."

"I'm curious, what did they think?"

Olivia looked at her playfully, "Honestly, they thought you were an idiot."

"They got it right."

"No they didn't," Olivia said, wrapping her arms around Frankie. "I didn't have to push you into Laura's arms, remember? I don't think any of us knew what to do."

"I'm glad we got through it, and right this second we're in one another's arms and I'm going to kiss you like my life depends on it, because it does." She leaned down and pressed her lips tenderly to Olivia's, then harder and harder until their bodies molded together and their tongues danced with abandon. They finally parted both panting looking intensely in the other's eyes speaking without words.

When Frankie could finally speak, "I'll walk you to your car."

"That's a good idea," Olivia said breathlessly.

At Olivia's car, Frankie pulled her close. "Do you mind if we get dressed up for our date Friday? I mean, we've never really done that."

"I don't mind at all. I'm glad you work out because your heart may stop when you see me in a dress."

Frankie smiled, "My heart usually stops whenever I see you."

Olivia leaned up and whispered in her ear, "Mine does too." They held one another close for a moment.

"You fit perfectly in my arms," Frankie said nuzzling her neck.

"Mmm, hurry up Friday," she murmured, running her hand through Frankie's hair.

They pulled apart, want in their eyes. Olivia sighed, "Bike ride tomorrow?"

"Let's ride to the park."

"Sounds good."

Frankie leaned down and brought their lips together for one more kiss. "Text me when you get home?"

"I will."

∼

When she got home, she texted with Frankie and couldn't stop thinking about that kiss in the office. It made them both speechless. She got out of her clothes and was about to step into the shower when her phone buzzed. She smiled thinking it was Frankie, but when she picked it up, Jenna's name was on the caller id.

"Hey you," she said, answering.

"Hey yourself, how are you?"

"I'm good."

"Okay, I couldn't wait. I've been thinking about you since you left. How are things with Frankie? Please tell me she woke up and you two are together."

Olivia chuckled, "Couldn't stand it?"

"No, the idea of you up there, hurt. I just wanted to check on you and make sure you're alright."

"I'm good, really good," Olivia said, unable to hide the happiness in her voice.

"Care to explain."

"Turns out Frankie and I don't communicate very well because of fear."

"You aren't special, that happens to lots of people."

"It's not going to happen to us anymore. We sat down and talked honestly. She thought I had moved on the day I told her goodbye."

"What? Why would she think that?"

"She saw me with my boss at a swanky restaurant right before I came down there and thought I was on a date. Then she saw me the day after I got home with her again. Her mind was as messed up as mine was when I told her I'd back away."

"So, what you're saying is that both of you are idiots."

"Were. We are no longer idiots. We have learned how to ask questions and communicate."

Jenna released an audible breath over the phone. "That's good for Frankie, but bad for me."

"Jenna—"

"Seriously Olivia, I am very happy for you. You are obviously in love with her and she'd be crazy not to be in love with you. I'm not fooling myself that there was anything between us, but..." she trailed off.

"Incredible sex! I don't know about you, but damn Jenna!"

"I know! It was incredible for me, too. Wasn't it obvious from both of us?"

They both started laughing. "I will never forget that night."

"Me neither." Jenna paused, "Hey, that's not going to cause a problem for you and Frankie is it?"

"I hope not. I wasn't planning on telling her. Because I don't even want to think about what she was doing with Laura. However, I'm pretty sure nothing happened between them. She said she knew within a couple of days that it wasn't going to work."

"Well, I'll do whatever you need me to."

"I did tell her that you and Lucy were coming to the race. I'll be so glad to see you both, and she's excited to meet you."

"I'll be glad to meet her. As much as I wanted to fall for you and you for me, I know it ain't happening. We had some Earth-shattering sex when we both needed it."

"I agree. I had no idea it would be that good though," she replied, giggling.

"Me neither. When we were holding each other, I felt like we were in a halcyon cocoon where no one could hurt us. And I so needed to feel that at the time."

"Halcyon? Word of the day? I would never have thought of that but, you're right. It felt so calm and peaceful where no one could touch us."

They were both quiet for a moment, lost in the past.

"Okay, how's your training? Are you ready? Only a week and a half to go."

"Yes, Coach! I'm ready. Frankie and I are going on a long ride tomorrow after work and I'll swim in the morning. Only a few workouts left."

"I'm so proud of you, and Olivia?"

"Yeah?"

"I'm really glad we're friends."

"Me too, Jenna. They sent me to Houston to save a project and I think you ended up saving me."

"I think we saved each other. I'm going to go, call me anytime."

"I will and thanks."

"Love you, Olivia."

"Love you too."

∽

Olivia walked into the pool area and saw Stella sitting on the bench. When she looked up and saw Olivia coming towards her, a smile quickly appeared, brightening her face.

"You look much better than you did for our last swim."

Olivia grinned and sat down beside her. "I feel much better."

"I wonder why?" she said, teasing.

"Because of you! You're the one that made us stop acting like middle schoolers and actually talk."

"You weren't acting like middle schoolers. It's hard to be vulnerable and tell someone what you're feeling, even when those feelings are caused by a misunderstanding or incorrect interpretation. You didn't know what Frankie saw and you couldn't understand why she hadn't talked to you. I'm just glad you finally talked."

"God, me too. All these feelings I have for Frankie can go to her now. I don't have to try and hold back or wonder why. I can relish them, even wallow in them and feel good."

"I love that."

"And maybe even better is that Frankie isn't holding back either. I can feel ...," she trailed off.

"Love? Don't be afraid to say it."

Olivia smiled shyly, "It is love. I'm not afraid to say it. I love Frankie and have for a while, and I think she loves me too."

"Really? Of course she loves you too! But you haven't said it to one another yet?"

"No, I was about to the night we talked, but my boss walked in."

Stella chuckled, "I may have heard something about that."

"Yeah, we were in the middle of a, let's just say, life affirming kiss."

"Oh wow, that was some kiss."

"It was and most of them have been since. One thing Frankie and I can do is *kiss*," she said giggling.

This time Stella laughed, "It is so good to see you like this."

"Everything feels like it's in place now. Frankie and I are on the same page, my training is on point and I'm ready to make this triathlon mine! And two friends I made in Houston are coming up to cheer me on."

"Really?"

"Yes. One was my assistant on the project and the other was staying at our hotel. We'd meet up everyday after work. They made sure I got my training done before drinks or dinner. They claim to be my coaches now."

"I'm so glad to hear that. I was a little concerned about you. I didn't want you diving into work to forget about things here. That wouldn't have been good."

"They kind of helped me through it so I wasn't sad and miserable the whole time, especially since I didn't hear anything from Frankie."

"What'd y'all do? Anything fun?"

Olivia thought back to their happy hours, her night out with Jenna, and then the night they spent together. "It wasn't really the things we did, it was more about how they made me feel."

"What do you mean?"

"Between them and the success with the job I regained a lot of the confidence I left here when I got on that plane. Lucy and I were badass on the job." Olivia contemplated for a moment and then said, "And Jenna made me feel wanted."

Stella quirked her eyebrow, "Wanted, huh? That's a very powerful aphrodisiac."

"It is and sometimes hard to resist," she said wistfully.

"You know, it wouldn't be wrong if you didn't resist."

"What?"

"Who says you had to resist? The way things were with you and Frankie when you left seemed to be done. I mean, it wasn't unreasonable for Frankie to think you were out on a date. I know you so I knew there was no way you'd be dating that soon, but while you were in Houston and not hearing from Frankie, and someone made you feel desirable, why wouldn't you?"

Olivia sat there for a moment thinking about what Stella said. She turned to her and said, "Jenna is the woman that was staying at the hotel, she sat down next to me at the bar the first night I got there and bought me a drink," she said, looking away with a smile. "She was already friends with my assistant Lucy, but neither of us knew that at the time. Her wife died a year ago, so she's a widow at thirty-five. We became friends easily; I hope you can meet her next weekend when they come to the race. She liked to flirt with me and I liked it too," she said, looking back at Stella. "I told her about Frankie so she knew the situation. The last night I was there we all went out to dinner and Lucy was with a date, so Jenna and I went back to her room for a drink. She walked me back to my room and the want in her eyes for me made me pull her inside. I think we both needed to feel wanted. She hadn't even looked at another woman since her wife."

"I know how that is."

"Yeah, I knew you would. I don't really know why I'm telling you all this, but she stayed the night. I think her biggest concern was that I'd feel regret or that I'd done something wrong."

"I hope you didn't."

"I didn't. I don't regret it at all. It was a wonderful night between two people that needed one another. We're friends, nothing more. I love Frankie, Jenna knows that and she isn't in love with me."

"I'd like to meet her."

Olivia smiled, nodding her head. "I don't plan to tell Frankie. Should I? I mean, we haven't talked about what went on between her and Laura, and honestly, I don't want to know."

"Oh," Stella thought about this. "I'm not so sure I would either, but if you think she might find out, if it were me, I'd rather she hear it from me than from someone else."

"I don't know how she'd find out. Sofia knows, but she wouldn't say anything. Oh no, Stella I haven't put you in a bad position, have I?"

"No. You and Frankie weren't together, what you did on that trip is your business and no one else's. Jenna won't say anything?"

"No. We talked last night and she's the one who brought up that she hoped it wasn't a problem for us."

"You're sure she doesn't have feelings for you?"

"I'm sure. She said last night, as much as she wished she'd fallen in love with me, she hadn't."

"I understand that too. You have all this love for your wife that has no place to go and if her marriage was happy like mine, then you miss that feeling."

"I don't want to hurt Frankie and we certainly don't need any other problems right now."

"Even if you told her, I think she'd understand."

"I think it's time for a swim."

"Me too! You've got a triathlon to slay!"

19

Olivia woke up with a smile on her face. It was finally Friday! She had been looking forward to this date all week. Her work schedule today wasn't too hectic and she was taking off a couple of hours early so she could get ready. She wanted to make Frankie unable to keep her hands off her.

Frankie was picking her up at her house, so she cleaned last night and changed the sheets on her bed this morning. When she looked back on it, she and Frankie had felt the attraction from the beginning, but it had taken a few weeks of workouts and bike rides to get to that first kiss. And what a kiss it was! As she remembered she could feel Frankie's lips on hers. Then chaos had hit! But they had navigated through it and tonight she would both tell and show Frankie that she was in love with her.

She took one last look around, knowing when she got home all she would want to worry about was making herself irresistible. The thought made her smile.

The day flew by and she only had a couple of things left to do when she looked up and was surprised to see Elizabeth walk in.

"Hi Olivia, I want to meet with you on Monday morning at my office at 10:00, will that work?"

Olivia pulled up her schedule and looked, "That should be fine. I was working on revisions to the plans we discussed this week. That can't be the only reason you came by."

"No. I need a favor."

Olivia didn't like the sound of that. She'd be glad to help... just not today. "Okay, what's up?"

"I know you planned to leave early today, but I really need you to meet with a client that can't be here until this evening."

Olivia's heart sank, "Elizabeth—"

Elizabeth cut her off, "I know you have a big date tonight. Frankie could pick you up here."

"But I don't have my dress with me and I wanted to have time to get ready."

"You still can, that's why I'm here. You can leave now, and go get your dress and make-up. You can get ready here."

"Here? But what about the client?"

"I'll be here, too. I just need you to start it off and then I'll take over. Frankie can pick you up and you two have your date," she said smiling and nodding her head like it's all settled.

She thought about it and guessed it would work. One reason she wanted Frankie to pick her up was so they'd end up at her house. She guessed they still could; she'd just leave her car here.

"Okay Elizabeth, I guess that would work. I'll call Frankie on my way home to get my stuff."

"Oh thank you, thank you."

"This must be an important client."

"The biggest," she said, smiling like she was not telling Olivia everything.

"Right, okay."

"Scoot, go get your stuff," Elizabeth said, hurrying her out the door.

That was a little odd, but Olivia didn't have time to think about if she was going to make it home and back and still have time to get ready. She pulled Frankie up in her contacts and called her.

"Hello, my beautiful date"

Olivia laughed, "You sure are cheery."

"Am I not usually?" Olivia could hear the smile in her voice

"No, you are. I just thought there might be a reason for you to be especially chipper today."

"You mean because I have a date with the absolutely most beautiful woman in the world?"

"Wow, you're turning on the charm."

Frankie laughed, "You bring it out in me."

"Well, we have a problem."

"What kind of problem? We're going out tonight, no matter what."

"Yes, we are! No way we're missing this date tonight. Would you mind picking me up at work instead of my house?"

"Not at all, that's fine."

"There's some important client Elizabeth wants me to meet, but she said I only have to start the meeting and she'll take it from there. Of course they can't be at the office until this evening."

"It is not a problem, babe. You schmooze this client and I'll sweep you away."

Olivia giggled. She noticed what Frankie called her and liked the way it sounded. She could feel her cheeks reddening with the thought of Frankie sweeping her anywhere.

"Are you still there, babe?"

"Yeah, I'm still here, just thinking about you sweeping me away."

Frankie laughed, "I know that sounds kind of silly."

"Not at all. It sounds romantic to me and I'm wishing it was now."

"It's not too much longer. I promise it'll be worth the wait."

"Frankie Dean what do you have planned for me?"

"You'll just have to wait and see."

"I have so much anticipation I might explode!"

She chuckled, "Meditate. That's what you and Stella would tell me."

This made Olivia laugh. "Okay, okay. Well, I've got to run. I'll see you later."

"You sure will, and just so you know, I can hardly wait too."

"Bye," Olivia said softly with a sigh.

"Bye."

Olivia gathered her things, made sure everything was set at her house, then hurried back to work.

When she finished her work, she went to the back room of the house to get ready.

Her make-up was light and understated, but made her look fresh and vibrant. She let her hair fall softly in waves to her shoulders. It looked like a golden halo. Her sleeveless summer dress had a short skirt that showed off her tanned and toned legs that months of bike rides and running had formed. Her shoulders that weights and swimming built were exquisite, she looked in the mirror and applied a little lipstick, stepped back, and approved. Was it enough to stop Frankie's heart? She giggled thinking about telling her that earlier.

She stepped into the main area of the house. Everyone had gone home except for Elizabeth.

"Wow, Olivia you look beautiful. She's not going to know what hit her."

"Thanks. I have a question, why is there a notice closing 1101 down the street?"

"Uh, they were doing some work in there that needs to dry, so they made sure no one would come in and mess it up."

"Hmm, okay. Do you have any idea what?"

"Not right off hand. Don't worry about it."

"I'll check on it Monday. When is this big client supposed to be here Frankie will be driving up any minute."

Elizabeth checked her watch and at the same time the door opened. Frankie walked in and her jaw dropped.

"Oh Olivia, you look incredible."

Olivia smiled walking toward her, "Thanks, babe." She kissed her on the cheek. When she backed away, she noticed Frankie was also wearing a short sleeveless top that showed every muscle in her shoulders. It made Olivia hungry to kiss and nip the beauty of those chiseled muscles. She ran her hands up and down her upper arms and smiled. Her fitted pants left little to the imagination. Frankie had a beautiful body and Olivia couldn't wait to discover every inch of it.

"Uh, you look stunning," she said, finding her voice.

"Wow, you both look amazing."

Olivia was still staring at Frankie when she realized they couldn't leave yet. "Elizabeth, where is this client, we have to go!" Her patience was gone, even if Elizabeth was her boss

"Well, the client is here."

Olivia turned around and looked at her. "What? Where?"

"She means me. I'm your client," Frankie said, taking both Olivia's hands in hers. "I no longer want to live in my place. I want to build something new to start a life with you." Olivia's eyebrows flew up her forehead. "Wait, I'm not trying to overwhelm you, just listen a sec. You know I wanted a house, that's why you showed me around here in the first place. I meant it."

"I knew you did," Olivia said nodding her head.

"I have a reason to do it now. And who better to help me than you."

"Okay?"

"I've helped her get the process started, but she wanted you to see the house she chose and help make a few changes."

"So, you're in on this," she said, narrowing her eyes at Elizabeth.

She smiled at the two of them, "I'm going to leave you to it. Frankie has the rest."

Elizabeth left and then it was just them. "I'm not sure I understand," she said.

"You will. I need you to know that I don't want you to feel strange at my house because Laura lived there at one time."

"I wouldn't, that's the past."

"It is, but I don't want to be there. I want a house here. Would you go with me now and help me?" she asked with such hope in her eyes.

"Of course I will." Olivia had a feeling she knew which house Frankie had chosen.

Frankie leaned down and kissed her briefly but softly. "I promise I'll make it worth it."

"I know you will."

"Okay, come with me." Frankie took her hand and led her out into her Jeep. They drove down the street and pulled in at 1101. Olivia nodded her head now, understanding why Elizabeth had closed it.

They walked up the drive hand in hand and Frankie stopped. "I can still change the color of the trim out here, and thought I would."

She looked at Frankie and smiled, "I would too, if this was my house."

They walked inside. "If you'll remember there wasn't any furniture last time, but to make it look like my vision I staged a few things. I could use your help because I wasn't sure about some."

"Okay, why don't you walk me through it."

Frankie took her hand and walked her over to the dining area. "I know it's open concept, but I thought this would probably be the best area for a dining table. But tonight, without furniture in here, I thought it would be a great place to dance."

Olivia looked up at her, startled. "Dance? Are you going to hum for us?"

Frankie chuckled, "Not exactly. May I?" She opened her arms inviting Olivia inside. With a skeptical look Olivia placed her arms around Frankie's neck, allowing her to pull them close. Suddenly music began to play. Olivia looked into Frankie's eyes, pleasantly surprised. She pulled her closer and Olivia nuzzled her neck with a subtle moan.

She pulled away again so she could see Frankie's face. "I knew you were magical but, that's a good trick with the music."

"Thanks, I really wanted to hold you close so, what better way."

"You're full of surprises, aren't you?"

"Maybe." She leaned in and kissed right below Olivia's ear and heard her gasp.

"Careful, we won't finish this tour if you keep that up."

Frankie chuckled as she softly kissed her way along Olivia's jaw and paused at her lips. "My heart stopped when I saw you, just like you said it would."

"I lost my breath when I saw you. I really need you to kiss me right now."

Frankie gently placed her lips on Olivia's. She couldn't take it and ran her hand through Frankie's hair, pulling her closer and deepening the kiss. When the song ended the kiss continued. They stopped to breathe and fire was burning in both their eyes.

Frankie let out a breath she'd been holding with a whoosh. "My god, Olivia." She gathered herself then said, "Let me show you what I've done on the patio." She took her hand and led them to the back of the house.

The door was open and Olivia looked up and saw Sofia, Desi, and Stella out on the back porch.

"What are you doing here?" she said looking from one to the other.

"I'm the chef," said Stella with a little courtesy.

"I'm the bartender," said Desi, pouring them both a glass of wine on the elegantly set table on the patio.

"And I'm the DJ and ambiance."

Olivia raised her eyebrows. Sofia winked, "You'll see."

"I couldn't do this alone, so I got a little help from our friends."

"It's all so beautiful, thank you."

"You're the one that's beautiful, Olivia," said Stella, pulling out a chair for her.

"We're going to take off. If you need anything Frankie can take care of the rest," said Desi.

Sofia patted her shoulder and winked at Frankie as they walked by.

"How long have you been planning this?"

"Honestly, it was a dream at first because of what happened after we left here last time. But after you agreed to go out with me, I got to work. When I realized I'd need help to get it right, I knew they would all pitch in. Here we are. I hope you don't mind it's almost like you're at work."

"No, it's not. This is different. I'm getting to see a dream come true."

Frankie reached over and took Olivia's hand, "That's what you are to me Olivia. Do you remember that not long after we met, you said you weren't my type?"

"I remember."

"You were right that day. I thought, there's no way she would ever go out with me."

"Why?" Olivia said, surprised.

"Because, you are so smart and talented, and me? I own a gym. You could do so much better."

"That's ridiculous. I thought I wasn't your type because of the way I looked. We were both wrong."

"I want to make a toast," Frankie said, taking her glass. Olivia picked hers up and lifted it.

"To the future, let's jump in together and see where we go." They clinked glasses and Olivia leaned over and kissed her gently.

"Let's eat, this smells delicious."

"I have more music, let me start the playlist," Frankie hopped up and with dusk settling around them and music lilted in the air as they enjoyed the meal.

During dessert, Frankie asked, "One week until the race. You're not getting nervous, are you?"

Olivia reached for her glass and had another sip of the excellent wine. "I really don't want to talk about the race tonight. All I want to do is spend time with the beautiful woman across from me."

Frankie smiled and dipped her head, "Would you like to see more of the changes I want to make?"

"I do."

They both finished their wine and Frankie said, "Let's go in."

She took Olivia's hand and showed her a few other things she wanted to do in the living area and kitchen. Olivia couldn't believe the changes she wanted to make were all the same ones she would make, too. This date was not only eye-opening but reaffirmed how much they had in common. It made her fantasize about this being their house someday. Wisdom told her to slow those thoughts down, but it seemed like they had overcome so much to get to this point that she couldn't help herself.

They made it to the extra bedrooms and Olivia asked, "Do you still see kids in these rooms?"

"I do. How about you?"

"Yeah, I'd love to have kids."

"Do you want to have them yourself or adopt?"

"I think I'd like to try myself first then if that doesn't work I'd love to adopt."

Frankie nodded, looking around the room and imagining them playing with their child. It may be a dream now, but she was going to do all she could to make it come true. She looked up and Olivia was staring at her and Frankie knew she was reading her thoughts.

"I like that idea."

"What?"

"I have a pretty good idea what you were just imagining and I like it."

Frankie walked over to her and put her hands on her hips, pulling her close. "You know, I think there's only one room left."

"I think you're right," Olivia said with her hands on Frankie's shoulders. She wanted to devour them, and the thought made her heart speed up.

"You know, we don't have to leave here tonight."

Olivia looked at her with a puzzled look on her face. "What do you mean?"

"It's my house and if I want to stay the night I can. Let me show you," she said with a seductive smile. She took Olivia's hand leading her down the hall and opened the door to the master suite.

When Olivia looked inside she couldn't believe her eyes. The doors were opened to the patio and twinkling lights adorned the porch. She looked around the room and there was a beautiful bed in the exact place she told Frankie she'd put it weeks ago. And on the bed were dozens of rose petals that made the room smell exotic. She looked at Frankie in shock.

"Do you like it? You're not saying anything."

"I'm speechless. Frankie, this room is gorgeous!" she said, looking all around the room, spinning in a circle.

"I wanted it to be special like you, but also because this night is special," she said, knowing Olivia understood completely. "Shall we dance?" she took Olivia's hand and led her onto the patio. Wrapping her arms around her, she pulled her close.

They swayed to the music and Olivia leaned back, looking into Frankie's eyes, "I remember that kiss we shared right here, do you?"

"I've replayed it over and over again for weeks."

Olivia took her hand and cupped Frankie's face, staring at her lips. She traced a finger down her jawline and ran a thumb over her lower lip. She licked her own, and slowly brought their lips together. They met with tenderness, but passion was bubbling just beneath the surface, ready to erupt. Olivia was trying to go slow and enjoy every breath and every touch, but Frankie made it hard. She wanted her so very much and could feel the love radiating from her. Their tongues explored the other's mouth slowly and completely.

Frankie's hands roamed up and down Olivia's back, gently caressing and softly coming to rest cupping the firmness of her round behind. She lost her breath as Frankie gently sucked her tongue into her mouth.

They separated slightly, their chests rising and falling as their breath came quicker. Olivia took the hem of Frankie's shirt and slowly guided it over her head. When she saw that Frankie wasn't wearing a bra, the fire in her core burned hotter.

"You are beautiful," she whispered as her hands rested on Frankie's shoulders. She slowly glided both hands down her chest and cupped her breasts. Frankie sucked in a breath as Olivia ran her thumbs over her hardening nipples. She leaned in and lavished Frankie's ear with her tongue.

"Good god, Olivia."

"You taste so good," she said and trailed her tongue down Frankie's neck and nipped and sucked at her collarbone, all the while rubbing circles around her nipples. Then she bowed and took Frankie's nipple into her mouth, sucking it in and biting down gently.

Frankie squeezed Olivia's shoulders when she bit down and threw her head back groaning. Olivia continued to taste as she moved over to her other nipple.

She leaned back looking down at Frankie's pants, with her fingers in the waistband she unbuttoned and unzipped them smiling sexily with her lips and eyes. Before she could pull them down Frankie reached for the hem of her dress and mirrored her earlier move, pulling it over Olivia's head. She unclasped her bra, letting her round breasts free. Her nipples were already hard and Frankie bent down, gently taking one in her mouth and Olivia moaned; her hands on the back of Frankie's head, keeping her there. She looked down and watched as Frankie licked, sucked, and nibbled. Her love, hot with every touch; she'd never felt anything so consuming. Never felt so wanted and loved at the same time.

"Oh Frankie," she said breathlessly. "We'd better go inside."

Frankie stood up and before she could move, Olivia grabbed her pants and pulled them down so she could step out of them. She had on sexy black panties that Olivia reminded herself to appreciate later, but right now all she wanted to do is go inside and take those panties off and bury her head in Frankie's sweetness.

As soon as they cleared the threshold, Olivia crushed her lips to Frankie's. She'd never wanted anyone the way she wanted Frankie. Her love poured out and she wanted to fill Frankie with it, so she'd never doubt it was hers.

With her arms wrapped around Olivia, Frankie slowly backed her to the bed. "I want you so much Olivia, I can barely breathe."

"I know, baby, I know." Olivia sat down on the edge of the bed and Frankie kneeled between her legs resting her hands on her thighs. Olivia stroked up and down her arms gazing intently in her eyes. She'd never seen Frankie's eyes so green, and so brilliant against her tan face and dark hair.

Frankie picked up one of the rose petals and trailed it from the hollow of Olivia's throat down between her breasts, watching goosebumps rise in its wake. She smiled as Olivia's chest rose and fell faster and faster. Slowly, she circled each nipple following the petal with kisses. Olivia reached behind her and rested on her hands, intently watching Frankie's every move and feeling the love in every touch. She dropped the petal and ran her index fingers under Olivia's red pantie's waistband. Olivia gasped with the touch then raised her hips so Frankie could pull them off. She slowly glided them down her legs, caressing as she went. With the panties off, Olivia scooted up on the bed.

Frankie stood at the end of the bed, drinking in the sight of her lover. Olivia looked her up and down, her eyes resting at last on Frankie's sexy black panties. She quirked an eyebrow and Frankie began to slowly shed them.

She crawled onto the bed, slowly resting her leg between Olivia's, feeling her wetness on her thigh. They fit perfectly together, their bodies intertwined. Propped on her elbow she took her hand and traced Olivia's cheek with a finger. She looked deeply into her eyes and saw the deep brown richness reflecting her own fire kissed green.

"I'm in love with you Olivia. I know you know that but I'm filling your heart in every touch, in every kiss, in every moan, in every scent with my love for you and only you." Then Frankie kissed Olivia like she'd never been kissed before, it enveloped her in love, in passion, desire and need.

"Oh Frankie, I love you too. I love you so much."

With this confession of love, Frankie entwined their fingers, holding their hands on either side of Olivia's head. She kissed her way down and across Olivia's breasts and then releasing one hand she stroked Olivia's leg as she licked across her taut stomach. "So beautiful," she whispered as Olivia rested her hand in Frankie's hair.

She licked across the base of her stomach to where her light curly hair started. Olivia's pungent scent hit Frankie and she took a moment to breathe it in. She started low and licked up the length of Olivia, just grazing her lips and causing a loud moan. "Shit, Frankie," she said, shaking her head from side to side.

Frankie couldn't wait any longer; she had to taste the woman she loved. And taste she did, she ran her tongue through and among her folds, licking up the wetness that kept coming. Olivia moaned in delight as Frankie licked around her opening and then slid inside. From there she licked up and around her clit, over and over until finally sucking it into her mouth.

Olivia cried out, as much as she wanted her there, she pulled on Frankie's cheeks, "I need you up here." She buried her tongue in Frankie's mouth just as Frankie entered her with one finger relishing the velvety softness.

"Mmmm, that feels so good, baby," then she kissed her again. Frankie added a finger and began slowly moving in and out. Olivia joined the rhythm with her hips all the while groaning and pulling Frankie closer. She began to pick up the pace and Olivia moaned, "Yes, baby, yes."

Frankie thrust in deep and curled her fingers up as Olivia's sides clamped down on her tightly. Her brown eyes went wide and locked on Frankie's, Olivia cried out Frankie's name and held on tight as her orgasm ripped through, wave after wave. She finally let go, collapsing on the bed, smiling. She quickly grabbed Frankie and kissed her.

"I've never felt more loved."

Frankie smiled with such an expression of love and tenderness on her face, "Because you are loved so very much."

Olivia let out a big breath. "My god woman," she said giggling. "That was, everything. And if you'll give me a minute."

Frankie laughed, "We've got all night."

"Oh honey, this is going to take all night and more."

Olivia quickly flipped Frankie on her back and straddled her. Frankie's eyes were wide with anticipation.

"I can't wait any longer. I can tell you over and over that I love you, but words go only so far. I want you to feel my love for you. I want you to know that I'm giving it to you with my heart, my body, my soul, and my mind. I'm giving you all of me."

Frankie looked up into her eyes, cradling her face in her hands, "Make me yours."

∼

Olivia woke with her head on Frankie's shoulder and her hand resting on her stomach. She smiled as she remembered making love so tenderly and then the laughter when they shared a snack in bed. It didn't take long for that snack to be forgotten as their hunger for one another won out. As Frankie held her close, even in sleep Olivia could feel her love.

Olivia didn't realize she was tracing her fingers over Frankie's stomach until she stirred.

"Um, we fell asleep," she said rubbing her hand up and down Olivia's back.

"I don't think we could help it," she said giggling and raising up to see Frankie's face.

"That was the best workout I've ever had."

Olivia chuckled, "Said like the fitness instructor you are."

Frankie raised up slightly to look out the patio doors. The sky was beginning to lighten.

"There's something I wanted to show you."

"Do we have to get out of this bed?" she said, pushing Frankie back down.

Frankie giggled, "Yes, but I promise it will be worth it."

"You've said that to me before and it was true, so I'm going to believe you. However, I have no clothes in here."

"Ah but you do. I had Sofia pack you an overnight bag."

"You thought of everything."

Frankie smiled, "I tried. But you don't have to have clothes for this." She got out of the bed and reached a hand for Olivia.

Instead Olivia laid there, looking her up and down. "You are the most beautiful person - inside and out - Frankie Dean, and you're mine."

Frankie smiled shyly, "I am. Come on." She grabbed a blanket and wrapped it around them both as they walked out the patio doors. She guided them a few steps onto the patio and turned to her right.

Olivia gasped, "Oh my god, Frankie. It's beautiful." The sky was beginning to change from gray to a deep red. And as they stood there it burned into brilliant streaks of red to orange to yellow as the sun brought a new day, a day they welcomed together.

Olivia turned to see the sun on Frankie's face and when their eyes met, "This has been the best night of my life."

Frankie's smile widened and her eyes softened, "I hope this day is the start of many bright ones for us, together." She leaned down and brought their lips together and the kiss quickly escalated.

"I know how I want to start this day," Olivia said seductively.

Frankie turned them around, "Race you." They ran through the doors and jumped back in bed arms and legs everywhere. Frankie's last thought before kissing Olivia was 'I'm home'. Then she stopped thinking as she was surrounded by feelings, emotions, touches, scents; all Olivia.

20

Olivia smiled across the patio table at Frankie. "Brunch delivered, you really thought of everything?"

Frankie chuckled, "I tried to. Care to share that cinnamon roll with me?"

Olivia narrowed her eyes, "I don't know, this isn't usually on my training diet, so I may be a little selfish."

"I thought you didn't want to talk about your training. Or was that just last night."

This made Olivia laugh, "No, you're right, I don't." She handed Frankie half of the cinnamon roll. "I'll tell you what I do want to talk about. Those sexy, inviting black lace panties you had on last night."

Frankie blushed briefly, "You liked those, did you? Few people know that I like wearing sexy undies. I usually wear workout clothes all day long and my self-care includes lacy panties. I will admit I recently purchased those in hopes of driving you wild."

Olivia fanned her face with her hand, "I hope you could tell that they did."

"I noticed. I also noticed that palm tree tattoo on your hip."

Olivia smiled, "You worshipped it like you did the rest of my body.

All the imperfect curves and that extra layer that is still there. I could see in your eyes how beautiful I am to you."

"That's because you are! It doesn't matter how your body changes, it's you! You, Olivia, are beautiful; you're perfect to me! Don't you get that?" Frankie stood up, "I guess you didn't notice this." She turned around and pointed to the back of her legs.

"What?"

"Most women call it cottage cheese. Everyone has imperfections."

"I seriously didn't notice it, babe. But I don't care. I love it because it's a part of you."

"Exactly! You know how the emphasis on body image in today's world upsets me. We are more than just our bodies!"

"I know. You've changed my way of thinking. I don't really see these curves anymore. When I look in the mirror, I see a body that can do things that bring me joy. That's probably why I didn't even notice your cute little indentations on the back of your leg. I saw a body that I love and couldn't stop kissing. And now I know a couple of places that seem to drive you wild with the slightest touch."

"It's your touch. I don't think I've ever been that…,"

"What? Hot? Lustful? Happy? Content? Wanting more? Are you going to stop me?"

"No! Keep going, all the above."

Olivia giggled, "Just so you know, I've never, either."

"Do you have any plans the rest of the day?

"I do. Right now I plan to give some attention to those adorable legs of yours."

Frankie's smile couldn't get any sexier.

"You know, we haven't tried out the shower yet," she said standing up and taking Frankie's hand, leading her back through the door. "I love what you're doing with the place," she said, teasing over her shoulder.

After their fun in the shower, they were laying on the bed, propped on pillows and looking out the patio doors.

"You know, this really is the perfect place for this bed."

"You doubted my design expertise?"

"No. I just didn't realize it gave such a nice view of the backyard."

"When you move in you'll be able to see a few more of the design elements that are meant to make it special and not just a house, but a home."

Frankie thought to herself, she knew she'd found her home, in this house and in Olivia.

"Do you realize the two real dates we've had were both in this house. And now you've bought it. What kind of lesbians does that make us?"

"If you'd move in, I think it would make us perfect lesbians."

"Can we have a few dates somewhere else? Then by the time the house is finished maybe I'll think about it."

"That's a great idea. I'm going to say this and get it out in the open because we have been known to have communication issues."

"Okay, go for it."

"When you planned our first date and walked me through this process because you knew I would love it was a little unconventional. Would you agree?"

"I would. My thinking behind it was that I wanted to do something you'd never done before, that you would love."

"And you did. But that night, in this house, when we kissed right in that doorway," she said, nodding to the patio doors.

"I remember."

"I felt like I was home, Olivia. In that moment, I felt like I was exactly where I was supposed to be: with you. That one kiss was like a preview of what's to come though neither of us knew that at the time."

"Oh Frankie," Olivia sat up and reached for her hands.

"Last Monday when we worked through our communication issues," she said playfully. "You agreed to go on this date and I didn't have any idea where I was going to take you at the time. But, when I walked into my house later that night, it didn't feel like home. And I realized I haven't felt like I had a home since my parents found that letter and were horrified at the thought that I was gay. I've lived in many places since then and been with several women, but this house and *you, Olivia* are my home. So, when you're ready, this is your home too."

"You realize, as an architect that designs dream homes, that is the most romantic thing anyone could ever say to me."

She reached up with one hand and cupped the side of her face, "I love you, Olivia."

"Oh Frankie, I love you too."

∼

"So, are you going to give me all the details? You know I'm living vicariously through you right now." Olivia and Sofia sat on her patio having a beer.

"I don't believe that for one minute, Sof. Maybe you're tired of those hook-ups and it's time to find someone to actually date."

"Maybe, but I want to hear about your date. Frankie worked hard to set that up. To hear her tell it that house is special to both of you."

"It is and now she's bought it! I can't believe it! And she's making the exact changes to it that I would make if it were mine."

"I think that's the idea. You living there with her."

"I know."

"Is it too much? I mean, you just worked through everything."

"We spent a lot of time together before we ever had that first date. Frankie is not pressuring me at all. When the house is finished we're going to talk about me moving in. For now, our plan is for a real date that's not in that house," she said laughing.

"So, were you surprised? She didn't tell us everything she had planned but, it did sound special."

"I was incredibly surprised. And thanks for helping. It meant a lot to have our friends there."

"Highlights? And I don't mean the sex, you're glowing; that tells me all I need to know."

Olivia chuckled, "The food was amazing and we danced. We went through the rest of the house and had an interesting conversation in the spare bedrooms."

"How so?"

"We talked about kids. Frankie wants them and you know I do. It was surreal, I looked around that room and I could see our kids' toys and their cute little beds." She smiled, thinking back to that image in the bedroom.

"That's wonderful Olivia. I know how important that is to you."

"Oh, I remember what I wanted to ask you. When you said you were responsible for ambiance, would that mean the master bedroom?"

Sofia smiled, "Did you like it? I helped Frankie with the rose petals. It smelled amazing in there."

Olivia thought back to sitting on the bed and Frankie trailing that rose petal gently over her breasts. Her heart began to beat faster and her face flushed as her nipple hardened.

"You don't have to answer that, I think I can tell from the look on your face."

"It was amazing, you're right. And in the morning, we woke up and Frankie walked us out on the patio wrapped in a blanket. We weren't there for two minutes before the sky started to brighten as the sun rose. It was like she ordered this spectacular light show just for us. It was incredible."

"If I'm up for the sunrise it'd better be incredible."

"Right!" They laughed. "Then later in the morning the doorbell rings and it's breakfast! She'd arranged to have brunch delivered. She thought of everything. Oh, and thanks for packing me a bag."

"No problem. How long did y'all stay? Didn't Frankie work yesterday?"

"Nope. We left this morning when we ran out of food."

"This morning!"

Olivia looked over at Sofia. "We had a lot to talk about," she said, winking.

She laughed, "I know you did."

"God, I can't stop thinking about her."

"I'm not trying to be a downer but, what about Jenna?"

Olivia looked over at her, "What about Jenna?"

"Are you going to tell Frankie about your night with her?"

"I'm not planning on it. I'm excited for Frankie to meet Jenna and Lucy."

"Are you sure about that?"

Olivia sighed, "I don't want to hurt Frankie and that would."

"I get it. It's not like you were together."

"Now that I know what she was thinking while I was in Houston," she shook her head. "It would never have happened if we'd just talked."

"Do you feel differently about it now?"

"No. It was one of those moments, you know."

"Yeah. And what difference would it make. You thought she was with Laura and didn't say anything."

"Can we talk about something else?"

"Yes. Let's order food."

"You choose, you know where the menus are."

"Be right back," she said going inside.

Olivia was starting to get a bad feeling about Jenna. Not Jenna herself, she'd be glad to see her. When it came to the night they spent together, where before there was no anxiety, there was now. Everything would be fine. Lucy and Jenna would be there for the weekend, she'd race, introduce them to her friends, and they'd go back to Houston.

∽

OLIVIA AND FRANKIE pedaled along the lake road. They were enjoying a few days of bliss since their date. The path they followed to the lake was in sight. Olivia turned in first with Frankie trying to catch up.

"You've definitely gotten faster," Frankie said, pulling up next to her.

"I should have by now as much as I've been riding." She leaned over and kissed Frankie on the lips before removing her helmet.

"This is your last long ride before the race."

"Yep. I did a brick Monday, still not sure why they call it that. But I biked 10 miles then transitioned to run 2 miles just like in the race. And I've practiced transitions at home. I laid my helmet, glasses, and shoes on a towel. I pretended to come out of the pool, dry off my feet, put on my shoes and socks. Then put on my race belt, my glasses and helmet and grabbed the bike and pushed it away. I pretended to come back in off the bike, dropped the helmet and took off running. Who knew there were so many steps to this besides swimming, biking, and running?" she said laughing.

Frankie gave her a quick hug, "You're going to be great! I'm so excited for you!"

Olivia chuckled sitting down, "I'm excited too. The rest of the week should be easy."

"Don't you have volleyball tomorrow night?"

"Yes, we won last night."

"I know. You and Sofia have really helped Veronica's team."

"It's fun, we're loving it."

"So what are you going to do after the triathlon?"

"I don't know. Maybe I'll rest," she said chuckling. "I might take another class. I really liked that strength class I took when I first started," she said while her eyebrows danced up and down suggestively.

Frankie laughed, "You did? I'll let management know."

Olivia leaned back on her hands and threw her head back chuckling. "You know, this is one of our 'not a real date' places. I have a sweet memory here when you told me about your first love. And then I have that not so sweet memory when I stupidly told you I'd back off."

Frankie turned to her, "I have an idea." She leaned down and brought their lips together in an insistent kiss.

"Mmm, I like the way you think," she said pulling Frankie on top of her. "Wait, how many other girls have you made out with here?"

Frankie looked up as if she were counting. "None! This was my place until I brought you here."

"Really? I'm the first girl you brought here?" Olivia said sweetly.

Frankie nodded, "And the last." She kissed Olivia soundly. If either had any doubts, they were gone.

"As much as I'd like this to continue," Olivia said with Frankie kissing her neck. "This ground is hard and I'd like to be naked with you."

Frankie chuckled, getting up and offering Olivia her hand. "We're closer to your house. Race you!"

"Hold on, Wonder Woman," Olivia said holding on to her hand. "Will you stay the night?"

"I'd love to."

"Just so you know, you're welcome every night," Olivia said tenderly. "We can't race to my house because our cars aren't there, but I'll race you to the gym and we can go to my place from there," she said jumping on her bike and taking off.

"Hey, wait for me!"

They flew into the parking lot neck and neck, laughing the whole time.

"What a race! I think Frankie won," Stella said standing in front of the door on her way out.

"I'd better win, I've been at this a lot longer." She turned to Olivia, "I'll be right back, babe." She took her bike and hurried inside to get her bag.

"You look happy," Stella said to Olivia.

"I can honestly say, I've never been happier. Frankie is wonderful."

Stella chuckled, "She sure is and I'm glad you two found one another."

"Me too. Are you done for the day?"

"Yes. I'm going home to a glass of wine."

"Oh that's right, you love a good glass of wine. You and Jenna will get along great then. I'm okay with wine, but you and Jenna love it."

"I'm looking forward to meeting your friends and to your party Saturday night."

"I thought it would be a good way to get us all together. We can hang out in the backyard, eat, drink, and laugh."

Frankie came bursting through the door. "I'm ready."

Olivia chuckled, "Slow down, babe. We've got all night."

Frankie's face turned beet red as Stella laughed.

"Don't you dare be embarrassed. I've got you now and I'm not letting go," she said reaching for Frankie's shirt and pulling her into a kiss.

"You two have fun," Stella said walking off chuckling.

Olivia loaded her bike in her car and Frankie followed her to her house. They pulled into the driveway and got out.

"Do you want to get something to eat?"

"I can throw something together for us," Olivia said, opening the back door.

Frankie followed her in, "Are you sure?"

"I'm sure," she said, setting her things down on the kitchen island. Frankie did the same.

Olivia pulled Frankie to her, "I'd rather do something else before we eat though." She nibbled on Frankie's bottom lip before kissing her hungrily.

"Mmm," Frankie moaned as Olivia's tongue lavished her mouth with love.

Olivia took Frankie's hand and led her to the master bedroom. "Clothes off!" She pulled Frankie's shirt over her head giving her a quick peck on the lips. "I'll go start the shower." On the way to the bathroom she turned and looked at Frankie. "What are you waiting on? Clothes off. Come on." Then she took her own shirt off and giving Frankie the sexiest smile she'd ever seen.

Frankie pulled her shorts and bra off swiftly and followed Olivia to the bathroom. Olivia had her clothes off as the water warmed up. She turned and kissed Frankie deeply. She stepped into the shower taking Frankie with her. The warm water rolled over their bodies, mixing with sweat and desire as their lips met and Olivia pulled her closer and closer.

"I can't get enough of you," she said pushing Frankie against the wall. She took body wash and squirted some in her hands and rubbed them together. Then she slid them over Frankie's body, soaping her up. Her shoulders were Olivia's undoing, those muscles were so strong and beautiful; her hands ran down her arms to her sides and then came back up her stomach. Olivia could feel her quiver underneath her touch. She brought her under the water wetting her hair and rinsing the soap away. Then she pushed her back against the wall and looked deeply in her eyes. Frankie could feel her knees weaken under Olivia's fiery gaze. She nibbled on Frankie's ear and trailed down her neck with her tongue. Frankie's breath was ragged.

"Fuck, Olivia." She could feel Olivia's smile against her skin. Then Olivia's mouth was everywhere.

She circled Frankie's nipples nibbling on each. Frankie's hands were flat against the wall holding her in place. She couldn't believe she was still standing. She could feel wetness between her legs that had nothing to do with the shower. Olivia was tracing her tongue over her body in all the places she knew would drive Frankie wild. When she parted Frankie's lips and licked from her opening to her clit Frankie groaned louder. She could feel Olivia's love in every caress, in every touch, in every kiss. She could feel it in her fingers, in her tongue and in her lips. Filling her up, over and over until all that love burst into the fiercest orgasm.

When Frankie didn't think she could remain standing another moment Olivia held her up and pinned her to the wall with dark brown eyes. "I love you so much, Frankie."

Frankie's eyes softened, "Babe, I love you, too."

Their faces held such love for one another. They finished washing their bodies and hair. They dried off and laid on the bed.

"Do you want me to go make us something to eat?"

"Can we lay here a minute?"

"Mmm, we sure can," Olivia said snuggling into Frankie closer.

"Do you need any help with the party Saturday?"

"I'm not sure. If I do, you're the first I'll call."

"Good. Have you heard from Lucy and Jenna?"

"Yes, they'll be here Friday evening."

Olivia let out a big sigh.

"What?"

"What, what?"

"You know what. You sighed. Is something wrong?"

Olivia was silent for several moments. She closed her eyes and buried further into Frankie's chest. Then the words came tumbling out.

"I'm about to tell you something that I wasn't going to tell you, but now I think I should. And I'm afraid it's going to hurt you and I don't want to hurt you, babe."

"Breathe," Frankie said, rubbing her back.

Olivia sat up and Frankie started to follow but she pushed her back down. "I want you down. Something happened in Houston. I'm telling you this now while you're naked so you can't run away from me."

"I'm not going to run away from you, ever."

"I want to explain where my mind was at the time."

"Okay, I'm listening."

Olivia let out a deep breath, "While I was in Houston, I thought you were here with Laura…"

"Naked in bed," Frankie finished for her.

Olivia snapped her head to Frankie, "Exactly! And it drove me crazy. I tried not to think about it, but when I didn't hear from you my mind went a little crazier."

"Oh babe, I'm sorry I didn't call or text."

"I know that now. Did I tell you that Jenna is a widow?"

"No. Isn't she your age?"

"Yeah, a couple of years older. I'm thinking she and Stella may have a lot in common because she loves wine too. But Jenna and I became close. I told her all about you and she told me about her wife. She said she hadn't been interested in another woman since her wife died."

"I remember Stella going through that. But that all changed for Jenna when she met you, didn't it?"

"Yes."

"I'm not surprised." Olivia looked at her perplexed. "Olivia you are so approachable and giving, and you're kind. You can see the kindness in your face."

"The last night I was there, we all went out for drinks and dinner. Jenna and I ended up in my room and we had sex." Olivia looked at Frankie, trying to read her thoughts. When she didn't say anything Olivia continued. "Nothing happened before that because I was sure of the connection between us," she pointed from Frankie to herself. "Then when I didn't hear from you, I thought the worst. She needed me to fill the emptiness inside her, to know she could still feel. And she made me feel wanted; I could see it in her eyes."

"Do you see how much I want you, in my eyes?"

Olivia smiled, "I see the want, but in your eyes, I also see love. I see how much you love me and want to show me."

"I do."

"Jenna is really a great person and I wasn't going to tell you because it doesn't matter."

"And you thought I was here doing the same thing with Laura."

Olivia nodded

"Honestly, babe. We had one real kiss and when we did your face flashed in the front of my mind. I knew there was nothing. You are who I'm in love with."

Olivia smacked in the side of her arm.

"What was that for?"

"You should have called me! If I'd known that, then Jenna and I would have never happened."

"I know, I'm sorry."

Olivia fell into her arms, "It's not your fault, it's not anyone's fault. We're together now, that's what's important."

"How are things with Jenna now?"

Olivia popped up, "We're just friends. She actually was happy you came to your senses."

Frankie's eyebrows raised, "Oh man, they think I'm an idiot."

"Not really, I told them everything that happened. They thought I was pretty dumb, too. They're going to love you and you're going to love them, you'll see."

"Thank you for telling me. But now, I'm hungry. Can we please eat something?"

"Just how hungry are you?" Olivia said kissing Frankie's neck up to her ear.

"Mmm."

"That's what I thought."

21

Grace pulled into the parking lot and saw Frankie with two dogs waiting on her. She was happy Frankie liked having sessions while walking the dogs. It wouldn't be a surprise if Frankie took one home with her someday.

"Who are we strolling with today?"

Frankie handed a leash to Grace, "This is Nora. She's a dachshund as you can see. And I have her friend Samson that is a little dog mix."

"Little dog mix?"

"That's what the manager said," Frankie chuckled.

"Okay then, let's stroll." The dogs led them away from the shelter with smiles on everyone's faces. "Catch me up, how are things?"

"Things are wonderful."

"Wow, tell me more."

"Neither Olivia or I communicated well and we made each other miserable. Before you ask, here's what I now know, you cannot stop communicating with someone out of fear. We have talked, really talked and now are not only on the same page, but happily together."

"Good for you both. Communication is tricky, that's for sure."

"You remember she went away for work?"

"Yes."

"While she was gone, I didn't text or call her; thinking that's what she wanted instead of simply asking. She didn't contact me because she thought my silence meant that I was back with Laura. By jumping to conclusions instead of asking we both caused heartache."

"But, you've talked and gotten past it."

"Yes. One thing did surprise me. While she was gone, she made friends with two people at her hotel. One of them was extremely interested in her."

"Uh-huh."

"They ended up having sex."

"How did that make you feel?"

"Surprised. And then she explained where her head was and also about the other woman."

"You weren't angry or hurt?"

"Well, no. She explained that she thought I was with Laura and this woman was a widow and hadn't been with anyone since her wife died. Olivia told me it felt good to be wanted."

"Of course it did. Isn't that what we all want. I'm sure she was very vulnerable at the time as well as the widow."

"Yeah. She wasn't going to tell me because she didn't want to hurt me. But when she explained the situation, how could I be mad?"

"But were you hurt?"

"Not really. We both have a past and exes. It feels more like that."

"Good for you. Does it bother you that she wasn't going to tell you?"

"No, because she did. We are both making every effort to communicate. Unlike with Laura, I've told Olivia how I feel and where I see us."

"Care to share?"

Frankie chuckled, "I'm buying a house in the subdivision she designed. Not just any house, a house we both looked at together. I've told her when she's ready that I want it to be her home too."

"Wow, that's putting it right out there."

"I know, but I love her and want to spend my life with her. I've told her no pressure."

"You can say no pressure, Frankie, but, buying a house. That's a big deal."

"I know. But I'm trying to be open and communicate."

"You are! What about this other woman? Is she in the past?"

"Actually, I'm meeting her tomorrow."

"What?"

"The two friends she made are coming to the race this weekend."

"And how do you feel about that?"

"Good. I'm glad to meet them; they helped her through a hard time. They are friends, that's all."

"Wow, all this maturity and adulting. You may not need me anymore."

"I still need you. Talking to you helped me to be open and now Olivia and I are together with a bright future."

"I'm glad. Nothing makes a counselor happier than a happy client."

"Let's give two more dogs a walk. We still have time."

"Time to go back, Nora. Your little legs are probably tired."

∽

"I'd better go. Don't we have something in the morning," Frankie looked up, pretending to search her memory.

"Ha ha," Olivia deadpanned. "Only the biggest race of my life!"

Everyone was visibly surprised. "Okay, maybe not the biggest, but it's a big deal to me."

"It's a big deal to us too," said Lucy. "We didn't swim all those miles, bike with you, and run along beside you for nothing."

"So, your memory is a little different from mine." They all laughed. "You're right, I should probably try to get some sleep. Come on, I'll walk you out," she said taking Frankie's hand.

"It was nice to meet you, Frankie," Jenna said. "Good luck tomorrow. Now that we know you're not an idiot, we'll be cheering for you too."

"Aw, thanks, Jenna."

"Yeah, we were pretty sure you weren't an idiot because who could let this one go?" Lucy said smiling at Olivia.

"Come on, you're embarrassing me."

They walked to Frankie's Jeep hand in hand.

"Are you getting nervous?"

"A little."

Frankie leaned down and kissed her. "You'll do great."

"Hmm, that kiss seemed to help," she said wrapping her arms around Frankie's neck and pulling her in for a deep, long soulful kiss. "I'm going to miss you tonight," she said breathlessly.

"Mmm, we wouldn't get any sleep," she said, holding her close.

"Who needs sleep when we could be doing this," she said, kissing her deeply again. "Okay, I'll let you go, just for tonight." Olivia opened the door and Frankie got in.

"I'll meet you in the morning so we can put our bikes together."

"I'll be there." Olivia watched her drive away and went back inside.

"She's really great, Olivia," Lucy said. "Why in the world would you give that other woman a chance?"

"I know! We both messed up, but everything is good now."

"I'm glad. You both look so happy together," said Jenna.

"I never dreamed it would be this good."

"So what do you think this big meeting is about with Elizabeth on Monday?"

"I have no idea. She told me about it this morning. I told her you were spending the weekend with me, but she didn't say anything else."

"Guess you'll have to wait. Can't be anything bad, can it?" asked Jenna.

"No. I can't think of a thing. Well, I've got to get my stuff together for the race and try to sleep."

"Can we help?"

"No, I'm just double checking everything. Do you need anything? I hope you don't mind sharing."

"Not at all. It's fine," said Jenna.

Olivia went to her room and checked her bag for the third time, making sure everything was in there.

"Hey, I just wanted to say good luck tomorrow," said Jenna standing in the doorway.

"Thanks."

"Frankie knows, right?"

Olivia turned to her, "Yeah, I told her. Didn't really mean to but I did. Everything is fine, really."

"What a relief. It would kill me if I messed this up for you two."

"We didn't do anything wrong," Olivia said sighing.

"I know," Jenna said holding her hands up. "You two are perfect for each other."

"I love her so much."

"It shows. Goodnight. Try to sleep."

"I will. Goodnight."

∼

"Who knew triathlons started so early in the morning," Lucy said sipping her coffee.

"I know! Whose idea was that?" Sofia said as they watched Olivia go through a quick pre-race inspection of her bicycle with race officials.

"I'm sure it's to get it done before it gets too hot."

"You're right, Jenna. That's exactly why," said Stella.

Desi walked over after having her bike inspected, "We're going to set our bikes up together as soon as they get through inspection. If y'all will wait here, it won't take us long."

"Okay. Do you need any help?" asked Stella.

"No, transition will be busy, we'll help Olivia."

They all followed the three with their eyes. They went through the entrance to the transition area and found a place that all three could fit together. Olivia hung her bike by the seat on the stand and laid her towel down on the ground to the side of the front tire. She placed her glasses in her helmet along with her race belt. At the front of her towel she placed her shoes with her socks inside them. On top of the shoes she laid a small towel. She would use this first as she came out of the water to dry her feet. She looked at all her gear and made sure it was just like she practiced. The idea was to come in quickly and change to her gear for the bike leg, then come back shedding her helmet and taking off for the run to the finish line.

"All set?" Frankie asked.

"I think so. Take a look, I didn't forget anything did I?"

Frankie and Desi both looked at her towel making sure she had everything she needed.

"It looks good," Desi said, putting an arm around her and giving her a little squeeze. "You are going to do great! I know it!"

"Thanks Desi. I'm nervous."

Frankie smiled at her, "It's good to be nervous. I am, too. It'll go away as soon as you hit the water."

They walked back over to where their friends were and waited for the opening ceremonies. The event leaders welcomed all the athletes, volunteers, and fans. They explained a little about the programs the entry fee supported; the money going to help others in need. It was time for the National Anthem and they all sang along.

Olivia went through waves of nervousness. One moment she'd be fine and then the butterflies would go crazy in her stomach. She practiced the three deep calming breaths she learned from Stella months ago. Frankie gently took her hand and stood alongside her trying to calm both their nerves. Olivia looked up at her and smiled, thanking her with her eyes.

"This is it, we have to line up to be ready to start with our group," said Desi.

"How many people are here?" asked Jenna.

"Around seven hundred signed up," said Stella.

"Wow!" said Lucy.

"I know! That's why I'm starting near the back. I don't want to get in anyone's way," said Olivia.

"You won't be in anyone's way, I promise," said Frankie.

"Hey, thank you all for coming to cheer me on. I'm hoping to be done in an hour and a half. So, see you at the finish line," she said high fiving each one.

"You'll hear us along the way," said Jenna.

They walked down to the back of the mass of people lined up to start. Large markers were floating out in the lake for them to swim around and back to shore totaling 300 meters. From there they would walk or run to transition and get on the bike for 10 miles. Then back to transition for a two-mile run.

Olivia kept taking deep breaths as the people continued to enter the water and she got closer to her turn to start. She knew this would be a race with herself, where she would be pushing herself and pacing herself, and talking to herself the entire time.

With only a few people in front of them, Frankie turned to her and said, "You got this, babe. I'll see you at the finish."

"Okay," she reached up and kissed Frankie for luck.

"Here we go!" yelled Desi as she dove in the water. Frankie was next and then it was her turn.

Her swim hat was bright pink and her goggles were snug as she ran into the water and started swimming. She was panting for breath and knew she had to calm down. She needed to swim stroke by stroke just as she'd practiced so many times in the pool and here at the lake.

After a few moments, she settled into her rhythm and began to relax. She could see swimmers ahead of her and went around a few. Just as she was beginning to enjoy it, someone swam right over her. What the fuck! Couldn't they see her? Stella had warned her this would happen, there would be arms and legs coming from all directions. She pulled her head up and looked around and could see a path ahead. With a big breath she put her head down and resumed her swim. She made it around the buoys and before she knew it, she could feel sand under her feet.

She walked out of the water taking a big breath and could hear her friends cheering for her. Frankie was waiting to go to transition with her.

"You aren't supposed to wait on me," she said.

"I'm not. I finished and you were right behind me. I'm so proud of you!"

This made Olivia smile; she'd made it through the swim.

Stella walked beside them, "Good job staying calm when that jackass swam over you."

"Good thing she couldn't hear what I was saying in my head," she laughed.

They made it to their bikes. Desi was just leaving when they walked up and gave Olivia a high five. She sat down, dried her feet and put on her socks and shoes. "That was so fun. A little crazy, but fun!" She stood up and grabbed her race belt that had her bib and number attached to it. She put her glasses on and then her helmet.

"Okay babe, you're doing great. You know where the big hills are," Frankie said taking her bike off the rack.

"I remember," she said clicking the strap on her helmet and grabbing her bike.

"I'll see you at the finish," Frankie called over her shoulder. "I love you!" She was so proud of Olivia, she thought her heart was going to burst.

"Love you too!" Olivia called back as she jumped on her bike and took off. I'm doing this, I'm really doing this, she thought to herself. The swim was the part that she was the most nervous about and it was done. She felt most confident on the bike. The big hills weren't for a few miles so she could relax, catch her breath, and enjoy it.

She breezed along and looked at her watch. The swim had taken nine minutes, just as she expected. She had no idea how long she'd been in transition, but she tried to hurry. If her calculations were right, she was on pace to finish the bike in around 45 minutes, just as she had hoped. It won't be long now until the first big hill. She took a minute to think about how happy she was to see Frankie's face when she came out of the water. And then to hear Jenna, Lucy, and Sofia cheering made her almost tear up. So many volunteers were along the course encouraging them, it was amazing.

Biking up hills was not one of her favorite things, but flying down them was! Some of these hills were really challenging though, she shifted to an easier gear over and over until she cleared the hardest one. It should be clear sailing from here. Then she heard shouting.

"Come on Olivia! Way to go! Looking good!"

She looked up in time to see Lucy and Sofia waving and cheering her on. This gave her an extra burst and she waved back. Forty-three minutes after leaving transition she steered her bike back to her towel. She wondered how Frankie was doing. Desi could run like the wind so she knew she was probably almost finished.

She put her bike back on the rack, took her helmet off and drank one more big gulp of water. Her legs felt like bricks when she tried to start running. Maybe that's why they called those practice sessions bricks! She heard Stella and Jenna encouraging her when she left transition

"Look at you Olivia! You're doing awesome!" yelled Jenna.

Stella ran beside her for a moment, "I'm so proud of you! This run is yours! Make it your bitch!"

This made Olivia burst out laughing. When she looked at Stella she was grinning from ear to ear. No doubt, she had the best group of friends.

At this point, she didn't care about her time. She was tired and the run was hard after swimming and biking. She tried to think about anything but running. The idea of crossing that finish line with Frankie and her friends waiting was what got her through the first mile. Then she began to look at what she was doing.

A few months ago she couldn't run a quarter of a mile much less bike five. And here she was about to finish a fucking triathlon. The woman she was madly in love with was waiting for her just up the way along with her very best friend in the world. And there were new friends waiting too, new friends she couldn't wait to become old friends.

And then she heard them, "Come on Olivia! You're almost here! Way to go!"

And then she saw them, Frankie was jumping up and down waving along with Sofia and Lucy. Desi was waving her in and Stella and Jenna were clapping. She felt so loved! But also ready to end this damn race!

She heard the announcer call out her name and number as she crossed the finish line. A volunteer put a medal around her neck and another handed her a bottle of water. And then Frankie had her arms around her, smiling in her face with such love in her eyes

"You did it! I'm so proud of you!"

Olivia hugged her back and kissed her full on the lips. They walked over to where everyone else waited, each giving her a congratulatory hug.

"Ugh," she breathed out. "That was awesome! But, I'm glad I'm through!"

Everyone laughed.

"Let's get something to drink," Desi said, leading them to a table set up with fruit, snacks, and drinks for the athletes. They finally found an empty table where they could all sit down.

"So, tell us about it?" said Stella.

Olivia smiled. Frankie had an arm around her and she could feel the pride oozing with her touch.

"You get so excited you have to calm yourself down. It's crazy. There were a couple of women that were racing together that were about my pace. We would pass one another and encourage each other. It helped keep me going."

"Did you think you wouldn't make it?" asked Lucy.

"Hell no! I'd put in so much time training there was no way I wasn't crossing that finish line!"

This brought another round of cheers.

"What about Frankie and Desi! They finished too!" This brought cheers from the group.

"Aaw, thanks Olivia," said Desi.

"And thanks for not waiting on me. I know that killed you. But I had to do it myself," Olivia said to Frankie so everyone could hear.

Frankie beamed, "It was brutal! But it made me finish faster so I could be here waiting on you."

"Yeah, when she finished the bike, the first thing she said was, 'How was Olivia'," Stella said laughing. "Then when she finished the race, same thing. 'How was Olivia starting the run'."

"I couldn't help it. All these months I'd been telling you how great it was and I didn't want you to kill me when you came in if it wasn't wonderful. Was it wonderful?"

Olivia smiled at Frankie with such love, "It was everything you said. When I'd get tired, I would stop and talk to myself and say 'You're doing a triathlon, bitch! That's something!'" Much laughter followed. "But you're right, crossing that finish line was incredible!"

"They've opened transition so we can get our bikes," said Desi.

"I'm starving for real food, but I'm also nasty," said Olivia.

"Who cares! Get your stuff and let's meet somewhere and eat," suggested Stella.

"Sounds good to me, where to?" said Frankie.

"Let's meet at the gym and we won't have as many cars."

"Okay!" everyone said in unison.

They all had lunch together and split up after for the racers to clean up and rest before everyone was coming to Olivia's for the party that evening.

22

The party was in full swing at Olivia's. She looked around her backyard at her friends and was filled with such joy. She was grateful for every one of them. How her life had changed in a few short months.

"How are you feeling? Are you tired?" asked Stella.

"Not at all. Well, maybe a little, but I feel great. Hey, I got you and Jenna a special bottle of wine. Did you see it inside?"

"I didn't."

"Come on, I'll show you," she said, leading her into the house. In the kitchen she found Jenna opening the bottle of wine.

"Hey, I didn't think you'd mind. And this is a really nice bottle. Did I rub off on you?"

Olivia laughed, "No, I got this for you and Stella. You two are the wine drinkers. I'll drink it occasionally but not like you two."

"What does that mean? Are you calling us winos?"

She chuckled, "You know better. Let's see, how would you say it, the two of you have more sophisticated palates than I do."

"Hmm, okay, I'll take that," Jenna said, handing Stella a glass.

"Thanks," Stella said nodding her head slightly with a soft smile.

"Olivia, we need you out here," Frankie yelled from the backyard. "Desi is trying to mess up the grill."

"You'd better go. Des is a great person, but backyard chef she is not!"

Olivia laughed and ran out the back door.

"Hey, this is good. At least she knows how to select a good bottle," Stella said sipping from her glass.

"I may have given her a few pointers. It's amazing what you can talk about when you're sitting in a hotel bar with no place to go. And with two architects I might add. I had to steer the conversation into something I understood," Jenna said chuckling.

"You three became fast friends."

"We really did. Lucy is about to move to her new house so I'm not sure what I'll do."

"How long are you staying in Houston?"

"It's an open-ended consulting job at the moment. I go back home to check on things occasionally. I'm actually trying to find a place to relocate."

"Forgive me for being so forward, but is it because of your wife?"

Jenna smiled, "Olivia told you?"

"I hope you don't mind. I've been through it too."

"She told me. To answer your question, yes it is because my wife died. Things don't feel the same at home and it's all so sad sometimes. Moving may be my best option."

"I get it. All the places that you used to love suddenly make you sad."

"How did you get through it? I work long hours so I'm exhausted and fall into bed."

"I did that for a while, but you can't sustain it."

"When I met Lucy at the hotel and then Olivia, I slowed down the work hours because I had someone to spend time with. Being alone is better now, but,"

"But you still get lonely. So do I and it's been five years. I will say this, someone or something will come along and you'll be ready. You won't know it, but suddenly you'll be interested in something and not as lonely."

"What did that for you?"

Stella chuckled, "For me, it was yoga. I've taught it for years, but I immersed myself in the mind part of it and my pain began to ease. I still miss her as much as ever, but, I can live."

Jenna studied Stella for a moment. "Did Olivia tell you anything else?"

Stella smiled and nodded, "I'm glad you could be there for one another."

"Me too," Jenna said as her face reddened.

"There is no reason to be embarrassed. It's a good thing," Stella said reaching out and putting her hand on Jenna's forearm.

"Hey," Sofia said, walking into the kitchen. "Oh no, I didn't interrupt something, did I?"

"Not at all," said Stella. "You want to try a glass of this excellent wine?"

"Oh that's right, she shopped especially for you two."

"Then try some, it's good," said Jenna.

"Okay, I'd love to," said Sofia as Jenna poured her a glass.

"Did Olivia save the grill? I heard Desi was being Desi."

Sofia laughed, "She did. For Desi to be so talented I'm not sure grilling is in her wheelhouse."

"You couldn't be more right."

They walked outside to join the group as Olivia put the burgers on the grill. The aroma was heavenly as the meat sizzled.

"We're having burgers because I haven't had one in ages since I was training for this triathlon. I do have grilled chicken for those of you that do not want to indulge, but I highly recommend the burger. If you thought I could design a house, just wait until you taste one of my burgers."

"I can vouch for her! They are the best!" Sofia spoke up.

"While everyone is gathered around, I wanted to thank you all for being here and helping me the last few months. I'm not talking about the triathlon, either. When I came to Your Way, I was overweight and thought a number on the scale would change everything for me. I thought that number would make me attractive. And someone tried to tell me the first week that it's not about the number on the scale, it's about what's inside," she said, looking at Frankie. "At that time, I couldn't see what was inside, but Frankie, Stella, Desi, and Sofia could. As my muscles became stronger, so did my self-worth. And that wouldn't have happened if the people around me hadn't believed in me. Because you did, slowly but surely, I began to believe, too. Your Way has changed my life and brought me so many new friends and the most beautiful girlfriend," she said, putting her arm around Frankie's waist. "It has to be magical or Sofia certainly wouldn't have kept going." She looked at Sofia and they shared a laugh.

"And because of this renewed confidence I made two new friends that I think fit right in with our group," she said, looking at Lucy and Jenna. "Y'all need to think about relocating to North Texas. You have a family waiting."

"That's a great idea," said Frankie.

"Maybe that's what our big meeting is about Monday, Olivia. Maybe Elizabeth wants me up here with you," said Lucy.

"Wouldn't that be fun!" Olivia exclaimed.

"I thought you were leaving tomorrow," Stella said to Lucy and Jenna.

"No. Lucy has a meeting with Olivia's boss on Monday so we're going back after that," said Jenna.

"What plans do you have for tomorrow?" Stella asked Olivia.

"None."

"Let's all go to the lake. We can swim and paddle board," suggested Stella.

"That's a great idea. I have two boards," said Olivia.

"Me too," said Stella.

"I have one too," said Desi.

"That's plenty, we can take turns," said Olivia.

"Let's do it!" Everyone agreed.

Later that night, everyone was full of good food and good spirits as the laughter continued.

Olivia came back outside from walking Stella to her car to find Lucy, Jenna, and Frankie sitting around on the patio. Everyone else had already gone.

"Stella said she invited you to spend the morning with her while Lucy and I are at the meeting, Monday," she said to Jenna.

"Yeah, she asked what I was going to do and I didn't really know."

"You'll have fun with her. She can show you around the gym, maybe it'll make you want to move here," she said. She took Frankie's hand and pulled her up and led her inside as Lucy and Jenna continued their conversation.

She pulled her down the hall to her bedroom and closed the door. When she turned around, she pulled Frankie to her and crashed their lips together in a torrid kiss.

"I've needed that for the last few hours," she said breathlessly. "Will you spend the night? There's more I need from you," she said seductively.

"Are you sure?"

"Yes, I'm sure. Do you not want to?"

"Of course I want to. I've been struggling all night to keep my hands off you."

Olivia giggled, "We've got it bad."

"Yeah, we do," Frankie said, bringing their lips together again.

With their lips still connected Olivia pulled them over to the bed and plopped down pulling Frankie on top of her. "Mmm," she said holding her close. "Just a few," she brought their lips together. "More," she kissed her again. "Kisses," she said this time, deepening the kiss to Frankie's moan.

After several minutes they broke apart and Olivia said, "Okay, let's put the food away and get back in here."

Frankie jumped up, "Race you." Olivia erupted in giggles as they raced down the hall.

On Monday morning, Olivia pulled into the Your Way parking lot to drop Jenna off.

"Are you sure you don't mind hanging out here with Stella?"

"Not at all."

"I don't know how long this meeting will last, but Lucy and I will come back to get you as soon as we're through."

"It's okay, Olivia. I'll be fine."

"Okay, text me if you need us to come get you."

"I'll see you when you're done. Good luck you two." She got out of the car and went into the gym.

"I think she'll be just fine. She and Stella seemed to be having a good time yesterday at the lake," said Lucy.

"I noticed. That was such a fun day. You want to know one of the best parts for me?"

"Hmm, let's see. I'm guessing it has something to do with Frankie."

"Haha but, yes, it does. She is Miss Athlete America and she hasn't been on a paddleboard much. So, it was fun for me to teach her a few things and for her to sit on my board while I paddled us."

"Y'all are too cute together."

Olivia smiled thinking back to yesterday with Frankie and her friends at the lake. It was the perfect day.

She pulled into the subdivision and noticed Elizabeth's car wasn't there yet. "Elizabeth isn't here, let's drive to Frankie's house. We might be able to get in."

They drove into the driveway where two work vans were parked. When they got out, a woman with a tool belt on walked out.

"Good morning, would we be in the way if we did a quick walk through?"

"Not at all, watch your step," the woman said smiling and walking to one of the vans.

"Wow, maybe I'll ask Elizabeth for a transfer here," Lucy said discreetly watching the worker.

Olivia chuckled, "Come on, I'll show you around." She gave her a quick tour. Olivia had been to the house several times since Frankie purchased it and couldn't keep the smiles and good memories that flooded back.

When they got back in the car Lucy said, "That house is perfect for you."

Olivia looked at her confused, "What do you mean?"

"I mean that would be a perfect house for you and Frankie. I could see you there with little kids running around."

"Whoa!"

"You know you've thought about it. And if you haven't, what's wrong with you?"

Olivia chuckled, "You're right, I have thought about it."

"Okay then. I'm just saying, I could see you there."

Olivia nodded and pulled into the driveway at the office at the same time Elizabeth did.

"Good morning," she said getting out of her car and noticing the direction they'd come from. "I don't guess you were checking on the progress of a certain someone's house were you?"

Olivia chuckled, "I was showing Lucy."

"Good morning Lucy, good to see you again."

"Hi Elizabeth, nice to see you, too."

"Let's go in and talk."

They followed her into the office. "Anyone want coffee?" asked Olivia. She got everyone their preferred drink and they went into the private office. Olivia and Lucy sat on the couch while Elizabeth sat across from them.

"I was very impressed and pleased with the work you two did in Houston," Elizabeth said as Olivia and Lucy smiled at one another. "So much so that I have an opportunity I want to offer you both. First, let me explain it's not a package deal. You do not both have to accept."

They looked at one another. "Okay?" Olivia asked questioningly.

"There is a project north east of Austin that is about to enter the third phase."

"The one near Georgetown?" asked Olivia.

"That's the one. The project manager and I think you would be perfect to lead this next phase, Olivia."

Olivia's mouth dropped open and her eyes grew wide in surprise, "Me?"

"Yes you. And Lucy, with your experience I think you could handle the project design."

This made Lucy gasp in surprise. "Wow, that's quite a step up for me!"

"Do you not think you're up for it?" Elizabeth asked.

"Not at all," Lucy said, sitting straighter. "I am."

"You are Lucy. You can do it," added Olivia.

"So can you, Olivia. You'd be such a good leader," replied Lucy.

"That's why I chose you," Elizabeth said looking at them both.

"Of course, there will be quite an increase in your salary and profit sharing that goes along with the promotion. There will also be some added perks like, oh, for example your gym membership. I can get you a list of those with Human Resources."

Olivia couldn't believe it! The lead project manager of the entire phase! She'd dreamed of what it would be like to do that exact job at this subdivision.

"The project would likely take five to ten years depending on sales, of course."

Olivia nodded thinking about the area.

"You would have to relocate," Elizabeth said, focusing on Olivia.

Move! That's what Olivia heard. Six months ago this wouldn't have been an issue, but she could feel her face getting red thinking about leaving Frankie now.

"Let me show you the layout. I brought the specs over Friday so we could look at them," she said, getting up and going to the conference table. Olivia and Lucy followed, looking at the drawings spread on the table as Elizabeth explained more about the project. She studied the drawings and let Elizabeth's words sink in as she described Olivia's dream job. There was only one problem, it was in Austin! She tried not to worry about that part just yet.

"Do you have any questions? I know it's a lot to consider. You have a few days to think it through, but before you decide, I'd like for you to drive down and look at the site. I know you're going back to

Houston today Lucy, and you have a full schedule the next couple of days, Olivia. Do you think you could meet there say, Thursday?"

They both considered this and nodded.

"I could go Thursday," they both said.

"Okay, that's all I have for you today. Look it over and I'll answer any questions you may have. Take your time."

"Thanks Elizabeth, and thanks for the opportunity," said Olivia, feeling a bit overwhelmed.

She smiled, "You deserve it." Then she looked at Lucy, "You, too."

"Thanks," said Lucy as Elizabeth left them. She turned to Olivia, "Holy shit!"

"I know!"

"Did you have any idea?"

"Not at all."

"What do you think?"

"I think this is what I've been working for, that's what I think," said Olivia, shaking her head as she continued to look at the plans.

"It's a lot to think about."

"Yeah, it is. Do you have any questions? I know you and Jenna have to get going."

"I'm sure I'll think of a ton on the way home. I'm glad we drove; I'll have plenty of time to think about this."

"What do you think?"

"Unlike you, I don't have anything holding me in Houston. So, it looks incredible. Imagine us teaming up, Olivia!"

"I know! We'd be a force," she said giggling. "Come on, we'd better get Jenna."

They walked into Your Way and Frankie was the first person Olivia saw. Her face lit up when she saw Olivia coming toward her, but it fell to concern as she got closer.

"What's wrong?"

"Nothing," Olivia said, leaning up to kiss her.

Frankie tilted her head, "Are you sure?"

"I'm sure, nothing is wrong."

"Did your meeting go okay?"

"Yes, I will tell you all about it, but Lucy and Jenna are about to leave."

Lucy, Stella, and Jenna walked over to them.

"Hey, would you want to have an early lunch before we hit the road? Stella said there's a place nearby that's quick," asked Lucy.

Olivia turned to Frankie, "Could you join us?"

"Babe, I can't, I have a class in a few minutes."

"Okay," Olivia said, sighing. Turning to the others she said, "Y'all go ahead and save me a seat, I'll be right there."

She took Frankie's hand and pulled her into the office. "I know you only have a minute, but the meeting was about a promotion."

"That's wonderful!" Frankie said, pulling her into a hug.

"Can we talk about it tonight? I have a lot to tell you," Olivia said subdued.

"Sure, sure. Come by here after work. Why do you not seem excited?"

"I am excited, babe. It's like a dream, but, let me tell you all about it later. Okay," she said kissing her.

"Okay." Olivia started to walk off but Frankie grabbed her arm. "I love you."

Olivia turned with the sweetest smile, "I love you, too." She brought their lips together again and was gone.

Frankie had an unsettled feeling as she watched Olivia go.

23

Lucy explained the job offer to Stella and Jenna at lunch. They were extremely excited for them both.

"You're kind of quiet, Olivia," said Stella.

"There's so much to consider," Olivia said coming back to the conversation.

"Hey," Jenna said, covering Olivia's hand with her own. "I'm here for you if you need to talk."

Olivia smiled, "I know and I appreciate it."

Stella apprised Olivia, "I know what you're thinking and you don't have to turn it down because of Frankie."

"I'm trying to let the shock wear off and then I'm going to look at it from all sides. I'm keeping an open mind until we go there on Thursday."

"Frankie will support you all the way," Stella said.

"I know. I can hear her already, 'we'll make it work, babe'."

"That's exactly what she'll say."

"We're talking after work. She doesn't know all the details yet."

"I, too, am here for you," Stella assured her.

"Thanks."

After lunch Olivia took Lucy and Jenna back to her house to get their car for the return trip to Houston.

Lucy hugged her and said, "Let me know what you think, I'm leaning toward going, but like you, I do have things to consider. I'll see you Thursday."

"Okay. Drive safe." She walked around the car and Jenna softly pulled her into an embrace and held her.

"I know this is hard. I'll talk it through with you, anytime," she whispered in Olivia's ear.

Olivia pulled back with a sweet smile on her face, "I'll call you."

"By the way, I'm so proud of you competing in that triathlon. You're such a badass!"

"Thanks again for coming, it meant the world to me."

"And thanks for introducing me to Stella."

"She's amazing. I knew you'd like her. Maybe I'll be seeing you again soon then?"

"Maybe," she said getting in the car.

"Text me you made it home safe," Olivia yelled as they drove away waving.

She decided to take the rest of the day off to look at her options. A little later she texted Frankie and told her to come to her house after work.

In the middle of the afternoon she was laying on the couch looking at the Austin area on her iPad when she heard a knock at her front door. It was too early for Frankie. But when she answered the door, there she was. She was so glad to see her that she flew into her arms and held on tight.

"Wow," said Frankie holding her. "That's a welcome!" She pulled back and looked into Olivia's face, gazing over all her features. She leaned in and hovered her lips over Olivia's. "We've got this," she whispered before kissing her tenderly. She felt Olivia relax in her arms and deepened the kiss.

"Why are you here so early," Olivia asked.

"With a welcome like that, who cares," Frankie chuckled, walking inside. "I asked Desi to take my last class because I knew something wasn't quite right this morning when you told me about the job. Are you alright?"

"I'm better now that you're here." Olivia almost decided right then and there that she wasn't taking the job.

Frankie sat down on the couch, pulling Olivia down beside her. "Tell me all about it."

Olivia took a deep breath and filled Frankie in on the project, where it was, and that she would be leading the team for the entire phase of the subdivision.

"Wow, that's awesome! I'm not surprised though. You are so good at what you do."

Olivia smiled at the praise but looked down.

"Are you going to tell me or make me guess?"

"What?"

"You haven't told me everything."

Olivia sighed, "Have you ever thought about adding a second Your Way location?"

"What?"

"Baby, I'd have to move there or be there all week, at the least."

"Hmm, so we may have to do long distance for a while?"

"Unless you want to open a gym there," Olivia said, teasing.

Frankie smiled, "I'm not sure that could happen. Look, we will do whatever it takes. Do not worry about us. We will make this work."

"I knew you would say that."

"Tell me about the job. You'd be in charge of the whole thing?"

"Yes." Olivia went on with more specifics and described the things she'd be able to do that she couldn't do in her current position.

"It sounds like the dream job you described to me not that long ago."

Olivia nodded, "It is."

"Then take it. What's holding you back?"

"If I moved there, my life would be work. I know you would come visit and I would come here, but, I don't know that I want to do that. The project will last five to ten years," she hesitated for a moment.

"And? Don't be afraid to tell me what you're thinking."

Olivia looked deeply into those green eyes that had given her such joy, "I don't want work to be my life anymore. I have you and," she took a breath. "And I want kids with you."

Tears sprang to Frankie's eyes; she didn't think she'd ever heard anything that made her happier.

Olivia put her hand on the side of Frankie's face, "If I take that job, it would be hard to do that. I know we've talked about the future, but that's commitment, babe."

"There is nothing I want more than to have a family with you. You know that; I bought a house," she said chuckling. "What if I moved with you? Do you think it's the job that would keep you so busy or us being apart?"

"You'd do that? You'd leave your business and move with me, when you're buying a house?"

"If it's the best option for us and our family, I'd do it in a heartbeat."

Olivia was shocked for the second time today. She never considered Frankie coming with her. They looked at one another for a few moments as thoughts ran through Olivia's head.

"Lucy and I are supposed to go to the site Thursday and look it over. Let me do that and think about it. I mean just because it was my dream job at one time doesn't mean it necessarily is now. Okay?"

"Okay. That sounds like a smart decision, a good plan." She took Olivia's hands and looked around, "Did you have anything you were doing right now?"

"No. I was waiting for you to get here and thinking about this damn job."

"Would you like to take your mind off it for a bit?"

"I sure would," Olivia said nodding her head.

"Well, we haven't really been alone in days," Frankie drew out the last word dramatically. This made Olivia smile.

"No, we haven't."

"Well, it's just you and me here now and we can be as loud as we want," she said suggestively.

"Frankie Dean, are you trying to seduce me?"

"I'm trying to be a good girlfriend and relieve your stress."

"Relieve my stress, that's what you're calling it?"

Frankie nodded her head seriously.

"Then you'd better take me to that bedroom and have your way with me."

They jumped up and started shedding clothes as they ran to the bedroom.

∼

OLIVIA LAID in Frankie's arms and could feel her gently playing with her hair. She could stay here just like this forever.

"You are the best stress reliever ever. Don't tell Stella, but you're better than meditation."

Frankie chuckled, "Your secret is safe with me."

"We've had some big decisions to make. You buy a house, me with this job."

"Yeah? Are you going somewhere with this or is it just an observation?"

"Some people would say we're rushing things and that we don't know one another very well."

"Uh-huh, and who would those people be?"

"No one in particular, just in general."

"Olivia, what are you trying to say?"

"Do you think we're rushing into this? I don't want to pressure you into anything."

Frankie wondered where this was coming from but calmly said, "We're not rushing for me. You know my last relationship wasn't going anywhere and that's why it ended. Just because this one is moving fast doesn't mean it shouldn't. Do you think we're rushing?"

"No. I know we're in the middle of this new relationship and everything is beautiful and sexy and wonderful right now. And I also know It won't always be that way. But I have no doubt in my mind that you are who I want to live my life with and want to raise kids with, so why should we wait around a certain amount of time to live the life we both want?"

"I couldn't agree more. You do remember that I'm older than you," she teased. "Some people would say I'm too old to have kids."

"Who said that?" Olivia said sitting up and staring at her.

"I'm sure there are people out there that feel that way. But what I mean is maybe this is our time for our kids. I'm not saying we have to jump in and start having babies, but for us it will take some time to do that and if we're certain then why wait? It's our life, babe, no one else's."

"Then, we're on the same page. Life together, kids."

"Same page but, you left something out."

Olivia looked puzzled, she counted out on her fingers, "What did I leave out?"

"How about marriage? Do you not want to marry me?"

Olivia looked at Frankie like she was crazy, "Of course I want to marry you!"

"Well, you never said it," Frankie said, sitting up.

"This is not a marriage proposal," Olivia said firmly.

"It better not be because if you were asking me to marry you, well, I thought you'd do a better job," Frankie said teasing.

Olivia grabbed her and kissed her, "You'll never know it's coming."

They laughed and Frankie thought this is going to be fun to try and outdo the other proposing. She kissed Olivia, feeling so grateful.

∽

Olivia was true to her word and hadn't thought too much about the job until Thursday. As she pulled into the area north of Austin, she found the office and went in to find Lucy. She'd received a text that she'd be waiting.

She went inside and found Lucy and met the current project manager. He gave them a run down on what the next phase looked like and then took them on a tour of the property. They looked at the first phase and through the second that was nearing completion. Then he took them to an area where streets were being completed, ready for new construction to begin.

"I'm going to leave you with the golf cart. Feel free to look around and when you're done come back to the office and I'll answer any questions you may have," he said as a pickup truck pulled up to take him back.

They rode around, both deep in thought; seeing their vision as homes appeared in their minds on the lots. Olivia tried to see herself here. She was excited when she pulled in and thought the area was beautiful. The location was perfect and should easily sell. This job was indeed what she had always dreamed. But she didn't feel comfortable, it didn't feel like home. She knew right then, there was no way she could take this job the way it was presented.

"What do you think?" she asked Lucy.

"I think it looks like an incredible opportunity for me. I also think there's no way I'd be getting it if it wasn't for you."

"Wasn't for me?"

"Yeah, if you hadn't come to Houston and trusted me as your assistant there's no way she would've thought of me for this job."

"You earned that all on your own."

"Maybe, but you gave me the chance."

Olivia parked the golf cart and walked around. "There's no way I can do this and move here."

"What do you mean?"

"Well, you know me. Trying different things. I've thought about this all the way down here. And now that I've seen the layout, I've got an idea of how I may be able to do the job and stay where I am."

Lucy's eyes widened, "Tell me more."

"Do you have your phone with you?"

"Of course."

"Let me get my iPad," Olivia said, going to the golf cart. "I'm going to Facetime you."

"Okay." Lucy picked up when her phone trilled. "Hey there!"

Olivia laughed, "Here's what I want you to do. Show me that lot two spaces down."

"What? Show you," Lucy questioned, then she got it. "Oh! Okay." She walked to the lot and using her phone she gave Olivia the tour.

"Let's go back to one of the houses and see if this works."

They drove back to the construction area and with Olivia still in the golf cart, Lucy went inside. Olivia asked her to show her various parts of the construction and lot. Then she asked her to come back.

"We do so much remotely now, I don't know why we couldn't do this too."

"So, what's your plan?"

"I'm going to go back to Elizabeth and see if I can sell her on this idea. I'd still come to the site from time to time, but I really think this could work. One reason they want us for this project is because we are talented, so if we can give them what they want why should they care how we deliver it?"

"Brilliant!"

"Would you be able to do this? A lot of the day to day at the site would fall on your shoulders."

"Hell yeah, I can do it!"

"I thought you'd say that."

"What now?"

"I'll present this to Elizabeth in the morning. You start thinking of the best way for us to show her because we'll need a kick ass demonstration when I do."

"Okay, let me think about it and you do the same."

"I'll call you when I get home and we'll plan it out."

∽

Olivia and Lucy worked on the presentation until late that night. Frankie marveled at her skills. Watching her talk through issues and come up with a solution, even though Frankie wasn't sure what it all meant, she was still mesmerized. Olivia looked over at her and smiled. She disconnected with Lucy and told her they needed a break.

"Whatcha looking at?" she said playfully.

Frankie gave her a seductive smile. "You have no idea how hot it is watching you work through this project."

Olivia's eyes widened, "Oh really?"

"Really," Frankie said nodding her head fervently. "If this wasn't so important to you, I'd have been over there telling Lucy you'd call her back."

Olivia chuckled, getting up and walking over to the couch, "Well, I needed a break and might have time for a little…" She didn't finish her statement as she straddled Frankie and put her arms on her shoulders. She leaned over and captured her lips with a searing kiss. A few minutes later her phone trilled. Olivia sighed, "Gotta get back to it."

"I'll be waiting for you in the bedroom."

"It may be a while."

"That's okay. Wake me when you come in."

Olivia watched Frankie walk down the hall as she connected the call. This was a crazy idea, but it just might work. She knew there was no way she could leave Frankie; she didn't want to and she wouldn't need to if Elizabeth took a chance.

∽

Elizabeth walked in and sat down across from her. "So, you wanted to see me."

"Thanks for coming out today. I've been thinking about the project and as you know, I toured the site yesterday. If you would've offered me this six months ago I probably wouldn't have thought twice. But now, my life is much different. And as I looked at the opportunity, the increase in pay and benefits, and the area, one thing kept coming to the front of my mind."

"What's that?"

"You told me once that you had to stop traveling and step back because you wanted to be present with your family. If I move there, that job would take all my time and I wouldn't be able to have a family."

"But you're young, Olivia."

"That phase could last ten years."

"I really hate to see you turn this down."

"Well, I may have a way for me to stay here and still run the project."

Elizabeth tilted her head, "I'm all ears."

Olivia presented her idea and showed how it would work with Lucy. They demonstrated several different examples of design issues that could arise along with solutions. When they were finished, she disconnected the call and sat back, trying to read Elizabeth's face.

'You've given me a lot to consider. Let me ask you one question: why not just turn the job down? Why go to all this trouble?"

Olivia smiled, "You know I love a challenge and being in charge of that project would be so… but I've found my love and we want to have a family."

"I'll get back to you."

"Thanks Elizabeth, for coming down here today and for the opportunity."

Elizabeth nodded and left.

Now Olivia had to wait.

She didn't wait long because that afternoon Elizabeth called her and approved the idea. There would be guidelines and it was a pilot program, but it had the potential to be groundbreaking. Olivia disconnected the call and sat back, looking at her life. What a difference a few months could make, what a difference love could make, what a difference community could make. She smiled to herself, got up and went to her car. She was going to get her love and celebrate!

EPILOGUE

Six Months Later

WITH ELIZABETH'S approval it didn't take long for the project to begin in Austin. Lucy moved there and set their office up to her liking since she would be spending more time there than Olivia. The lots were being purchased quickly and construction had already begun on several homes. Olivia came to the site when needed and would often bring Frankie. They would stay for the weekend and make it a mini vacation, exploring Austin and the surrounding area.

Today was moving day though, and Olivia thought back to the day Elizabeth approved the project. She went to Your Way and picked Frankie up.

"Where are we going?"

"To your place?"

"To my place? Why?"

"You'll see." They drove up and walked on to the porch. Before

Frankie could unlock the door, Olivia took her hand and turned her around.

"We're here so you can pack a few things." She placed her hands on either side of Franke's face and looked into those green eyes that had become hers, "I want you to move in with me until the house is finished."

A huge smile lit Frankie's face. As she began to answer, Olivia put her finger over her lips.

"And when the house is finished, I want us to move into our home together."

Frankie stared into Olivia's soft brown eyes thinking, *you are my home*. "That would make me the happiest person in the world." Olivia returned her smile as she brought their lips together in a tender kiss.

A couple of months later, on a beautiful autumn day, Frankie took Olivia to what had become their place on the lake and proposed. Olivia was surprised and had planned her own proposal, but Frankie beat her to it. When Frankie slipped the engagement ring on her finger, Olivia held it up and stared, eyes wide. Then she jumped up and ran to the Jeep to get her purse. She came back and slipped Frankie's engagement ring on her finger. It was Frankie's turn to stare.

From time to time Olivia would still catch Frankie staring at her ring and smiling. It was in those moments she knew exactly how she felt; they shared so much love for one another. And every day they created more that was meant for the kids they'd raise together someday.

And now, six months later here they were on the last load about to move into the house where they shared their first kiss, where they made love for the first time, and where together had designed a home.

"Do we have to start unpacking today?" Frankie asked.

"Do you really think I can sit around with all those boxes staring at me and not unpack a few?"

"Of course you can't," she said chuckling.

"I know you're tired. So am I, but we have to at least make a path to the bed," she said looking at Frankie as she turned into the subdivision.

"Well, I can help with that." They both chuckled.

As they drove down the street, "Never did I imagine when I started this job in this subdivision that I would live here.

Frankie smiled, "The first time I rode through this subdivision I could see me living here. I just had to find the right architect. And let me say," she said reaching for Olivia's hand. "That you have built the perfect life for us."

Olivia kissed the back of Frankie's hand. She looked up as they drove in the driveway, "What's this?"

They got out of the car, Frankie came around and arm in arm they looked at the porch. Under a banner that said "Welcome Home" were Stella and Jenna on one side waving and Desi, Sofia, and Lucy on the other.

They turned in one another's arms and with tears in her eyes, Frankie said, "We're home."

ABOUT THE AUTHOR

Jamey Moody is a small town Texas girl that loves romance. She lives with her little terrier Leo that brings her toys every time she walks in the house. If she's not reading or writing you can catch her on her bike, paddle board, or in the middle of an adventure.

Jamey would love to hear from you! Join my mailing list at my website here:

Jameymoodyauthor.com

Or email me here:

Jameymoodyauthor@gmail.com

If you would be so kind as to leave a review I would be most grateful. This will help other readers to find my book and will help me to become a better writer. Thank you, Jamey.

Printed in Great Britain
by Amazon